THE SERENITY NEARBY

THE SERENITY NEARBY

EVE MORTON

SAPPHIRE BOOKS

SALINAS, CALIFORNIA

Dedication

For my Father

5

Acknowledgments

I wrote the first draft of *The Serenity Nearby* during the beginning of 2018. It stayed on my computer, in a draft state, until the end of 2019. When I picked it up again, I turned it into more than just a short novella about an academic conference gone bad; it now was a murder/ghost story with a hopeful romance at the end. What happened between those two points? A lot of things. One was that I got married. The other was that my father died.

I didn't really know my father that well; we'd been estranged since I was twelve. Yet I was the only living family member who could claim his body. So after decades of not having, not thinking about my father, I suddenly had one—at least on paper—all over again. He felt so much more like the shadow images that Bo collects in her shoebox (don't worry, this is not a spoiler) than anything flesh and blood. And as I figured out what to do and how to do it, I ended up thinking of these characters and the claustrophobic atmosphere of that conference. I extended it out, and to my surprise, found a lovely heart in the centre of the story. It was alive again, while some things in the past could never quite be that way.

In a way, I need to thank Emily Dickinson. Her poetry is the backbone of the conference in the novel and was deeply influential to the images used in its pages. Her poems *Because I Could Not Stop for Death* and *I Had Been Hungry All the Years* represent the two poles of the story: darkness upon darkness, then suddenly a light. I also derived much inspiration from the short stories of Raymond Carver and Leslie Jamison's understanding of Alcoholics Anonymous's role in literature in her book *The Recovering*. The title is a reference to Rebecca Solnit's *The Faraway Nearby* (which is how Georgia O'Keeffe used to sign her letters) and the serenity prayer from AA (written by Reinhold Niebuhr and memorialized for me in Kurt Vonnegut's *Slaughterhouse Five*). *The Serenity Nearby* is a dark and ugly book at times, but I swear, it does get better.

My family—Sandy and Travis—were also huge supports. I can't wait to share another work with them, as well as with everyone else who's reading.

Chapter One

*W*here is Jonathan?

Veronica Hockmeier was alone in the café. Aside from the woman working the counter at the front, Veronica was the only soul here. Once she'd surveyed the woman's short bob and the towel hung over her shoulder like she was some 1950s car mechanic, Veronica searched past the café's black walls and through the dark purple booths for her colleague Jonathan Morris. She could have sworn she'd seen his reddish hair and gangly frame from the window outside when she stepped down from her bus. Her dark hair may have been obscuring her vision, but she saw what she'd seen.

Right? No. Maybe. Where is Jonathan?

Veronica blinked three times. She thought she saw a body in the back booth, but once again, there was nothing. If anything had been there, it was now gone.

"Miss?" The woman behind the coffee bar placed both hands on the counter. "Can I help you find anything, miss?"

Veronica flinched. *Miss.* It was somehow too young and too old at the same time; it made her feel like she was back in the classroom. She always told her students to call her by her first name. "No, I'm fine."

"Can I get you something then?"

"Oh. Sure." Veronica remembered that she was not a teacher here. She was not a PhD candidate. She was just a customer, and for once, she was going to be served. Even if Jonathan wasn't here yet and the motes of her eyes had deceived her, she figured she could get a coffee. There was always time for coffee.

"Black but with no sugar," she said. "Large. Nothing fancy."

She smiled briefly as the woman gave it to her. Then, their short interaction now over, she moved to sit at the front window.

A warm feeling bubbled over her as she gazed outside. The sun was still in the sky, though it was past dinnertime now. The clocks sprang forward only a couple of weeks ago and the equinox had only just passed, along with Easter in Southern Ontario, but Veronica felt the hope of upcoming spring. The world was taking a deep collective breath, or at least, her small world of teaching and academia was. University classes were over now. She had grading to do tonight for her Intro to Literary Studies class, sure, but the last essays of the year never took as long as the first ones. She knew her students now, so she could understand if their comma splices were ignorance or arrogance or simply typos. Her English classes never had exams, either, so she was free from the drudgery of walking up and down the aisles of a stress-filled gymnasium of students as squeaky chairs and whispered comments made her feel too tense. She was free from all-nighters and red pens and lesson plans—free for coffee in the middle of the week just to talk.

Just to talk! Oh, Veronica couldn't imagine the luxury of that suggestion until Jonathan had emailed her earlier in the week. *Wanna get coffee? Just to talk and catch up, nothing too big.* She'd written *yes, yes, yes* before she could even notice his own comma splice. She hadn't even really read the email at all; she was too enthused by the prospect of a coffee date with a colleague. *No, a friend.* Because they were friends. *Right?*

Now Veronica wasn't so sure. Fifteen minutes passed, and he was still a no-show.

Jonathan Morris was a fellow PhD student in her program, another scholar of American literature, and another person also working with her own supervisor Stella Flanders. The two had been her research assistants for a paper Stella had written early in the academic year. Brianna Murphy, Veronica's best friend and comrade in the English Department, had also been selected as a research student, but she'd been sick that entire week, so the bulk of the scansion and journal comparison exercises had fallen on Veronica and Jonathan's shoulders. At first, Veronica worried about this task. Like any group assignment in high school, she'd had a sinking feeling that she'd be left alone with all the work, and because this was serious and she couldn't let Stella down, she'd do it all herself.

But Jonathan had surprised her. He may have been a man in academia, and men in academia were often notorious for steamrolling the accomplishments of women and outright mansplaining basic terms to experts in their own field, but Jonathan had been a delight. An utter delight. In between their nearly all-night working sessions, he'd gotten them pizza and diet Coke. Though Veronica, claiming to be sick like Brianna, would throw up the pizza come morning, she knew the gesture had been nice. When the publication had been successful and Stella approved of their work, Veronica had shifted Jonathan from man in academia to colleague, comrade in her mind. Her memories of Jonathan were cemented: he was one of the Good Guys.

He was still one of the Good Guys, Veronica was sure. Veronica pulled up the email on her phone. With one hand on her coffee and another busy on her device, the waiting seemed less intense.

After she'd accepted his offer for coffee—which was the right date, time, and place she'd now confirmed—his tone turned serious. *I need to talk to you about something pretty important. I'm hoping that you'll have noticed the same thing I've noticed. And well, maybe if we both see things, it'll start to make sense. I don't mean for all of this to sound cryptic,* he'd added as if he could have felt her heart pounding, *or like I'm trying to ask you out. I'm not. I just really need your opinion on something, and the only way I can do this is in person. Feels like the only safe way, no matter how many times I change my email password.*

Goose bumps pulled tightly at Veronica's skin. How could she have missed this for so long? She'd just been so enchanted by the hope of company, even something like community, celebration, that it surely slipped her critical gaze. Especially as Brianna seemed to get sicker and sicker and wanted to go out less and less and especially when Stella always seemed fussy and like she couldn't be bothered with anything as trivial as coffee, especially in the month of April, Veronica was in desperate straits for attention. At most, she'd figured this kind of email would lead to some sort of academic collaboration or discovery. A lost Emily Dickinson notebook? A new library to visit? Thoughts on the new movie about Dickinson's relationships with women? What else could she and Jonathan have in common, really, aside from research? He was from another province, straight, over six feet tall, and a serious ginger. Veronica was from a town outside the Toronto area, barely five feet, with dark features, and she was a lesbian—and very happy that most people in her department seemed to know that last fact in particular. She was off the market. Not for coffee dates, only for research dates.

Yet it was so clear now that what Jonathan wanted to talk about was not research. Why be cryptic about research? Her skin pulled taut again. Veronica touched the back of her neck. She turned around. She sought for the source of her bad feeling but found no one staring at her. Her stomach sank.

Where is Jonathan?

For a moment, Veronica felt as if she was in that Edward Hopper painting *Nighthawks*. In the image, there are three customers at the diner bar in 1940s America. One man is working the bar area and seems to be making shakes for the couple seated in front of him. The painting is done in dark colours, just like the sky depicted outside the diner. Veronica looked down at her coffee cup, realized it was no longer steaming, and felt as if she had been etched into the immortal image of the painting itself. There was an emptiness to *Nighthawks* that Veronica always liked, even if she hadn't thought of it in years.

Now, as she leaned back and embraced the feeling of emptiness inside herself, she realized the painting was the reason she was here in the first place. The painting had been in one of the first university lectures she'd attended in her undergrad. Veronica was not an art major, but this particular English professor used a lot of paintings in her lecture slides. She said it was boring and confusing to give walls and walls of text as she spoke. "So," she'd said in lecture as she gestured to *Nighthawks*, "I may as well give you some nice art to go along with it and hopefully illuminate my concepts."

After *Nighthawks*, there was *Christina's World* by Andrew Wyeth, which was then followed by numerous Georgia O'Keeffe's. Veronica loved every minute of it. She'd started to think in paintings, think in pictures—up until Stella Flanders, at least. Veronica had never sought out that other professor with the paintings, let alone remembered her name now, because only a week after that lecture, Veronica would see Stella on stage. She'd go to her office hours. And well, Veronica's investment in her university education had been sealed. With Dr. Flanders, Emily Dickinson, her hymnal poetry, and the American landscape of the Transcendentalists, rather than... whatever that other professor studied. She wasn't quite sure anymore.

Veronica suddenly wanted to know. She turned to Google but froze in the text box because she didn't know what to type. Professor who liked paintings? Yeah, that was not going to cut it, even if she did include the institution and what she could remember of the course code. She looked up Edward Hopper instead, then Georgia O'Keeffe. It was a distraction now, pure and simple, because Jonathan was not showing up. No one was coming into the café, either. The server washed the same counter, anxious. She wanted to go home. She wasn't part of the *Nighthawks* fantasy anymore, a landscape that would remain the same and pristine even in the current digital era. This server was bored. Veronica was bored. Classes were over. There were no emails in her inbox, not even an apology from Jonathan. What had he'd wanted to tell her? She didn't know. Now there was no bother in knowing.

She just wanted to go home, too.

She left her coffee unfinished by the window booth. The sun had set. Lights flicked on in the apartment building across the way. She briefly thought of the other painting by Hopper, the one with the sad girl in similar apartment windows, but she pushed it away.

⚘ ⚘ ⚘ ⚘

Veronica ended up at Stella's house. Her two-story, recently remodeled house was at the end of a cul-de-sac in one of the first suburban enclaves close to the university that wasn't overrun by students. Veronica could feel the noise in the area shift and change as she stepped off the bus and onto Stella's neighbourhood sidewalk. The crinkling of beer cans and cacophony of club music suddenly muted into Brahms, Haydn, or just plain silence. Even the air changed, going from cigarettes, garbage, and vaping to crisp and clean bonfires and evergreens . Veronica gulped as if she'd been drowning. This was where Stella lived. This was where she wanted to be.

But will Stella be home? Veronica wondered. And will she want to see me?

Her breath halted. These worries were more complicated. She and Stella usually had a complicated system of code words and calling to make their dates. It was necessary, Stella insisted, because of the academy politics and litigious policy makers. Veronica nodded along, not really understanding or caring, as long as she got to be with Stella.

Veronica knocked anyway. She wanted to fiddle with her phone again to keep herself company, but the battery was dying. She stared at the blue door. She waited. It was so quiet she swore she could hear her own blood pound in her ears. A minute passed, maybe two. She was about to knock again when Stella opened the door.

"Veronica." Stella said her name in a rush. She smiled wide, bright, and genuine. She wore her pale white silk robe; it was her after-teaching attire or what she wore when she did the laundry. Since it was the middle of the week and Stella liked to fold clothing during Charlie Chaplin films, laundry day made the most sense. Thursdays and Wednesdays, she'd said in afterward pillow talk, were the most cinematic days. Veronica never asked why, only nodded with profound understanding.

"I was just about to call you," Stella added.

"You were?"

"Yes. The conference emails have gone out."

Veronica's sudden euphoria became blotted out with tension. She'd wanted Stella to be happy to see her because she was her, Veronica Hockmeier, twenty-five, a Virgo through and through, but still just as whip smart as Dr. Stella Flanders, forty-eight, a woman who never read her horoscope or claimed not to, but who was on the cusp of a Pisces and Aries when Veronica had checked her license after their first liaison. The two had been having an affair for months now, yet Veronica still felt as if she was vying for her attention in almost every single spare moment. If not directed on Stella's research, her documentaries, her art and book collection, and her environmental concerns—then maybe, maybe, she could give Veronica some attention. Some satisfaction. Some love?

Not in this moment, anyway.

Tonight was all about the annual conference of Emily Dickinson scholarship, which took place in Amherst, Massachusetts, where Dickinson's childhood home was. Stella was asked to be one of two major keynote speakers, so she'd already been planning on attending this year, but now the others who had submitted a conference abstract would know for sure if they could attend. Since Veronica had been glancing at her email waiting for Jonathan all this time, she knew it still hovered at zero. There was a fat chance in hell her work was accepted for the conference. The rejection stung worse than she anticipated. It wasn't just the conference experience, the line on the CV, or the chance to hobnob and network that disappeared, but Stella herself. Tears blotted Veronica's face. She tried to push them away, to claim allergies or something she ate, but Stella hushed her.

"Come inside. I'm sure we can get to the bottom of this."

Veronica stepped through the doorway, took off her shoes, and allowed Stella to take her coat. Veronica watched with half-watery eyes and full attention at Stella's careful gestures. Even something as banal as putting Veronica's coat on a hanger seemed high class and artistic. When Stella poured her a glass of wine and set out some cheese and crackers, it was almost too much. Veronica barely ate and only sipped at her drink. Words hardly formed. She struggled to say anything, every syllable seeming inane. This was not who she wanted to become in front of Dr. Stella Flanders.

"May I see the rejection letter?" Stella asked after she'd rubbed Veronica's back for what seemed like a precise four minutes. "Perhaps I can decipher what the problem is about which the committee concerned themselves. From there, we can workshop your work together, and this won't happen again. Next year, when you apply, we will go together."

Veronica liked the sound of that very much. Not the workshopping—that sounded like going to the dentist without novocaine—but Stella saying *together* in that tone of voice made her recall the first time she'd spent the night. "There are no buses right now," Stella mentioned after she'd returned from the bathroom. Her hands smelled like her soap and like Veronica, and when she placed them by Veronica's chin to cusp her face, it was like heaven, along with the words that followed, "so I think you should stay with me."

The memory was not nearly as romantic as Veronica had come to believe, especially to an outsider, but this was how Stella showed affection. She was efficient; she was responsible. Her tender gestures were timed precisely and came down to the language she selected and used. In that preciseness and language, Veronica knew, was a poetry. And that first poem, about staying the night because of buses, had been all for her.

Tonight, that poem would have to be about workshopping. Dangling modifiers and cherry-picking citations. It would be harsh, cruel almost. But it, too, would be all Veronica's if she allowed it to be.

Then Veronica remembered. "I have no emails at all."

"At all?"

Veronica confirmed. "None from the conference. Does that mean I'm not even worth a response? That workshopping is impossible?"

"No." It was all Stella said for some time. "It means that academia's clock is broken. Always a snail's pace for anything. I may have already heard from Jonathan and Brianna, but—"

"You heard from Jonathan? He was supposed to meet me, but he never showed."

"I see." Stella nodded slowly. "Well, his paper was accepted. A very good abstract indeed. I'm quite proud of him. Brianna, I'm afraid, not so much. I've already set up a time and place to go over her work, though." Veronica fought back a wave of jealousy for Brianna and Jonathan. She wanted the success of the conference, one that would allow her to go on a blissful vacation with Stella—but she also wanted that harsh critique that Brianna would receive to be all her own, too. Stella was either going to lick her wounds and only her wounds, or travel with her and only her to this faraway imaginary place she'd come to imagine the conference as.

But this was the nature of supervision: sharing. Maybe not sharing beds, no, Stella was just hers there, but sharing Stella's mind. Her time. Her precision. *Fine.* Stella had to tend to many students, many abstracts, many dissertations. These barely nibbled crackers and wine, however, were Veronica's. She was the only one to do this at Stella's granite counter, especially as Stella was still in her robe.

Stella leaned against the counter as she began to clarify her thoughts. The beginning of her cleavage was visible. Veronica wanted to pillow her head against those breasts. She wanted to fall asleep and dream about something else.

"I'm sure Jonathan innocently forgot to meet with you. He sounded so…consumed the last time we spoke; I'm assuming he wanted to start that first draft. Sometimes, he's distracted. He's not always the greatest with emails in that state."

Veronica remembered how thrilled Jonathan had been when their pizza had come and they'd given him an extra topping they didn't charge him for. He'd been vibrating with excitement, and it was nearly impossible to get him back on track with scansion. When she'd mentioned this to him, all he could do was sheepishly apologize. *I think I'm just thrilled it was green pepper because I need some veggies,* he'd said. *Pretty sure I'm getting sicker now that I'm at grad school. The immunity's going, and so, vitamin C is always good.*

Veronica was jostled from the memory by Stella's hand on her shoulder. "Clarify for me: you don't have an email at all? My apologies for fixating on this point, Veronica, but I'd like to know for definite since I'm deeply involved with the planning committee and blind reading process, and I hate to see someone on that project fail to follow orders to give out the acceptances or declines by today. It's irresponsible and not practical since we now must book a hotel."

"Right. Of course."

Veronica grabbed her phone again and logged on. With Stella over her shoulder, she became aware of how dirty the screen was. Had the screen been black, the state of the fingerprints and grease would have been so strong and apparent that Stella's image might not have even been visible in one corner. Veronica wiped her hand across the glass when she opened her student email. To be sure, she pulled down to make the app load again.

"See? Nothing. I just—" Before she finished the words, the screen changed; so suddenly and wonderfully, the number zero had slid to a one. An email. From the conference organizers.

"Well, what are you waiting for?" Stella asked.

Veronica sighed. She didn't want to confirm the yes or no anymore. She'd liked all the attention she was getting when things were harder to decipher. When she opened it, she held her breath. When it was an acceptance email, she realized she'd believed it to be a rejection at first. She wanted her wounds licked, knowing it would come with sex. She wasn't so sure how her successes measured yet.

"Well done," Stella said once she'd read the whole correspondence. Veronica was still stuck on the "thank you" in the reply. "I thought your abstract was very interesting."

"You did?"

"Yes."

"You didn't say so. I was so worried."

"You never know how these things will go. Your topic was interesting, but it is a bit unorthodox, especially for an Americanist to study. But I see the gamble has paid off." Stella tilted her head curiously at Veronica. She stepped closer, aligning herself between Veronica's legs. Veronica'd sat on the stool in Stella's kitchen with her wine, but now the glass was forgotten. So was the phone. So were the thinly veiled criticisms in her work. None of it mattered as Stella curled a stray strand of Veronica's dark hair around her ear. Her approval and praise were silent, but Veronica felt them. She crooned under the support. She bloomed.

When their lips met, it was like that first time all over again. It always felt like the first time all over again. Stella was so forbidden, Veronica never took anything for granted. Each kiss was the first, each kiss was the last. Even as Stella deftly commanded Veronica's arousal, coaxing her tongue from her mouth with practiced ease, it was still so much more like mind-reading than intimacy. Stella knew her so well. She knew her so well and with such little effort. The kiss grew heated, and Stella's hands slid to Veronica's waist. She tugged her jeans. She felt the small of her back, her kidneys, and butt, kneading the skin and causing Veronica to shudder. When Stella touched her breasts, it was softly and over the shirt. She hovered over the nipples. She tugged. She toyed. She kissed and kissed and kissed, all so intoxicating, yet so slow.

Veronica was still getting used to the feel of Stella's robe. She was still hovering over her wrist, the bare skin on her collarbone. Her blond hair, flecked with gray, and her soft lips. Veronica felt so new, practically virginal.

"We should go upstairs," Stella said. "It's uncouth to do this in a kitchen."

Veronica swallowed. She would do this anywhere. Bed, table, outside. Now, later, by and by. Her quixotic lust felt like a Dr. Seuss rhyming couplet, and then she laughed out loud because if she'd said this to Stella, she would have pronounced Seuss the right way. Not the common way.

"What's so amusing, my Veronica?" Stella asked. She held her hand, tugging her up the stairs.

Veronica bit her lip. "Nothing, nothing."

Stella's bedroom was the largest room on the second floor, an en suite at the end of the hallway. Her bed, as ever, was tightly made with hospital corners. The sheets were pale blue, the colour of robin's eggs. Everything was in its place—her dresser with a full vanity mirror, the armoire, the rustic bedside tables, and numerous rings she'd inherited from her family—everything was there and immaculate, a museum over a room, save for a closet door that was open a fraction of an inch. Its mismatch was so strange that Veronica almost lost herself in that small crack.

Then Stella turned around to face her. She dropped the robe and revealed her naked form.

Veronica blushed. She almost forgot that she was supposed to be naked, too. Clothing melted away from her. Stella touched the underside of her breasts and cupped them in her hands, basking before their mouths met. Then Stella was all she thought of, all she could become, and all she ever wanted to be until morning.

"You never told me," Stella said when they were through, "what was so funny?"

"Nothing," Veronica said. She caught Stella's gaze and took a deep breath. She was naked. She would never, ever get used to her nakedness.

"Tell me," Stella said. "Tell me everything."

Veronica bit her lip. Stella kissed the raw place on her mouth, then she found the cleft between her thighs and worked on bringing her to orgasm again, all the while begging for the truth. Each kiss, each caress seemed to now come with a claim for confession, a constant interrogation of desire, a begging of *tell me, tell me, tell me.*

As Veronica cried out with another climax, she finally gave in. "It's just sometimes," she said, "you are so beautiful I feel like I'm in a painting."

"That's not funny."

"It's not?"

"No. So I think you're lying to me, Veronica. But I'll accept this answer as truth for now."

Stella withdrew her hand. She rose from the bed, slipped on her robe, and headed into the bathroom. Veronica was left naked, the blue robin's egg sheets suddenly cold. Her heart hammered in her chest. She'd done something wrong but couldn't parse it out. She wanted to throw up, but there was nothing.

She stared at the closet for another minute before she stood. She walked to the bathroom down the hall, not bothering to get dressed beyond her sweater. If someone had asked her what she was going to do, only one part of herself knew the truth. The other was silent. The other part lied—not just to Stella, but to everyone.

Veronica stood in front of the toilet bowl and shoved her fingers down her throat. Her heaving was sudden, revolting, but she felt so much better when she was done.

She found her phone after she'd brushed her teeth. A message cascaded on the screen, this time from Brianna. Veronica wanted to mute it; she didn't know how to break it to Brianna that she'd gotten into the conference while she had not. She wanted no bad news, no rejection, to linger. Veronica was about to mute the alerts when she actually read the message of her email. It was not about the conference at all. It was about Jonathan. Veronica opened it fully to read—and then reread—the message several times.

Then she wanted to throw up all over again.

Veronica, I don't know how to say this, Brianna wrote, *but Jonathan is dead.*

Chapter Two

In her first year of university, Veronica's exams had begun just after Easter. Since then, she realized she'd been thinking of that period as the redemption time. Classes were over—but the final assignments were not handed in, and the grades were still up in the air. *Anything can happen,* one of her teaching assistants in her first-year psych class had said. A student could still fail—or a student who was failing, like she'd been that year—could somehow suddenly rise again. *Just like Jesus, obviously,* the TA had said, *except I didn't tell the prof I mentioned Jesus.* Religion was forbidden in university, but redemption was common. Common as the B- grade, a pitiful seventy-five on the final. That year, Veronica entered the rank of the common student and passed all her classes with an average grade. She'd not failed. She'd redeemed herself.

Even as a teaching assistant with her own class and no longer a failing student, she still thought of this period as the redemption. It was the time when things could be undone—for the better or worse, and she tried to impart those graces that had been given her in her own undergrad. She tried. She really did.

But Jonathan Morris's death made everything feel like a lie. Not only was he dead, Veronica soon realized from her numerous correspondences with Brianna, but he had died by suicide.

Jonathan's super had found his body. He hadn't only missed the meeting with Veronica, but several of his students had said he was a no-show for their meetings, and he'd failed to schedule a final exam—or grade final assignments—on time. The super wouldn't have cared about these deadlines, especially since the rent was paid, but there had also been a deluge of phone calls from Jonathan's parents, demanding a wellness check. His folks were in Nova Scotia, several time zones difference, and not hearing from their only son could easily mean he'd been with his girlfriend all weekend—or that he was seriously hurt. So, finally, the super went inside, thinking he was going to calm down some down-home Podunk parents, and instead found Jonathan hunched over his desk, cyanide leaking the oxygen out of his bloodstream. Dead. Gone. And definitely not a mistake, an accident, or a careless way to store chemicals. He should not have had cyanide; he should have still been alive. He should have been having coffee with Veronica, meeting with his failing students, or answering his parents' phone calls—but he'd already been dead for days.

Veronica couldn't handle it. She'd spent so many sleepless nights trying to find out as much as she could between her rounds of grading. By the time she and Brianna had pieced it all together, though, Jonathan was gone and then *gone* gone. Not a week after his body was found, his parents had flown in, scooped up his stuff and his body, and taken him back to Nova Scotia.

That's it, Brianna had texted. *No funeral. No nothing. How is that fair?*

Veronica hadn't answered the text. She threw up again, this time not even needing to tickle her uvula, and then she tried to work. She could only see the face of that TA from her first year, however, and she just wanted to scream. There was not—and never had been—any such thing as redemption. Her TA should have never mentioned Jesus or even given her the idea. If he hadn't, maybe she'd feel a lot better now, rather than feeling utterly haunted.

She tried to go back to work. She tried to be kind to her students, but the month of April was now part of the dead time. Everything normal and life-sustaining was peeled away. The final grades she assigned belonged to ghosts. The university became a haunted house. And so, she spent as little time there as possible. She graded with zero feedback, posted it, and logged out of her school accounts. She bought frozen pizzas and doughnuts and ate them in a fury and threw them up again. After three days of this, she felt stretched out, too thin in her shoulders and collarbones yet too fat in her stomach. She shivered during the day and sweated at night. After a week passed and her pants didn't fit, she wanted to go to campus just so she could run on the track, make herself feel useful now that she was not grading, but her legs hurt. Her body hurt. All the buses were empty, reminding her it was the dead, dead, dead time all over again.

And she was just so afraid.

⚜ ⚜ ⚜ ⚜

One afternoon, Veronica lost an entire six hours combing through the university's website and her colleagues' Facebook pages. She hadn't known, really, what she was doing until it occurred to her that Jonathan had wanted to tell her something. That was why they were meeting, right? She went back and reread his email and copied and pasted it into a Word document so she wouldn't have to deal with student emails. She studied his words like they were a passage to deep read—but she could see nothing there that was too illuminating. She forsook this activity to go back to Facebook lurking, pretending to be a quasi-detective all the while. She traced Jonathan's friends online while drinking mug after mug of black coffee and feeling more like she was on the cover of a pulp novel as she did. Soon, she started to notice a trend in her caffeine-induced delirium. Almost everyone, save for herself, Brianna, Jonathan, and one more student from their academic start year in their PhD, had dropped out of the program. That was at least six students, if she remembered orientation correctly. Over half the cohort was no longer around.

Granted, this was a common phenomenon all over. Academia was hard. The wages sucked, the work was strenuous and sometimes took too long, especially for people who were marrying and child-having ages. Now in her third year, Veronica had watched several people withdraw, sometimes without explanation or notice, merely disappearing from the department faculty page past a certain point. Once the course work was complete, next came the exams in particular fields, followed by a proposal that must be approved, and then the years and years, and sometimes nearing a decade, of dissertation writing and defending. There were many twists and turns to become lost in, many differing corridors of the school that had to be explored and passed through successfully. People simply became lodged in one of them, and seeing no exit, constructed one for themselves by quitting.

Getting married. Working in a different industry.

Or simply disappearing.

In one of the first PhD orientations Veronica attended, a professor Stella's age with purple hair (who Stella would refer to as "cotton candy" instead of her name in their closed-door conversations), said she had seen one student who had been at the school for nearly nine years turn in a progress report. Everyone had forgotten about him, including his supervisor. The only signs of life he'd made were his tuition payments and this one lowly report.

"It was nearly blank," cotton candy said in an overextended gesture of her hands. Her nails were bright pink. "There was only a note that said 'still writing.' Don't be like him. Don't become Mr. Year Nine."

The story of Mr. Year Nine was repeated the next year and the next, but without adding another year to make up the difference. The colour of cotton candy's nails and hair changed, but Mr. Year Nine was staid and resolute, a tale from out of history, academia's mascot. Veronica imagined him at a dead end of a school hallway, writing his dissertation on a typewriter, a stack of paper next to him that grew and grew and grew.

Deep down, though, and especially in the wake of Jonathan's more permanent disappearance, she wanted to know whether Mr. Year Nine did eventually graduate or if he was still working. Finding any information on this would be impossible, though. He'd become Ahab, and the school was Moby Dick, and this was what needed to be imparted to students, apocryphal or not. *Do not turn this degree into something that it is not. There is no revenge story here,*

*no redemption arc, no biblical allegory. Find your area
of study. Pass your exams. And get out of here.*

Veronica heard the "get out" as a haunted chorus
as she tracked down the other students from her cohort.
One moved across the country to be with his fiancée
in Vancouver when she got a better job. Veronica
read his latest status update, which proclaimed he
was beginning another degree in another field. There
was another woman who decided to get a job in the
commercial sector, using her knowledge of scansion
to write ad copy and jingles; another student took her
analysis of David Mamet plays and used it to consult in
career firms. In her last years of undergrad, Veronica
had been approached by one of those exact career
consultants, telling her that with an advanced degree
in English, you can do anything because everything is
in language itself. She wondered if Delia was saying
the same thing, but perhaps adding that PhDs were
for closers only.

Veronica wanted to share her joke—but,
of course, she couldn't. She laughed alone in her
apartment instead.

The more Veronica sleuthed online, the more
she realized Delia and Christine and Margo were the
lucky students. Another student from her cohort had
left after she'd failed her first set of exams, unable to
please her committee with her answers and revisions.
On a way back Facebook post, Sara ranted that it
was a conspiracy, that she should have passed if not
for "personal vengeance outside of citations," and
there was no point in redoing something that was
only going to fail once again. Stella had been on her
committee, so Veronica had disabled notifications
when the first stirrings of animosity had begun, and

she hadn't seen anything from Sara since. Or Lucian, another student who'd failed his proposal writing and dropped out when funding ran out. He stopped posting about school after he'd said it was a waste of time and money; he only seemed to come online now to sell video games. Even now, as she combed through Sara's new life as a museum admin worker or Lucian's numerous consoles, Veronica was uneasy. She didn't want to think the system was rigged because that would mean she and Brianna had passed their exams and proposals by goodwill and not self-will. They had not spent months poring over *Moby Dick*, *Walden*, *Sister Carrie*, and the other tomes of great American literature to be told they'd done it all by sheer luck.

Veronica rubbed her eyes. She'd been doing this for so long. Her fingers were red, especially around the knuckles. Her neck was stiff. And her fridge was empty, so she couldn't even dull the icky feelings of her life in academia with the icky feelings of bulimia. She had papers everywhere, all of them student work, group work, attendance forms. She felt haunted now, through and through. Just because someone else had offed himself, she tried to recall, didn't mean that she had to sink into despair. It sucked. It always sucked.

But what had Stella said? What had she told her when Veronica showed up teary-eyed and despondent over Jonathan? One night, Veronica had managed to put on tights, an oversized T-shirt, and lipstick and wandered to Stella's house again. After inviting her inside, Stella had shut off her TV displaying *City Lights* and told Veronica she looked like hell.

"Of course I do. It's the dead time," Veronica said.

Stella had huffed and told her there was no such

thing. "If anything, you should be feeling joy."

"Joy?"

"Yes. The death of the semester leads to the birth of conference season. And Emily Dickinson awaits."

Veronica had nodded. The two had kissed. They made love twice, then Veronica had left in the morning with the promise of working on her paper. She did no such a thing. She binged and purged and played detective online. She repeated the same day, over and over, hoping that in some magical way, Jonathan would spring to life. The world would turn into a painting. She'd be free.

That was not how it worked.

There was no such thing as redemption anymore.

All this came back to Veronica now. She saw her life as an outsider might witness it, as a doctor who would report all her neuroses back to her parents like that one time she was institutionalized, and she grew cold. She swallowed. She may not have wanted to be as callous as Stella, as cold and intellectual, but she could—at the very least—clean out the ghosts that persisted in haunting her. She could not redeem herself—the past was the past was the past—but she could, at least, try for a future.

Yes, yes, Veronica thought, now gathering up the papers strewn all over her apartment. She was going to engage in some spring cleaning.

Then, and only then, would the ghosts go away and the dead time come back to life.

❧ ❧ ❧ ❧

By the time Veronica finished clearing all the old papers, grades, and even some of her first-year graduate work from her apartment, it was nearing a reasonable morning hour. The grey clouds misted away, and the sun came out. The sky was blue. Bright blue. *Spring?* Veronica stood under a ray of sunlight by her apartment's back door. She felt like she was at summer camp again, a place where anything could—and definitely did at age twelve—happen. The weather made her feel so strong and powerful, she suddenly found the energy to get herself on a bus to go into the campus. She could clean out her office desk. It wouldn't be as hard now, she was sure. It would be okay.

On the bus, she noticed a group of people surrounding one of the universities. The city where she lived was not Toronto—but it still boasted numerous schools. In addition to the university she attended (which was known for its interdisciplinary studies), there was a vocational college, a seminary, and another university (which was known for the sciences) all along the same street. It was at the other university where this crowd gathered. When the bus slowed for a stop, Veronica noted the main parking lot was flooded with people. Red and blue signs swayed as if some Jasper Johns flag painting had come to life. Veronica craned her neck, but the bus darted by so quickly she didn't have a chance to figure it out. Normally, she would view all types of protesting as pure show and nothing but. *Just hot air*, Stella might have said, *just students practicing their lungs, like babies do when they first breathe. It will pass.*

Now Veronica was more enchanted by the colours, by some signs of life. The university was within walking distance of her office. *Maybe I'll walk there on my way home. Go to a different bus stop.*

Just pass by. She nodded, deciding it was the best course. Green patches of grass at her school made her feel better, anyway. She didn't even mind that when she arrived at her office, her cellphone's signal was immediately blocked by the thick concrete walls. At the best of times, her phone's lack of signal in the corridors made her annoyed; at the worst, it made her feel unsafe.

Now, it was familiar. Almost like coming home.

When she slid her key in the office door, a startled cry emerged. And again, she didn't feel worried, concerned, or annoyed. She was practically elated: a noise meant someone else was in the office, which meant that Brianna was there, too.

"You!" Veronica cried out the moment she confirmed her suspicions.

"And you!" Brianna said back. She rose from her desk against the wall, combing some of her curly hair behind her ear as she did. Her glasses seemed to dwarf her face, especially as it seemed like she'd lost ten pounds in the last two weeks. Her face was gaunt, cheekbones sharp, and her skin was a pallid grey. It wasn't the newly chiselled face of someone getting healthy, shedding the extra weight around the middle through good choices, but a sustained illness finally showing up in someone's features. Brianna's illness was nameless still, even after numerous doctors' visits, celiac tests, and vial after vial of blood being drawn. Veronica had hoped that Brianna's lack of mentioning her queasiness in their texts meant she was getting better, on the mend, or something else encouraging. She saw now that she was wrong but was unsure how to mention it.

So they hugged. It was a long, sustained

embrace, one done from pure friendship, while also mixing with concern and empathy. After only two seconds of holding on, Veronica was so surprised to find tears coming to her eyes. She pulled away from the embrace, muttering her apologies, only to find Brianna doing the same.

"Oh, sweetie," they said in unison. They laughed. Soon, they cried even harder, now not bothering to be proud or ashamed. Brianna sat in the office chair, and Veronica sat across from her. She opened her drawer and found a tissue box they could pass back and forth. Their words were clipped as they cried and spoke of all that had happened. Veronica talked about her emails with Jonathan, how she'd wanted to see him, and now she was desperate to find out what he wanted to tell her. Briana nodded along, excusing herself several times to get water from down the hall. "I'm still pretty weak," Brianna said, finally broaching the subject of her illness. "But I needed to come to the office today, no matter what."

"You don't have to do anything," Veronica said. "I'm sure they'd give you an extension on grades—"

"I needed to," Brianna emphasized. "I'm… Jonathan wanted to talk to me, too. He said the same thing in an email to me."

"That something was wrong?"

Brianna nodded, though the action seemed to make her nauseated. She opened her own desk drawer and pulled out a booklet before passing it to Veronica. She blinked several times before recognition dawned. It was their comprehensive exam booklet from a year and a half ago.

"Oh, don't show me that. It's like war flashbacks."

"I know. Same here. But I think Jonathan was

looking through it."

"Through the university's exams?" Veronica asked. "Was he helping a new student prepare?"

"Maybe. He asked me about comps a while ago. But I think he was looking through mine specifically. This." Brianna gestured to her desk drawer. "It was all messed up when I got here today. I thought it was just me forgetting how I left things—some of this medication makes me foggy and I forget—but I think some parts of the exam are missing."

"What?"

Brianna peeled back the exam booklet where she'd answered her questions. Comprehensive exams were typed on a school computer and took place over four hours, so there was a lot of material that Brianna had—yet it was clearly not all of it. At least half of her pages were missing. Brianna also showed Veronica the question pack since her exam had been in a slightly different field, so her questions reflected her specific area. While Veronica specialized in American poets, Brianna was focusing more on religious tracts. "So was Jonathan. He was combining a bunch of American religious narratives. You know, like Mormonism."

"Right. I think he mentioned something like that when we worked on Stella's article," Veronica said. "He called it Bible fanfiction."

"I think it's more like American cults, though. That's where I think he was going with all of this. At least, that was what it sounded like the last time we talked."

"When was that?"

"Before your meeting. Failed meeting, I mean." Brianna coughed. "I think I was the last person to see him."

"And the last thing he wanted to talk about was cults?"

"Yes. At least I think so. I'm not sure. I had so many questions…"

"Me too." Veronica felt that same goose bump feeling on the back of her neck. Cults. And cults used cyanide, like the Peoples Temple in Guyana. She struggled to remember more of that conversation about Mormonism the two had shared. All she came up with was her own obsessive Googling of the uses of cyanide and how Jim Jones's followers had put it in Flavor Aid, not Kool-Aid, like everyone thought.

"Oh, God," Veronica said. "Did he… Was he drinking…?"

"I have no idea," Brianna said, knowing what she meant right away. They were quiet for some time, before Brianna shifted the attention back on to her exam and the booklet. "Part of this is missing. I remember writing about Joseph Smith, but now that section is gone."

Veronica looked at the pages where Brianna gestured. They didn't match up when read together, meaning that several in between were gone. "And you didn't throw them out?"

Brianna shook her head.

"So you think Jonathan grabbed them?"

"Maybe." Brianna shrugged. She went to bite a nail, suddenly nervous. "There's not much of a market for stuff like this, you know? They don't even do the exams in this manner anymore. It's all take-home now."

"So we suffered through four hours of writing at once for nothing?"

Brianna shrugged. "I…don't think Jonathan

passed."

"What?"

"The comps. He failed the second round."

"What?"

"The oral exam," Brianna said, as if Veronica could forget the gruelling second round. "He didn't pass his. He wrote it, and the committee said that was sufficient, but they questioned his oral defense."

"That doesn't make sense," Veronica said. "The same person wrote it. So he should get it."

"I know. But sometimes, you don't pass."

"What does that even mean?"

"Sometimes, you don't pass," Briana said the words so formally that Veronica wondered if that was what Stella had said to her about her abstract. Sometimes, you get rejected. Sometimes, you don't pass.

Veronica still struggled with this new understanding, though. It was difficult to truly fail in academia, especially once you had gotten so far. Especially if you knew your stuff, which Veronica had seen from Jonathan firsthand when she worked with him. She'd never read his written work, not that closely, so how could something be so good on paper, but in person it falls apart, and then have that be enough to keep him back?

"Oh," Veronica suddenly said.

Brianna nodded. "Yeah," she added. "Everyone thought he stole it."

"Everyone?"

"Well, not Stella, I guess," Brianna said. "But I don't honestly know what happens behind closed doors."

Veronica nodded. There was so much to unpack

in that single sentence, so many various meanings, but she couldn't go there. She could only focus on the kiss of death in the academy: plagiarism. It was a death sentence—more than that, it was an utter annihilation of the self. To be in a place of higher learning, a place where your thoughts were what mattered, and to then be accused of plagiarism was the worst thing that could happen. Your thoughts were not your own. They were someone else's. Your career was over, even if plagiarism was proven to be mistaken or undeserved. No matter; it was academic suicide.

It was literal suicide.

"I can't believe this," Veronica said. "There's just no way."

"That's the thing," Brianna said. "Jonathan didn't do anything wrong. He said he was fighting it, convinced that someone just made a mistake, a misunderstanding. All in good faith, he kept saying good faith when we spoke. I…I think he wanted to see how I answered the same question on my exam and whether or not they counted anything against me. I said I couldn't remember, that I would have to check my notes. But now…the notes are gone. And…"

"And?" Veronica repeated when Brianna drew quiet. "What else aren't you telling me?"

Brianna sighed. "There was a note."

"A note here?"

"No, a suicide note. It said he wasn't going to apologize."

"For what?"

"That's the thing, no one has any idea," Brianna said. "All I heard was that Jonathan's suicide note had in bold letters *I will not apologize.* That's it. Nothing more."

Veronica swallowed. The goose bumps returned. She wondered if this was going to be her constant state now any time she heard about Jonathan. Goose bumps. Guilt. And a deep sinking feeling of fear. She wanted to find a painting to match this scenario, so she could understand it, but there was nothing. Just a dark void.

"And now I'm here," Brianna said and brought Veronica back to the present. "And all of this is really weird. I don't know what to do with it."

Veronica swallowed. Her mouth felt dry and disgusting. Her room was stuffy. There were so many ideas that flitted in her mind, but nothing remained at the forefront for longer than two seconds. She pushed out a breath in frustration. "I wish there were security cameras here. I don't know what it would do, but—"

"I wish there were different keys," Brianna said, suddenly frustrated.

"Keys?"

Brianna held up the brass set that opened their office doors. "These open all the doors on the hallway. Anyone could have come in here and taken this part of my exam. Anyone—"

"What?"

Brianna tilted her head. "You didn't know?"

Veronica shook her head. "My keys said *Do Not Duplicate.*"

"Yeah, because they open everything on this floor."

"Oh, God." Veronica stifled the urge to vomit. How many nights had she spent in this office, knowing Brianna was long asleep or sick somewhere, and so, in her privacy, she thought of Stella? Masturbated to Stella? Watched or consumed or done something questionable behind closed doors because she thought she had the privacy to do just that? Hell, she'd even told Stella to come by one day so she could fulfill a fantasy of fucking on a desk. They'd gone to Stella's place instead since Stella seemed to turn her nose up at the state of the grad student offices. At the time, the rejection had stung; now Veronica was relieved they'd not fucked in that office because apparently everything here was on display.

Not only was redemption a dream, but so was privacy, secrecy, and decency.

"I can't believe this." Veronica started to open her desk drawers. She dug through the contents and swallowed hard when she unturned the ipecac bottle. She shut the drawer without looking further.

"Is something missing?" Brianna asked.

"No. I don't know. I just...I still can't believe anyone could walk in here and take stuff. This is insane."

"Not anyone," Brianna said. "Only those with a key."

Veronica caught Brianna's gaze. After a split-second nod, they grabbed their keys and walked the two doors down to Jonathan's office. His name was still there. So was the other PhD student's name who shared it—Michael Kramer, the only other person from their cohort left—but it was still eerie.

"We should knock," Brianna said. "You know. Just for..."

"Sure."

So she did.

No one answered.

"No one but me has been here all week," Brianna said. "But still. I had to be sure."

She slipped her key in the lock. Veronica knew it would fit now, but it was still shocking as the door swung open. They stepped inside. Veronica was holding her breath. When Brianna hit the light, she was still holding it. She held it and held it. She had no idea what she was waiting for. The office was normal. Cramped. Shitty posters on the wall, the exact same kind of average paintings that were put in dentist offices, just like the ones that were in their office, too. Books lined the wall, most of which were the free textbooks publishers gave to anyone teaching in a university with hopes of getting the book added to a syllabus. There was a jar full of pens, a few snapshots of a family that had all dark features, which meant these images belonged to Michael, and there was a phone on a desk. Jonathan's desk. The phone was off its cradle, but there was no noise on the other side. It had been disconnected.

Veronica was suddenly bothered by this fact. She plugged in the phone. She held it to her ear. The dial tone came back, as did a flashing light. A message?

Brianna and Veronica look at each other again. Veronica stepped forward. She dialed into the inbox and allowed the message to play since there was no password necessary. There wasn't even an intro message to say whose inbox this was. But there was no mistaking the voice that came on the line next: It was Jonathan. Slightly nasally, slightly twanging from his Nova Scotia roots. He addressed himself, speaking a to-do list of sorts, and recorded for later.

"My phone is out of storage space, so this will have to do," he began. "All right, before tomorrow, be sure to read over comments, message Stella, maybe go get drinks. Buy a nice wine. Submit abstract. Is that it?

Oh, research the type of cyanide used in Jonestown. Apparently, there is more than one type! That's it? Oh, funding form extension. And appeals process. Stella says it's on a different part of the website but easy enough to find with skilled searches. Yep. I think that's it."

The message beeped off. Veronica wanted to listen to it over and over again. Brianna's face became pale; she seemed to want to delete the message with how sick it made her appear. She sat in the cushioned chair used for students while Veronica sat in Michael's desk chair. Jonathan's remained empty. The office layout was exactly the same as theirs but inverted. It felt so familiar, yet so strange.

"I guess that's it," Brianna said.

"What?"

"He did it. He was researching cyanide. He did it. He—"

When Brianna burst into tears again, Veronica was at her side. She cooed and comforted, until she couldn't believe in it herself anymore. The voice she'd heard on the machine was not the voice of someone who was going to die by their own hand. He wasn't sad or morose or out of hope—he was vindicated. Righteous. He was going through an appeals process, and if that was for plagiarism, he sounded like he was going to win. He was making to-do lists, even if his phone was out of storage space. He was going to do something big, huge—she could hear it in his voice.

But he was not here anymore. And it was incredibly hard to argue with that fact. Whatever had taken him had taken him. Jonathan was gone.

"I don't want to delete it," Brianna said. "But I don't think Mike should have to hear."

"I know," Veronica said. "What if we just switched the phones?"

It seemed like the best idea they'd ever come up with. They switched the office phones, so it was now them who had the last recorded words of Jonathan Morris. It was the only right thing to do, Veronica knew—yet it didn't seem like enough. Not nearly enough.

Suddenly, Veronica couldn't stand not knowing her colleagues. The names on the doors they'd passed by were unknown to her; they were other students from other years. She'd seen their faces before, but who was Carl? Andrea? What about Julie and Divya? She wanted to put faces to names, and then voices to names, and then put all of it together in her mind to keep forever. Then she thought about the handful of other people she'd tracked down on Facebook. She may know who they were now, but she'd been lurking that entire time, remaining invisible, as she became a sleuth. They didn't know who she was anymore—and why would they, when academia put them in one of the most barren hallways, in offices without windows, yet gave them keys that opened everything without telling them? If any one of these people, these names and faces, had been accused of something horrible, and then killed themselves over it, would she have cried just as hard?

She wouldn't have, no.

But she wanted to now. She wanted to feel part of something more than sorrow or dead voices on machines.

"We need to have a mourning ritual," Veronica said. The idea coalesced and presented itself like a beacon, the only point of hope in darkness. "For

Jonathan."

"You mean like writing? A writing ritual?"

"No, not morning like daylight, but mourning like grief."

"Oh." Brianna thought this over for a moment. "I suppose a mourning ritual, whatever it could be, would raise awareness for mental health on campus."

Veronica nodded but didn't understand why it couldn't just be a mourning ritual. Why couldn't it just be about grief? Why did their sadness need to become political?

Brianna was still talking. "Yes, this is a great idea. The issue is getting out of control. Have you seen that piece in *The Chronicle of Higher Education*?"

Veronica shook her head.

"You should read it. Jonathan is not the only one to commit suicide during a PhD. This is an epidemic."

Soon enough, Brianna was on her computer and Googling all the stats about mental health, specifically mental health in their city. It didn't take her long to find three names of undergrads who had died by suicide on campus that year alone, though one was a suspicious death from over-drinking during St. Patrick's Day. It didn't matter anymore; to Brianna, it was another name in an epidemic, another way to take something that was deeply personal and make it systemic. She opened a Google Doc and wrote a list of names with Jonathan's at the top, a sort of annotated obituary of fallen students as if they were soldiers in a war on mental health. Everything came together quite quickly. Brianna forwarded the list of names to the head of the English Department—cotton candy—and the dean of Graduate Studies, along with a suggested meeting time for a candlelight vigil, and *The Chronicle of Higher Education* article for good measure.

Veronica watched her work silently, not adding much herself but her own ghostly presence. "Is that it?" Veronica asked after an hour. "Do we just wait now and twiddle our thumbs?"

Brianna shrugged. "Kind of the point of the bureaucracy."

"We should just do it now." Veronica's heart fluttered with the memory of those primary-coloured signs she'd passed on the way here. "Did you see the protest? We should do that."

Brianna narrowed her gaze. "Do you know what that was for?"

Veronica shook her head. "It doesn't matter. I like the energy. We shouldn't be waiting around. We should be doing something. I'm so sick of doing nothing. I…I just want to say goodbye to Jonathan."

"I get that. I really do. But you don't want to be Melanie Knight."

Veronica blinked. There were so many names, so many names in the past hour alone. Yet this one was utterly unfamiliar, even more than the unknowns on the doors. "Who?"

"Melanie Knight," Brianna repeated. When it was clear that Veronica was truly clueless, Brianna explained. The protest at the university up the street was about a grad student (Melanie Knight) who had taught something controversial in one of her classes, so she'd had a meeting with her department, where they'd bullied her into changing her position. When she refused to do that, claiming she'd merely wanted to facilitate discussion, she was sent to another meeting higher up the academic food chain. They heard her plight for free speech but still claimed she was making the classroom unsafe by using incendiary material to prove her point. They demanded she apologize, change her syllabus, redo the class, or lose her job.

"And so on and so forth," Brianna said. "She continued to refuse, so they stripped her of her teaching privileges. She'd already recorded one of her meetings, however, and when no one seemed to want to help her at the school and it looked like her academic career was at risk, she released it to the media."

"Wow."

"I know."

Veronica and Brianna were quiet. It was hard to tell who was on what side in this debate. Were the protests for Melanie's right? The school's right? The incendiary material? Free speech? It was hard to say. Veronica was suddenly so desperate for Stella's opinion because she'd know it'd be the right one. Brianna seemed quiet, too. Veronica realized she was looking at the phone and the recorded message of Jonathan. She stared so long and hard she saw blond hairs tangled inside the telephone keys from past uses; the phone was so old and contained so many different people's histories—yet Jonathan's had been stopped before it had even gotten started. He would never get a degree, let alone a protest in his name.

Or had his body been his final protest? Veronica swallowed. If the options, when forced into a corner like that, were either capitulate or die, capitulate or protest, Veronica wasn't sure what she'd choose.

Brianna seemed unsure, too.

"He was a good person," Veronica said instead. "I don't think he did anything wrong."

"I know. Me too." Brianna bit her lip. Her finger.

"So why are we scared?"

Veronica couldn't answer. Brianna's computer made a noise, and they both jumped. The sound had been an email alert. The dean and graduate department both wrote back at the same time. They liked the plan. It was good. The school knew, deep down, that they'd have to capitulate, too.

Everyone, really, should have been happy with this arrangement. An announcement was put out by the dean that listed the school's counselling services and the other measures available to students if they were feeling "overstressed." The vigil, the dean suggested, was better to keep as a private affair, so only the English Department was emailed. It would be a service and ceremony for Jonathan Morris alone.

"What about the others?" Veronica asked. "We don't even have a body for Jonathan."

"So we create it from other bodies," Brianna said. She cited Michel de Certeau's *Walking in the City* where the city itself is made through objects that the city produces. Jonathan's body would be made from the voices of those inside his death, the ones still surviving, and walking with his ghost.

Veronica knew it still wasn't enough. But it was all they had, so she believed it was the right choice. An hour later, when she realized she was too tired to keep going, she took the bus home. The protesters outside the school had dispersed. Only a single sign remained staked into the soft grass that said, "No apologies for free speech."

Chapter Three

The night of the mourning ritual, Veronica believed she was strong enough in her convictions to show Stella the Facebook posting about the cause. Over a glass of wine, Stella looked over the event with a keen gaze, her face fixated like a Gorgon. "I don't understand," she said after several long seconds. "What exactly are you raising awareness for?"

"Mental health in academia."

"And what does raising awareness do?"

Veronica's face felt hot, her skin tight. Her words fell out of her mouth like Babel. She stuttered with "it" for a while, before moving on to other conjunctions, each one like a broken limb. Everything about de Certeau was gone, eroded from memory. Brianna's talk about system power structures now seemed feeble, along with the issues concerning Melanie Knight. Even though Veronica had understood that controversy and was sure she was coming down on the side of the students—not just the grad students whose careers hung on stuff like this, but the students who were affected in her class—it didn't seem to matter. Who really cared about something as fussy as classroom politique? Veronica suddenly felt silly for even thinking in sides, in rights and wrongs, true or false. There was only ever what was in front of you to grade, to measure, to weigh. And this pithy Facebook message, no better than It Gets Better, was all that was there.

And that was nothing. All theory was now gone. Melanie Knight was a Jane Doe. So was Jonathan, for that matter. He was just a ghost.

Stella stopped Veronica's babble with a careful hand on her shoulder. It felt like a bruise and a caress at the same time.

"Most people are aware of mental illness in academia. They just don't talk about it."

"Then I suppose I want people to talk about it. Jonathan is dead. Other people have died. I know it. I..." Veronica grasped for her notion of the dead time and how the dead time now literally contained ghosts and how the university itself felt haunted, but she was silent. She thought of Stella's words: *You look like hell.* She felt like hell, and not some fancy Dante Alighieri Hell, but the hell that was sleep paralysis and bad breath. She didn't want to speak of her dreams of Jonathan she was having now in regular intervals or that failed coffee date, either, for fear that Stella would tear apart Freud's role in shitty dream interpretation.

The silence between them was heavy, like stones, before Stella finally spoke.

"Well, that is interesting. I suppose I see the merits here. We live in an age of confession. Of emotional capital and emotional exploitation under that capital. Confessions are wounds, and wounds are currency. So I'm sure you'll get people to attend."

Veronica knew this was Stella's most polite way of supporting her while also declining. If other people were surely going to attend, then Stella need not be present. She was not being cruel in her silence or even her own disregard of mental illness. She understood, she knew and had felt the waves of mental illness in the academy, if only from Veronica's own strange habits around food and sudden disappearances into her studies. After all, Stella reminded her over and over that you couldn't be a professor this long and not come across a student with some type of mental illness. Veronica knew this—not only from the small but distinct vantage point of having her own class and seeing her own students fall apart at the seams—but from the intimate spaces she'd shared with Stella. She'd seen her fold over accessibility studies letters, then heard Stella speak of the diagnoses in a hushed tone. It was not that Stella was ignorant, no; it was just that Stella preferred not to comment on it, like she preferred not to comment on gender studies or post-colonial studies in her own academic work. She was Bartleby on this, and many other fronts, simply preferring not to.

It should not have hurt as much as it did, but that was the truth. Stella was not coming. Even if Jonathan had been her student, she'd had students like this before. Students dying, students attrition-ing, students failing and failing. There was only so much she could do. *Boundaries my dear,* Stella had said during one of their first meetings. *Boundaries will always keep you safe. Know when to erect them and when to tear them down, and you will always, always be in control.*

Veronica had never felt so un-boundaried in her life. So uncontrolled, unwieldy. She'd thought feeling her emotions—especially her sadness and confusion over Jonathan—would make her feel better. Allow her to be freer, to be in her own skin. But no. It was just un-boundaried. Something had once been there, blocking her from painful experiences in the academy, and now it had been ripped away. She was sure, though, that if she went to this event, she could put all the pieces back together.

Maybe.

When Stella hugged her goodbye, Veronica fell apart at the seams herself. She couldn't put the pieces back together. They were too bruised, too ruptured, and like her favourite pair of jeans, they simply wouldn't fit anymore.

"Stella…" Veronica said, her voice weak.

"It's okay," Stella said. "I will have dinner for you when you get back. If you want dinner, that is. I know you and Brianna might have plans."

Veronica didn't know how to answer. "Maybe. I...I don't know yet."

"When you do, you'll let me know."

Veronica nodded. She wasn't sure if that was an invitation anymore, or if something had been retracted now. She swallowed. What did it matter? She grabbed all the parts of herself she could manage and walked out the door and into the city centre.

❧ ❧ ❧ ❧

Dozens of people were already there when Veronica arrived. They held candles for Jonathan. Some were shaky; wax mixed with puddles from a late afternoon rain. Brianna had the mic for most of the night, acting as the unofficial emcee. She listed the names of those who could not speak for themselves, lingering on Jonathan Casey Morris, then reading a poem from Adrienne Rich before she handed off the mic to others. Everyone formed a circle to stay warm and to mimic the AA structure without conscious awareness. Veronica could only think of Stella's words about confession; they passed around the mic like a collection plate and added their wounds. People spoke about lost loved ones, their own struggles with mental health and addiction. They spoke about everything and nothing at all. All the stories were the same yet brand new. Veronica felt Stella's hand on her shoulder like a shadow, a bruise that would never heal if she kept poking at it.

When the mic got to her, she felt at a loss. The entire time she'd been rehashing her own story in bits and pieces. Her own mental illness was vomit she induced, food she chased, and the depression dreams that would not relent. But what did that matter here? It was the ending—or boring middle—of a story. She could peel back to the beginning, the origin where it had started in a cascade of piano keys and wandering hands, but again, what was the point? She wanted to quote William Faulkner's words on the past never being past, but instead she fumbled with the mic.

"Jonathan was my friend," she said. It felt so trivial. "A good friend." She sighed. She'd somehow made it worse with redundancy. "I will miss him very much."

She passed the microphone. People clapped as if her words were worthy. Were they? She didn't think so. She didn't even say her own story. Her courage had been an illusion.

In a blink, the night was over. Brianna invited her for coffee, but she declined. Coffee made her feel like a painting and reminded her of Jonathan. "I think I just want to go home."

When she arrived at her apartment, she realized

she'd eaten nothing all day. It was not deliberate. It was an accident. But in spite of herself, in spite of all she'd just heard from others, she smiled in satisfaction. Her hunger was her only triumph of the day, the only facet that she knew definitively she'd done good. Right. Well.

Her hunger reminded her of teaching students. Especially on the first day of classes, the room would be so quiet and still. Thirty pairs of student eyes would be so needy as they looked at her. They were all there for her. She was in complete control. And if she filled this silence with her voice, she had been a good teacher. She imparted all her knowledge. She would be empty at the end of two hours, with nothing left to say, but her students would know something. And she would also remain hungry, as a way to extend that feeling. By avoiding food, only sipping on coffee or water, she'd fill herself back up with knowledge. She'd read book after book after book, allowing the letters to break off and fill her as if it were a feast.

Then she'd wake in the middle of the night, ravenous, and spread out peanut butter on crackers and dates and bananas, open boxes and boxes of cereal, wash it all down with a pint of soda, a never-ending conga line of food. She'd fall asleep with a half-eaten bowl of popcorn on her bedside table. She'd munch her way through half a pack of bread, the rest of it going stale because she'd forget to put on the twist tie again. She'd wake with all her cupboards open and empty like she had once felt.

Then she'd teach again, try again.

The cycle would repeat, endlessly. Coffee and water and talking, knowledge as food, food for thought, then the bingeing of ravenous fury. Knocking back carbs like pain and memories. A hunger that could only be put off, put off, put off like a meeting, but never fully abated, a hunger that was never ever satisfied because there would always be one more thing to do, to eat, to learn.

Veronica moved to her cupboards and opened them. It felt like a wing of a flapping bird, terrified and afraid. She found a can of soup. She brightened at the thought of a comfort meal, then shut the cupboard just as fast. She closed her eyes and remembered every item of food she'd stuffed into her face the night before. She didn't want to start that cycle again. *Persephone ate in the underworld, and it was what trapped her there,* Veronica remembered. *I cannot eat anything else here, not in the dead time.*

Veronica grabbed her keys and found an Uber to take to Stella's place. It was not the underworld, so it was the only place where she could avoid the endless cycles of hunger and satiation, of bloat and rot and bones.

Stella answered in her robe. She was drinking wine. The entire scene was familiar and, for a while, made Veronica go back in time. Jonathan was still alive—in her mind—the last time this happened. She wanted to let it happen again.

"How was the vigil?" she asked but already seemed to know the answer. Stella always knew the answer.

"It was fine."

They kissed. The robe fell down and away. Veronica licked and touched and tasted Stella on her knees, making her come once, before she decided she wanted to eat food. Real food.

Stella's cheeks were tinged pink as she led her

into the kitchen. Her robe was tied again but loosely. Her dinner leftovers were already wrapped and put on her favourite blue plate. Stella explained that, with the conference tomorrow, she didn't want to cook, so she ordered out. The portions at a family-owned Italian place around the corner were always too big. The osso buco alla milanese still seemed untouched, straight from the order. Only the trails of sauce on the edge of the plate showed that Stella had also eaten this food.

"Is it okay?"

"Yes, yes," Veronica said. In spite of the gnawing hunger, she picked at the meal. Everything tasted so sweet yet so salty. Stella sat at her laptop computer, across from Veronica at her table. She had her glasses on her nose, meaning that she was working on her paper. Veronica's stomach sank. The conference. It was this weekend. Over ten hours away by car.

"We're still going together, right?" Veronica asked.

Stella looked up from her reading glasses. She smiled. "Of course."

The last day of April was tomorrow, which meant that it was the last day of dead time, too. She and Stella would drive out of the country, be in another location, another time period, another life. Veronica rested easy knowing that they would be giving birth to academia's new life on the road and leave the shells of its destruction behind. Conference season meant spring was coming. It meant the darkness would relent.

And so, she finally allowed herself to take a bite.

Chapter Four

Stella drove. There was no insistence, only an obvious delegation of roles. Come morning, Stella rose at six to rent the car, and Veronica tagged along with crust still visible at the corner of her eyes. The bright lights and kelly greens of the Enterprise rental made her feel queasy. When Veronica swayed at the front desk, Stella reached into her purse and produced a muffin. Veronica smelled the cinnamon and sugar and knew it was the kind Stella often made during her bouts of insomnia, a recipe she claimed she found out of Dickinson's journals.

"No thanks," Veronica said, realizing she still felt half-asleep.

Stella held it out again, unmoving, until finally Veronica took it. She nibbled the edges as Stella spoke in a lucid tone to the rental agent. To her surprise, Stella put Veronica's name down as a second driver. She would not drive it, not likely, but it was a nice touch. On paper, they were equal.

"Good luck and enjoy your trip, ladies," the rental agent said from the window. Stella barely acknowledged the greeting and pushed the automatic button to block him out. She withdrew sunglasses from her jacket's front pocket and put them on over her nose. "Buckle up," she whispered to Veronica.

Veronica did as she was told, though her fingers felt like butter. The muffin made her stomach feel like a concrete slab. She still had two bites left and hoped Stella wouldn't notice her hiding it under the seat. If she did, she said nothing. They packed in silence and continued to drive in mute until they reached the highway, and then crossed the border without fuss or fanfare. It was only when they got on the road and the yellow lines of the American highway—so similar yet so magical—blurred together that Veronica felt as if she wasn't spinning in place.

Stella fussed with the visors on the car, blocking out the sunlight as she turned, and it hit her vision from a new angle. Though it was clearly frustrating, Veronica was also bemused. The sunlight, after weeks of nothing but rain, made it seem as if Stella's hair was gold threaded with silver.

"Feeling better?" Stella asked when she noticed Veronica staring.

"Much."

"Good. I think that's the first time I've seen you smile since mid-April."

Veronica wanted to turn away, embarrassed at her obvious emotions, but Stella put a hand on her knee. "I haven't had anything to smile about."

"Until now."

"Until now," Veronica confirmed.

Stella squeezed Veronica's knee before continuing. "You know why I got an SUV?"

Veronica shook her head. The night before, Stella had murmured something about wanting a rental so her Prius didn't have to take the trip, but that seemed like a reasonable, rational excuse, and not the romantic one that Stella's voice indicated now. Nothing but a façade, a disguise on Stella's true motives. Veronica sat up straighter in the car, desperate to witness a rare moment when Stella's personality came out through actual articulation, not a miasma of ambient intimacy they shared through proximate space.

"I'm up high in an SUV," Stella said, gesturing around her. "I can see everyone on the road. Into their cars, into their messy backseats, and I know what type of driver they are, while they know nothing about me."

Veronica waited for more. Surely, there was a poem she was going to reference, a Rilke line about observation and the witnessing of a new life. When there was nothing, just Stella on high, Veronica smiled. "You know, that reminds me of when I was a kid. I used to walk around my neighbourhood at night. I looked into people's windows. I wanted to see what they had on TV, if they had a TV. What was on their bookshelf, where they ate dinner. I never looked into bedrooms, though, of course."

"Of course." If not for the sunglasses, Veronica was sure Stella had winked. "But even if you were caught, no one would suspect anything of you—of me, either, for that matter. We are so small that people assume we can't harm. Women don't look into windows, become Peeping Toms, most people think. But sometimes, they do peep, but for other reasons. You have your windows. I have my SUV—if only for a weekend."

"It's nice," Veronica said. "Sometimes, I felt like I knew them."

"It's not about knowing. It's about seeing."

"What's the difference? Isn't seeing believing?"

"That's a cliché. You should know better."

"Right."

Veronica swallowed and nodded. She did not

add anything. She may have thought she and Stella were talking about the same act of witnessing, but it was clear now their intentions were different. One was about desire, closeness, intimacy, while the other was about power. Wasn't that always the case? Veronica sighed. She thought of that first-year lecture with paintings where that one prof spoke about John Berger's *Ways of Seeing*. What was that line? Men do the looking; women watch themselves being looked at? Something like that? The professor had thought it was garbage. She had thrown up O'Keeffe's work as a rebuttal. Clearly, O'Keeffe was doing the same act of art, the same act of seeing, and coming up with beauty. She was more than just a witness; she was a creator.

At the time, Veronica had thought the professor correct. Now, years later and with Stella in between her, she wasn't so sure she understood anything anymore.

When Veronica had gone searching into houses as a teenager, she'd wanted to see if she could find women together. Did women get married, share space? If she had been taller, if she'd had her own SUV, she would have looked into bedrooms and backseats just to see if what those women did together was what she had already done with her best friend. Was there more sub rosa knowledge she could glean from their desire, then mimic later on? Had she been a painter, she would have painted her imagination, but without seeing it first, how could she even imagine two legs, two sets of breasts, and two lips together? She had to go looking. She had to go exploring.

But in doing so and in learning from that space, she would also feel powerful. Surely. She'd gone walking, and peeping, for power. Veronica was also small, even smaller than Stella's five-foot-five height, and wanted to indulge in Stella's sense of extended power through the car and the space it took up on the road.

So maybe, Veronica reasoned, both were correct. You could look at something as the witness, as the subject, as the object, and something else altogether.

"What did you find when you looked?"

"What?"

"When you looked in houses," Stella said. "What did you find?"

"A lot of families," Veronica answered. After a moment, she added, "Most people didn't seem happy."

"Most people aren't. But it's good you looked and found out for yourself."

Veronica wondered what Stella's response would have been if she'd been caught under the gaze of a stranger. If Stella knew she was being watched, would her smile now be the same smile then? Veronica remembered the door to Stella's university office. She conjured the door's slow eclipse of space, moving from open to closed, acting as an invitation inside and then to a desirous privacy they could share together.

Veronica and Stella's relationship was never solely about academics, but it was easier at first to pretend that it was. Veronica had hovered around Stella's door during office hours out of intellectual curiosity. Her obsessive note-keeping during her lectures was done as a scholar, not a hopeful lover or even potential daydreamer. Veronica wanted Stella so much it kept her up at night, spilling herself over books and trying to consume all the knowledge of the world to impress her, but with the backup story that all this effort was done so Veronica could be a better academic at heart, so she could go to graduate school, get a PhD, and become a doctor. Stella was a mirror, a role model, not anything more, and Veronica's obsession was only because there were simply so few female scholars on which to base her own career aspirations. Even when Stella seemed to show just as much desire and energy for Veronica during these office hours discussions, Veronica was sure it was Stella trying to do her very best pedagogy, maybe reap the benefits of a staff award, perform her necessary service hours. Deep down, however, Veronica was sure Stella wanted her so much because when they were together it was like the song of a theremin. They created something beautiful without touching, without sense of timing or rhythm, but by sheer proximity. Academic or not, sexual or not, they had to keep meeting because good things could occur.

Veronica fell into the memories of those good things. She thought back seven years to her undergrad and her first meeting of Stella—then Professor Flanders—in Introductory Studies in American Fiction. The class read Steinbeck and Melville and Hemingway. On the lecture stage every Tuesday afternoon, Stella summarized the plots and spoke about these men with a sense of staid acceptance; these were the authors who built the foundations, yes, yes, yes, even if it meant leaving some women behind.

"But there are always hidden figures," Professor Flanders said. This was a time well before the nonfiction book and movie of the same name. "There are always hidden bricks in the wall of that foundation. Their backs bear the most weight, and they are the most silenced."

Mary Rowlandson was one author she'd come to

that term, followed by Eudora Welty, Louise Erdrich, and Kate Chopin among others, but it was Emily Dickinson who made Stella's eyes light up the most. Veronica had never paid attention to Dickinson before. She seemed strange and odd, another madwoman in the attic, a boring stereotype from another time, and poems that were creepy rather than inspiring. After Veronica had taken Stella's literary theory class and another class on American history Stella co-taught with someone else, it was finally time for Veronica to enroll in a reading course she was doing that was Dickinson and all Dickinson and taught by none other than Stella Flanders.

The class turned out to be her and two other students, alone in a room with Stella for her entire fourth year of university. All other classes took a backseat as Veronica was fully swept up into the aura of Stella Flanders. With so much attention fixated on Veronica's scholarship, she rose to the occasion. She impressed Stella so much with her attention to detail that graduate school was obvious. She allowed Veronica to stay after their reading course session was over so they could prep her application together. A future plan of study was needed and so was a five-year plan, along with applications for grants with names that were simply a string of letters like OGS and SSHRC. Suddenly, the remaining years of Veronica's twenties were filled. And Veronica couldn't have been happier.

"You will apply elsewhere, of course," Stella said during one afternoon session.

"But…shouldn't I have you as my supervisor?"

"Perhaps. There are lots of Emily Dickinson scholars out there. An entire conference is devoted to her every year in Amherst."

Veronica didn't want a roomful of people who knew what she knew, though. She wanted to know what Stella knew. She said as much, couched in the language of academia, until Stella eventually nodded. "You should apply elsewhere for your MA then. It looks poor if you do all your degrees at the same school. If you wish to study with me for your PhD, then elsewhere for the MA is imperative. You will need to get a job after all of this, and this is simply the best way to ensure your future. One of many options, at least...but I will be here should you wish to return."

The slight hesitation in her words became all Veronica needed. She applied to a different school, did a course-based MA, met another woman with whom she briefly fell in love but never acted on it. She found other women at clubs and had one-night stands, imagining their faces as Stella's when those unions occurred. There had never been so much as a touch between her and Stella at this point, but Veronica knew. Coming back to the school, after proving herself in the academic world, would matter. She had to be a scholar, then a lover. This could happen.

It was slow, but she was right. She was always right when she did her homework.

After a year of course work, when supervisors were declared, Veronica had a reason to haunt the hallways around Stella's office. Their meetings stacked up like fortune cookies. They went longer. The crack of the door became smaller and smaller. When it was shut for a month, the distance between their bodies became smaller and smaller. Finally, Stella invited Veronica to her house. No mention of work contained in the invitation. Just a house visit, a chance to catch up over wine. Halfway through their conversation on Dickinson, of course, Stella put her hand over Veronica's.

Then it was easy. Then everything made sense. All the shades had been drawn; there was no one peering in. They were safe together and so could be together.

Stella's house became as familiar as the lines of poetry; the dashes in Dickinson's work were like the wooden floors, stiff and creaking come morning. Talk of The Master just like the smell of almonds that permeated Stella's work room, the coconut body lotion, magnolias on the windowsill, paintings framed in the upstairs hallway. Persistent, present, up for interpretation. Coffee and marmalade in the morning, followed by muffins Stella always baked from a recipe rumoured to be from Dickinson's old journals, permeated the expansive house, only to become blotted out by the bitter taste of ipecac that brought it all up again.

At first, Veronica said she'd never throw up in Stella's place. The walls were too lined with art to sully with bulimia, the books too ancient and beautiful to mar with the persistent need to throw up.

But it happened. It always happened.

Some weeks, some months, some days were better or worse than others, but Veronica eventually learned to live with the inconsistencies of her desired self and her actual self. Her imagined bony body and the body that Stella grasped in the night. Veronica got what she wanted—Stella—and she was still doing a PhD, but sometimes, it felt like she was eating words and bringing them all up because she wasn't smart enough to be here. Then she was bringing up the words because she had too much to say, her genius caught in her throat like Dickinson's was in that room, like Sylvia Plath with Ted Hughes. Then sometimes, Veronica threw up because there was nothing left to do at all because the haunting lines Dickinson said about death led her to this inevitable space over a toilet bowl.

Veronica knew if she quit one activity, she'd have to quit the other. PhD and Stella, both or none at all. So she made sense of herself as a fragmented being, just as jumbled as Dickinson's lines and the burned last entries of Plath's journal.

Veronica used to think of this as a lament. Dickinson and Plath, along with dozens of other women, were kept out of the spotlight and not given their deserved recognition until after their deaths. But now she wondered what the act of witnessing truly got you. Power or desire, subject or object? She shuddered as Jonathan's face interrupted her thoughts. What would Jonathan's room look like if she had peered inside moments before the writing of his note and the last gasps of his lungs? She hated to think of this, yet all she could do was think as the SUV moved along on the highway. Would she have used her power to stop his actions or been too consumed by a curious desire to watch his own exit? She didn't know. She wanted to ask Stella, but Veronica was mute.

"There's also the scenery!"

"Hmm?" Veronica said.

"The hills." Stella gestured to the green patches of the American landscape outside. "It looks the same, but it can't be."

"Like an Emily Carr painting."

"Precisely," Stella said. "The Canadian Group

of Seven painters were obsessed with landscape, but it could never be this land. No, there are no great landscape painters to capture this. Only the Transcendentalists and their poetry. I like that more. It allows me to see it all for myself and to sit above it like an omniscient narrator."

"Like God?"

"Sure."

When their conversation quieted once again, Stella put on the radio. Veronica was relieved to not be alone with her thoughts, memories, or speculations anymore. Traffic reports fizzled, so she switched to NPR. When even that crackled out, Stella went to classical music. The crescendos were familiar to Veronica: Bach, Haydn, Chopin, Mozart. She thought of her piano teacher and then pushed the memory aside, like the curtains closing on a former house she stared too long into. She made her fingers quiet; she squeezed Stella's hand over the emergency brake. She returned her palm to Stella's thigh as her hunger returned to normal and insisted they grab coffee and lunch at a diner.

"A Kerouac place," Stella said. "I'm not a fan, but I appreciate the Americana. Pie and ice cream—a must."

An hour and a half later, Veronica swallowed down the sweetness of dessert after a deli sandwich. She shifted in vinyl seats as they creaked. Her skin felt too tight. She'd eaten too much food the night before. And this morning. She'd forgotten about the muffin. The thought sat like a heavy weight, a chorus of *too much, too much, too much, you must*. She tried to focus on the food now, but the pie faded to memories she didn't want to think about. Despite the voice in her head telling her to stop, she continued to eat.

"You ready to go?" Stella asked. A crust of her pie remained. Veronica had to fight the urge to ask if she could eat it, too.

"Almost. Just give me a second."

Veronica gestured toward the bathroom. Before she reached the doorway, she knew she was going to throw up. The action was easy enough to do; her fingers remembered the tickling of a uvula as much as they remembered the warm-up scales for the piano. She retched. Her body slid over the toilet, her long limbs poised like some inversion of Rodin's *The Thinker*. Her nostrils burned. She did it again. Her eyes watered. Again. But she was empty. Done.

Her face seemed too red, too pink with shame when she checked herself in the mirror. She saw her face as an outsider must see it—and panicking, she checked each bathroom stall to be sure she'd been alone. *Who would notice; who would see?*

No one was around. Another customer came in but said nothing to her, barely meeting her gaze before disappearing into the same stall that Veronica had emptied all of herself into. She found gum from her purse. She snapped the mint between her teeth like some twelve-year-old girl as they got back on the road.

If Stella noticed anything amiss, she said nothing. She became consumed with scenery all over again. She spoke over the classical songs on the radio, repeating parts of her talk she wasn't quite sure about yet. She didn't quite ask for Veronica's opinion—Stella never asked for anyone's opinion—but Veronica listened as an audience member would, commenting on parts she found interesting and asking for more clarification on others without critiquing the language used. When Stella was quiet, it took Veronica a few moments to realize she was waiting for her to contribute. Not banal praise for her work, but her own academic interests. Veronica's paper was on Emily Dickinson's arms—a strange topic, Stella had said, but one she was sure she could pull off if given the chance. Now Stella was giving her the chance. She may have read the abstract, but she now wanted to hear more.

Veronica's mouth was dry. An abstract was so different from the real words on the page and definitely less intimidating than Stella's waiting silence. "Emily Dickinson's wandering arms," Stella eventually said. "Tell me about them."

"Oh. Um." Veronica coughed. She swallowed her gum. And her stomach roiled again. "Do you know the Grimm story of *The Wilful Child*?"

Stella smiled but shook her head. "I know *Hansel and Gretel*. The poisoned woods and enchanted house. But what is *The Wilful Child*?"

Veronica told her the story, parroting the version she'd gathered from Sara Ahmed, the person who got Veronica thinking about the way arms could symbolize far more than she thought possible. "In the Jacob and Wilhelm Grimm story, a girl child is too wilful and disobeys her parents, so she is punished over and over again until she dies. After death, her arm reaches out from the grave, refusing to go under, so the child remains wilful even in death."

"Interesting. Sort of like 'spare the rod and spoil the child,' is it not?"

"Exactly. Philosopher Sara Ahmed links the story to a kind of poisonous pedagogy parents—and some teachers—impart on their children."

"And how does this relate to Dickinson?"

"I think Dickinson's will trapped her in her room, but it also saved her." Veronica went over the bits and pieces she had stitched together to form her abstract and the bullet points she had set aside in her computer much earlier in the year. It was all a skeleton, still waiting to form into a full and complete paper. Anytime the stress of the conference bubbled up inside of Veronica, she calmed herself by insisting that she had time to write. She wasn't presenting until the second day, and there was always so much downtime at these conferences, a different type of dead time to fill in with work she could do.

But now it was May, not April, and she had suddenly wasted all she'd been given. She felt like she'd left something behind, and in spite of moving forward, now had to go backward. Her words became doubled in her head; she thought of ways to articulate her thesis statement and then revised it before it came out of her mouth. Stella was silent. The roar of the classical music was too much, and she turned it down. Too many threads converged in her mind. She was hungry again, despite having just eaten. She hated the way food twisted and doubled inside of her, too.

"It's sort of like...No, it's more like..."

Stella opened her mouth to speak but gasped. She swerved the car to avoid hitting something but only succeeded in hitting something else. A thwack echoed from the front of the SUV and continued to rattle around underneath it. The sounds were like something soft, muffled below, yet somehow hard and ricocheting between the metal and plastic of the car parts. In spite of being so high up, Veronica saw nothing from their position. She froze. She did nothing but felt the centrifugal force of the car as it swerved.

Stella swerved once again to bring the car to a full stop. They'd long since left the highway; they were only forty minutes away from Amherst, according to the car's GPS. The sun was still out, but the early spring chill seemed that much colder now. No other cars were around. The music played at a low din overtop of the dinging of the car's safety system.

"What did we hit?" Veronica asked.

Stella opened her mouth and closed it again. She composed herself through rigid motions as she parked the car on the shoulder. She put on the four-ways, shut down all the noise. When she stepped out, Veronica soon followed.

Torn fabric and garbled pieces of paper scattered across the road. The paper soon disappeared when the wind came up. Veronica examined the fabric—something torn from a shirt that had seen better days, perhaps—but she saw no blood. Another piece of fabric seemed to be the strap of a backpack. She thought of a hitchhiker, of a man standing around and waiting for someone to pick him up. Another conference-goer? She shuddered.

Stella was staring at the ditch close to the car. She was frozen, her face etched as marble. Veronica stepped closer, each gravel stone cracking under her weight as she did. She became ebullient with chatter as Stella seemed colder and colder.

"What's wrong? Did you find something? What's going on?"

"Call the police," Stella said. "There's a body here."

Chapter Five

The man had been dead a long time. His skin had been blackened by prolonged exposure to the sun and general decomposition. Veronica had been so convinced he was a black man until the paramedics arrived and turned him over. His shirt had risen up, exposing skin that was lighter in colour and not marred by anything other than decay. He was a white man, probably in his late forties, but identity was so hard to tell after death, especially without a wallet or piece of ID on his body.

"How long has he been there?" Veronica asked.

"Don't know. The body isn't a clock," the paramedic said. He was a boy, no more than twenty-one years old. His hair looked like it was cut by his mother in a kitchen. After some pressing, he and the other paramedic (an older man, greying hair and hands that shook a bit), eventually conceded that the man could have been there a few days at most, a few hours at least. His stomach had already swelled and descended, as if his organs were cooking in a poisonous soup. And skin didn't become that black without some hours passing uninterrupted. Whether he was sitting on the road or his backpack had been there and that had been what Stella hit, no one was sure.

But Stella had not killed him. That was the most important thing. When Veronica finally braved examining the car itself, there was no damage to the fender. When Stella tested the engine, it still turned on, and the paramedics, and then the police who showed up an hour later, said the car was still working and safe to drive. What they had hit had been soft, but it wasn't the man. If it had been, he would have exploded on impact, Veronica was sure.

The whole thing was grotesque. Abject. She thought of Julia Kristeva and Emmanuel Levinas and their thoughts on decaying matter and corpses. She thought of all the ways in which to turn this experience into something academic, something to report on, but it never made it past her lips. Veronica held her citations behind her teeth as Stella spoke with police officers. They exchanged information quickly and efficiently, and Stella barely looked up to meet the officers' gaze and their six-foot-plus statures. This was the smallest Veronica had ever seen Stella, the most under the spell of someone else's words. She was taking orders, not giving them. Even if she was not at fault and the man had been dead a long time, Stella exuded guilt and shame—the guilt and shame of a small child, her arm bent and reaching back out of the grave, begging to be seen.

"Is that it, officer?" Veronica took a stance by Stella's side, checking her watch dramatically. Time slipped by, yet moved so slowly. "We need to go."

"For now, it is." He finished his interview with a collection of personal and car information, then handed them back their passports and IDs. Veronica put a hand on the small of Stella's back and guided her back to the car.

"You drive," Stella said, quick and clipped.

Veronica obliged.

It was dark by the time they arrived at the hotel. The parking lot was filled with a dozen other rental cars, making it difficult to find a spot that would fit the wide berth of the SUV. It suddenly seemed like a foolish purchase, an indulgence that they should not have allowed, but Veronica kept the worries to herself. The front foyer of the hotel buzzed with chatter. There was a desk to their right filled with nametags and drink tickets, and a line of people stepped off the elevator in a flurry of greys and blacks and professional browns. A conference in full swing. Veronica reached out for Stella's hand, shuffling their suitcases to her other side.

Stella pulled away. She took her bag from Veronica and walked to the front desk by herself. Veronica, stunned for several seconds, had to hurry in behind. She tried to push away Stella's coldness as fear, as having just seen a dead body and dealt with the police, but that was unfair. Veronica had witnessed the grotesque objects, too. They should be bonding, sharing. Not treating each other like strangers, still running and trying to avoid danger.

"Hello. Yes." Stella spoke to the front desk clerk in a clipped fashion. "I'm checking in. Stella Flanders. Thank you."

The desk clerk had long dark hair and bangs. Her bone structure was delicate, yet austere; a pointed nose with a flat forehead seemed contrasted against fuller lips and cheeks. Her Asian features drew Veronica's attention to her eyes, which remained bright and cheery despite Stella's tone. She typed in Stella's information on a computer and brightened even further with a smile.

"Ah, yes. Welcome, Ms. Flanders."

"Dr. Flanders, please."

"Yes, Dr. Flanders. I have you with a queen-size bed on the seventh floor. Will you need one or two key cards?"

"One is enough."

Veronica startled. She turned to Stella, her eyes asking a silent but persistent question. *What about me?* Stella finished checking in and headed to the elevator. The attendant smiled at Veronica, but she did not return the gesture. Veronica darted after Stella instead.

"What about...?"

Stella turned to her, stopping her question before it was complete. "This is a conference."

"Yes."

"We are academics. We cannot be what we are at my home here."

"What?"

"You are my student. Not anything more here. I can't explain beyond that. I shouldn't have to."

The elevator pinged. Stella walked inside. She pressed the close door button without waiting, without eye contact or a goodbye. Veronica's red face returned. She wanted to sob. All the emotions she'd been keeping at bay, putting on a back burner to focus on Stella, came rushing forward. She thought of the man at the side of the road, bloated beyond recognition, of Jonathan at his desk and oxygen starved, and all the ghosts lingering in her office. She was just a student. She was always going to be just a student, trapped in a dead-end hallway during a dead time, with no hopes of becoming anything more.

"Miss? Are you going to check in?"

Veronica turned to see the hotel worker. She

stood almost a foot taller than Veronica; she had to crane her neck to meet her gaze, and as she did, she noticed spots on the underside of the woman's chin, old pock-marked scars beside youthful acne. She was still so young, yet marred by a professional gait and manner that seemed to transcend her skin. A nametag on her blue hotel worker uniform announced her name was Bo.

"I…uh…I don't have a room. I thought I was going to be sharing. So…" Veronica rustled into her purse, pulling out her wallet and her credit card. She calculated how much she had left on credit. It would be close, but she could do it.

The hotel attendant's face fell. "We're booked up. Unless you have a reservation, I can't do anything for you."

Veronica wanted to sob again. "There has to be something."

"Are you sure you're not sharing?"

"No. I can't. I'm…"

Veronica's stutters and stops were silenced by Bo's fingers over the hotel computer's keys. "We have one person who still has not yet checked in. His instructions say that he is coming with a girlfriend, but he does not give a name. Can you tell me if you know a Mr. Morris?"

"Jonathan?"

"Yes. That's him. Jonathan Morris, room 519. All paid." Bo made a face as she turned behind her, looking at a door over her shoulder. When she glanced back, her brows were knit conspiratorially. "Are you the girlfriend?"

Veronica wanted to say yes. She thought she was someone's girlfriend. She strained to remember who

Jonathan had been with. She surveyed the faces at the vigil. Was anyone crying more than anyone else? Was there a shadow presence, lingering, wondering why she had also been deprived of a funeral for her beloved? Was anyone else blonde, like the same colour of hair she found caught in his office phone?

She remembered no one in particular. Bo was waiting, her confidence ebbing away. This was a trick she was playing, something she knew she wasn't supposed to do, as well.

"Yes," Veronica said. "I'm his girlfriend."

Chapter Six

Veronica barely had time enough to put her bags in the room. That was all she wanted to do tonight, anyway. The crash had made them late; there was only fifteen minutes before the social mixer and the first keynote speaker would begin. Though she longed to have the night for her paper, especially after becoming so flummoxed in the car, she reminded herself that this was, in theory, never about the papers or keynotes or research at all. Not even a line on a CV was useful, unless it led her to create a network of people and colleagues, maybe even something approximating affection, which she could use to call in a favour at a much later date in her career.

"You will need a job someday," Stella had told her during one of their first closed-door meetings in her office. "Graduate school is the easy part, where all your needs are met by rote requirement. So use the time given and get good at talking. Remember the *manna* from that line of poetry in class?" She paused, as if to let Veronica fill in the citation from John Milton. When she nodded, Stella went on, "Manna from heaven, a gift given in the desert after years of famine. Manna is honey in the mouth, nice words spoken to people who have the entire hive of honey at their disposal but hidden. Use nice words, your manna, to get what you want."

Nice words were more than just the long,

complex ten-dollar ones that made Veronica seem well-read (but only if she pronounced them right out loud, something she still struggled with on occasion); they were compliments, questions, and intrigued statements she gave to people who held higher degrees and funding and reference letters in their back pockets. Sometimes, silence was a nice word, as long as it indicated interest, followed by acceptance. How you got ahead in academia was the same way you got out of the desert, according to Stella, and that was to no longer be satisfied with being a student, sucking manna from a benevolent God.

"It can be so easy to be taken care of as a student, so easy to slip away onto other people's syllabi and not make a name for yourself. But you have to find a way to get to the hive, to the source." Stella had gone on to talk about the influx of contract workers in the academy, describing them as parasites. Even if contract work wasn't the contract workers' fault, they should not take it in principle. "The parasite feeds on what little it is given, so you have to hunger it out. You have to dry up the work so the better jobs start to come."

Veronica's stomach ached now at the memory. She was sure that she'd been hungry in that meeting. Starving even, dull and persistent. Her stomach might have rumbled in the hallway as she sipped coffee and chewed gum endlessly, before it filled with butterflies as she entered Stella's office. She wondered how much of her hunger that Stella could sense back then. The desire between them had always been easy, even if they weren't acting on it yet, but the other hunger—the latent and pathological kind—could be so invisible if you didn't know what to look for. Despite Stella seeming to know everything, Veronica still didn't know if she knew the shape and sensation of hunger like this.

And confession of these feelings and the pain they wrought seemed pointless, especially right now. Veronica shucked her suitcase in the room that belonged to a dead student and shut the door. The door seemed to bang twice, as if it had been shut once by her and then another from a ghost. She gasped at the second noise. She closed her eyes and opened them. Waited. Nothing.

This was not a haunted hotel; it was a commodified one with the same triangle pattern on every space of carpet from the fifth floor that Jonathan had purchased on a credit card he was surely not going to pay off; it was the same triangle that would also be on the seventh floor where Stella would stay in her queen-size bed; the same carpet that went from the elevators to the stairwell to the emergency exit to the laundry room to the ice room and the gym. The hotel was not haunted, not haunted, not haunted, save by some retro nostalgia that still filtered through the guests as they went on vacation. Even these conferences were vacations to academics, right? Conference season instead of vacation season since academics had to work, work, work to get what they wanted. It was the same from state to state, hotel to hotel.

Veronica was suddenly overwhelmed by all that she had not been doing. Like her hunger, her work seemed to be bogged down by negative space. Her lacking paper. Her missing dissertation. The one missing citation that she'd forgot to include in her comprehensive exams but that no one had caught. The email she could no longer check on her phone because she was in the States and now roaming. Canadian texting and calling rates were too high, and she'd not thought ahead to get a cell package. She'd not thought ahead to get a hotel room, thinking she could share.

But she was a parasite, sucking manna without thinking of the hive.

She clutched her key card in her hand, wondering if she could go back inside and unpack her laptop. She could start writing the paper. But another bang scared her away, another echo that sounded like Marley's chains from Charles Dickens. She walked away from her door and toward the elevator. She needed to go to the mixer, even if her professional clothing seemed flat and lacklustre. She needed to make a name for herself.

She smiled at her reflection in the elevator mirror. Her cheeks still felt flushed red with heat, but her skin was pale and smooth. Her dark brown hair was frazzled by her part but easily fixed with the flat of her hand. Her wine-coloured blouse brought out the natural colour of her lips and dark brown eyes. She stood straight and stared at herself. She had felt so horrible in the bathroom on the interstate, but now she felt radiant. Could death do that to her? She flexed her shoulders forward to create a concave space in her collarbones. She touched the bones, the space below them, so much like a cave. She could spend hours in that space. She touched her ribs over her blouse and slipped a hand underneath to feel them against the skin. If not for the elevator announcing the ground floor, she would have lifted her shirt to see if the bones were still there underneath her skin, to see and make sure her stomach was not bloated like the dead man's.

But it was time to get off.

She walked out into the hotel lobby and followed the same triangles to the reception hall, where the nametag table and check-in station was. Her university affiliation under her name Veronica Hockmeier made her feel secure. The nametags were stiff, like the tongue of a shoe that had yet to be broken in. She hung it around her neck and fixed her hair. She stepped into another bathroom and gobbled up the space in the mirror to fix herself again. She counted collarbones and ribs. She glanced at the toilets, saw no one, and finally lifted her top to see her bones.

The relief that flooded her system was like a drug. In spite of the food, of the bingeing, and everything else, she was still thin. Still here. The sensation pushed her out the door and into the mingling arena. She smiled to everyone she saw and traded in her drink ticket for white wine in a plastic cup. A man in a corduroy suit spotted her right away. He smiled. He flirted. Said he'd gone to her university as an undergrad. She told him she had, as well. He made a joke as if they'd been there at the same time, though he was in his forties. After talking about Dickinson and the Transcendentalists, he moved on to someone else. She talked to another man, flirting with a professor emeritus she'd never met before, then got another drink.

It was easy to flirt. It was easy to be desired. She was so used to it, so numb to it, and so relieved by the fact that she only liked women. She could imagine the complex web of *maybes* and *do you wannas* that would be tangled in her throat if she also liked men. She could imagine being confused by intellect and job prospects, by flirtation and citation. But she didn't like men. She was using them to get ahead.

When she spotted Stella across the room, her stomach sank. She thought of the *maybes* and *do you wannas* again, even though Stella hated slang. When they texted, it was always in full words. Always without emojis. In that way, Veronica supposed Stella was being a professor, an adviser, a supervisor. Maybe she had been that all along and the things they did in bed with didactic handling of her own desire. Veronica wasn't sure. It just hurt. So she turned away and walked across the room, hoping to feel desired by someone for a little bit longer.

Instead, she heard her nickname. "Ronnie? Ronnie, is that you?"

She turned to face Samantha, though the name took a beat to remember. Her height made Veronica strain her neck once again to meet the blue eyes and freckled skin of her onetime study buddy during her master's degree. Samantha's red hair was darker than before, as if age had made her go brunette. She had different glasses perched on her nose, with a lighter and almost invisible frame. Her typical sundresses were swapped out for the standard conference fare of the professional skirt and jacket. Samantha looked good, classic. Where Veronica once thought Samantha was the perfect arty girlfriend, she was now the perfect colleague.

Which meant that Samantha was the perfect competition.

Veronica stilted her greeting for a moment before her affection won out. She gave Samantha a hug. "What are you doing here?"

"I'm presenting tomorrow! Nine in the morning, too. Super jittery about it. Hence my liquid courage." She winked playfully as she sipped her own plastic cup of red wine. "It's my plan to still be drunk as I give the paper. That way, I will be confident."

"I see." Veronica's potential jealousy ebbed away. She thought of what Stella would say: *Perfect on the surface. Underneath the suit, there is a child.* "What is your talk on?"

Samantha spoke in clipped sentences, hastened by alcohol and excitement, about the sadomasochistic dynamics of Emily Dickinson's writing and other queer approaches. "You know, building on the Camille Paglia reading."

She heard Stella in her head again, then spoke the words as if they were her own. "Isn't that more of a nineties fad reading?"

"Nuh-uh. There's lots more meat there. I want to dig into it."

Veronica suddenly saw how the whole paper would go. A non-paper, as Stella warned her about, where a cool item would be presented not for argumentation but for the coolness quotient. It would be a reading of the obvious, an assumption on the part that we were simply interested in the topic because we were here, not that you had to keep us interested because you have been called here. The panic of her own paper's potential caused the skin of her arm to ripple into goose bumps.

"And what about you?" Samantha asked. "Something great, no doubt. I hear you're working with Stella Flanders. She's giving the keynote."

"Uh-huh. Um."

Both of their gazes drifted to Stella again. She held herself regal, serene. She'd changed since the road and redone her makeup, now dressed in a blue jacket and skirt, with blue highlights over her eyes, as if she was torn from Picasso's period without being too sharp or misshapen. Over the course of Veronica's (and Samantha's) MA, there had been a time when the two of them had fawned over Stella. They both loved her as a scholar, then as an object worthy of desire, like she was right now. For a long time, Veronica was sure that she and Samantha could have been an item because their attraction for the same person would have kept them together in a triangle of desire.

But Veronica held out. She would always hold out for Stella, even when her blue radiance now was more like a hoary frost.

"I came in with her," Veronica said.

"You did?"

"I did."

Samantha grinned. She was not jealous. She praised "Ronnie" for her success. It was clear they were talking about sex and citations. "With her behind you, you will get a job anywhere."

"That is the hope."

Veronica wondered if anywhere included next to Stella. If the job she could have could be in the same department, contracts renewed, with the possibility of tenure. Or would moving in next door, no matter how permanent the placement, be living like a parasite again?

"Are you okay, though?" Samantha asked suddenly. Her attention fixated on Veronica with laser precision. "You're looking pretty skinny. You're not working all the time, are you?"

"No."

"No?"

"No." Veronica drank some of her wine. She felt woozy. When Samantha suggested they head to the hors d'oeuvre table, she said yes, though she hated the thought. Conference food was bad. Hotel food was bad. But she went and nibbled at it in small bites, still fearful that eating too much anywhere would make her feel trapped. She liked being in the centre of everyone, hearing stories and gathering her own intel, but her back was always close to the fire exit. When Samantha finally left her side, she felt stung by the words.

Skinny. Skinny. Skinny.

It reminded her of childhood bones, scraped knees, and sinewy tendons; it reminded her of dark fingers against white ivory, the blackness of a bruise from sitting against plastic high school chairs. It reminded her of bile in her throat and a sickening sense of sweetness that followed her around. The hors d'oeuvre felt hot in her mouth. She wanted to throw up again.

She turned and found Stella behind her. She stood with an empty glass. "We should talk."

"No."

Veronica ran into the bathroom. She threw up. Bitter and harsh, and so much harder to do with the wine. She was going to make herself sick beyond the vomit, she knew. This much throw up was going to corrode her teeth and fuck up her electrolytes. She made a promise to herself that she would eat nothing but bananas tomorrow, drink nothing but green tea. She was going to be balanced and whole.

Stella waited outside the bathroom. The doors to the conference area were closed. A hush had fallen over the other side, signalling the keynote was about to begin. Stella seemed as if she didn't know or didn't want to know. Boredom etched her face.

"We should talk, *Ronnie.*"

Veronica winced. Stella hated the nickname. *Ronnie makes you sound like a boy*, she had told her. Stella didn't want her to be a boy or to use her boyishness to get ahead. Veronica had wanted to tell her that her family had thought her a boy; the hope of the first child coupled with a wrong sonogram hastened their delusion until the first gasp of the nurse who delivered her. She was supposed to be Ronald, a Ronnie, after her father. Instead, she started to tell everyone to call her Veronica and only so.

"She's an old friend," Veronica said. "Her paper is going to be terrible."

Stella smiled. Just barely, just a hint. Applause sounded from the door.

"We should go in," Veronica said but didn't move.

"It's Henry Gable. We were at the same school, too. And his paper is going to be horrible. I think we're the only good ones here. So tell me about your paper." She gestured to the bar at the hotel, scattered with only two other visiting scholars who were playing hooky and a vacationing father in Bermuda shorts. "We never got to finish before. And if you were done telling me about those wandering arms, then tell me something else altogether. Either way, we should talk."

Veronica nodded and followed Stella's blue light to the bar.

Chapter Seven

Stella bought Veronica a drink at the bar. She did not say she was sorry, but the spaces in her language communicated her apologies. She claimed her separate room was for academic distance only since she could lose her job for sleeping with a student.

"Everyone in the academy is running around scared in the wake of certain other accusations," Stella said. "Every person confesses on social media now, and a hashtag can ruin someone's life, no matter the validity or inaccuracy of the claim. I can't take the risk of an outsider looking in and marking us without understanding."

"I understand," Veronica said.

Stella gave her the look that said, *no, you don't.* It was familiar from those early conferencing days in her office hours during undergrad, when Veronica tried to make her points about Steinbeck in a less than elegant way. This time, however, Veronica wasn't at fault. She could not understand—not in this way— because Stella had not told her. So Veronica sipped her drink, seeming to come to terms with the vagaries in her own language and how that silence marred.

Nine months had passed since that first blissful night with Stella, when their relationship had become something more. Nine months—and not a single fight, not a single crack in their relationship, in spite of Veronica's own foibles, all because Stella was still strong. That was what made today different, Veronica was sure: Stella had cracked. She was no longer the rock, the fixation that filled the negative space of desire, and now that she had faltered, so many more demons seemed to rush inside.

Stella sipped her own drink. She seemed to realize the cracks in her own façade and the way in which it twisted her normally beautiful countenance into something sinister. After a sigh, she asked, "I don't think I've ever told you why I study what I study, have I?"

"Emily Dickinson is one of American literature's hidden figures."

"No," Stella said. "That's ad copy. That's not real."

"Then no, you haven't," Veronica said, her voice flat. She waited a long time before Stella continued.

"I began my degree as a biology student. I put on my college applications the woefully dramatic story that I wanted to save the rainforest and cuddle wildlife. I did truly, but I also buried the lead. I wanted to study biology with a minor in chemistry because I witnessed a bad chemical spill in my hometown. Do you remember Love Canal?"

Veronica shook her head. Stella's face was stolid, expressionless as she explained a chemical disaster that happened in the New York area in the 1970s. Veronica had no idea why Stella had asked her if she remembered it, as if she had been alive to recall the black sludge that leached out of family backyards and public parks from a chemical company. Their twenty-three-year age difference seemed to disappear in that moment; Stella was in her youth again, a twenty-something like Veronica, and the two of them were sharing a casual drink rather than talking about one of the worse environmental tragedies in U.S. history.

"I grew up in Love Canal," Stella said. "I was the oldest in my family and watched as my brother and sister were born with defects. First we thought my brother was slow since it was something that had happened to the family before—a distant cousin who could barely read. My mother figured it must have been bad genes. We learned to live with David's handicaps and emotional outbursts, and we became stronger together. My mother became pregnant again. But when Gina was born with a cleft palate, we knew something was wrong. None of this had happened before, yet we weren't the only family in our neighbourhood with similar stories. Once we all started talking, so many stories came forward. And my family had been some of the luckier ones. David and Gina's illnesses and defects were okay to live with. I was shocked and horrified when my best friend's newborn sister was born with missing legs and another set of teeth. Something like that became so much more difficult to explain and rationalize away, nearly impossible to integrate. These chemicals are so strong. We realized we would never fully be rid of them, that we would have to move to be completely free. Our parents did not want to move, though, so they rallied around us, and we followed. And we were successful, more or less."

Stella took a drink. She reiterated the evacuation, the cleanup efforts, and the eventual settlement the chemical company reached with the townspeople. "I wanted an apology, though. I wanted someone from one of those plants to look at my brother and my sister and tell them they were sorry. That never happened, of course. To admit apologies is to admit guilt. So I went away to school and thought I would get it myself through a degree in biology, chemistry, or maybe even something like environmental studies, by way of apotheosis and redemption. I wanted to protest more places like the one I grew up in. I wanted to document the guilt, categorize and number it, and archive it to history, so no one could forget. Instead, I found myself inside a lab killing frogs with the same chemicals."

"What?" Veronica wasn't sure she'd heard correctly. Stella's voice had been devoid of emotion up until this part about the frogs.

Stella nodded. "It happens. You need to study death to prevent it. I would spend hours in the woods and bring specimens back to the lab, then kill them, examine them from the inside out. Even though it was no different than the death I'd witnessed in Love Canal, it started to wear on me. I went home for March break and found out my mother had cancer. Another lingering side-effect of our family home."

"I'm so sorry," Veronica said, but Stella shushed her.

"To say you're sorry is to admit guilt. And you are not responsible for the black sludge. Only the company is."

The rest of Stella's story was easier to follow and comprehend. Stella dropped out of school to take care of her mother, who died six months later from cancer spreading to her lymph nodes. Even with her mother gone, Stella had to remain home to take care of Gina and David. Her mother wasn't the only person to die in the town of cancer, either. More relatives and friends spilled in with the disease, all without a family history, all of them from exposure to the toxic black sludge David called "the ooze." Stella became a bed nurse for many more people, somehow being able to stand in the middle of all the toxic junk, the blackest ooze, and walk away scot-free. "I still get mammograms and ultrasounds now, decades later. I'm not sick. I don't know what I did to be so lucky, but I am not ill."

Veronica swallowed. She could taste her former vomit, like a childish dalliance in her throat. How could she throw up her food when Stella had suffered so much? And how could Stella think herself lucky in spite of everything?

"What happened?" Veronica asked. "You know, after...?"

"You mean after I walked away from the death and destruction?" Stella asked, then chuckled bitterly. "Eventually, an aunt from Texas came in and took Gina and David. Told me to go back to school, that I would be dishonouring my mother's memory if I didn't do what I needed. But biology as a research area didn't interest me anymore. I couldn't stand to keep killing what I sought to protect. Everything seemed so futile, so pointless. I thought of dropping out and running away, but I found an Emily Dickinson book my mother had by her bed when she died. At the time, I'd been too sad to read it, but I'd taken it with me back to school as a way to remember her. When I read it then, I understood that she had been reading it as a way to prepare for her own death. Then the deaths of others. More than anything, I saw our town, my mother, my brother and sister, and me at the centre of it all, represented through Dickinson's words. *I heard a fly buzz — when I died,*" Stella said and quoted the poem at length. She smiled, revealing a row of white and pristine teeth. She seemed happier than Veronica had ever seen her. "I understood that feeling. And I knew I could study that and make her proud that way. And so, I did."

"And you're a great scholar."

"Thank you. I know. The scholarship is important, of course," Stella said, her voice staid once again. "But I think I lost sight of the origin of my own desire for a while. It's easy to forget the past when everything is happening around you all at once. So easy to become distracted in this current age. But I need to keep that book in mind, its position by my mother's bed, the ooze, David and Gina. I need to keep it all in mind, or I fear I stare too far into an abyss of scholarship that has no ending citation in sight."

"The...man today?" Veronica asked tentatively. She saw his distended stomach, his stretched-too-far and blackened-by-the-sun skin, his idleness on the road and a mysterious backpack that was torn to pieces, a book bursting from its centre. No wonder Stella had turned away. No wonder Stella had become scared. She'd seen death on the side of the road, struck it with her car, and been made to feel responsible, if only for a second. Death, like Dickinson had once written, was trying to stop her, and Stella had remembered so viscerally that she'd wanted to chase it all along.

"Yes, that man..." Stella sighed. Veronica put her hand over Stella's. She allowed it to stay there, cloistered at the hotel bar where no wandering eyes could see. "I am not afraid," Stella said suddenly. "Please don't think I'm afraid."

"I don't. But it's okay if you were."

"I'm not afraid. It's...loving, actually."

"What?"

"Seeing that man today, remembering Love Canal, the poems... It all reminds me of taking care of my mother, her last days alive. It was horrible, yes, but in Dickinson, death is not horrible. He is a kindly Master. Death is a communal act, one that must be witnessed to be real. It's reverent in that way, deriving from the Latin and French terms for fear. Death can be truly terrifying, yes, but it's also one of the few times I've ever felt truly, utterly, and irrevocably loved."

"Loved by death?" Veronica asked. Her voice was small. She realized that in all the time she had spent with Stella, from that first moment on the stage to sharing a bed with her the night before, that they had not once said I love you.

Now she realized Stella probably never would.

"Yes, by death," Stella said, smiling. "Of course."

Chapter Eight

"Y ou should come with me," Stella said an hour and a half later.

Veronica met her gaze. This was an invitation to the room—not merely to share an elevator—and it was clear that she should not decline. Veronica knocked back the rest of her drink and then followed the silhouette of Stella's body three paces behind. The elevator made her heart jump as it rode up and up and up past her floor and opened onto the somehow more expansive seventh. The triangle shapes on the carpet were sharper, the doors more solid, and the ice machine somehow colder. Stella opened the door with a flick of the card and held it tight, allowing Veronica to step inside first. She closed the door behind her, their bodies touching. Sparks and sound erupted, a theremin of light.

Stella's mouth sealed Veronica's, taking her breath. A kiss became a swordfight of nerves, each one of them on a hair trigger. Veronica mewled and begged to be disrobed. She needed Stella's hands to run up and down her ribcage, her collarbones, the flat bones of her shoulders, and reaffirm that this was beautiful. Sharp and hard, but beautiful. Stella's naked body was just as thin, her skin pulled just as tight over her body, but now it contained more scars than had never been visible before.

Veronica pressed her mouth into the arches

of Stella's hands; she licked her palms, tasting the almonds and the oh-so-familiar sweet scent of coconut hand lotion. She sucked each digit, pushed it past her lips and let her nails nick her gums. Even as Stella's fingers hit her uvula, there was no sickness that followed. Veronica opened her mouth wider, ready and hungered, and Stella withdrew her hand to replace it with her tongue. Veronica groaned, shifted, and sucked between Stella's neck and collarbone. She followed down her body, counting ribs with her tongue, holding hips against the hotel wall, and slicking herself with more spit before she entered Stella's wet centre.

Veronica rarely fucked Stella; their lovemaking was almost always the other way around as Stella held off her own orgasm until the last possible moment, until Veronica was like butter in her hands after a long, satiated sensation enveloped her. It was different now, though, because everything was different now. Veronica could enter Stella first, with precision, because now she knew Stella's insides. She knew the story of why she had come here, been in this place, and in this period. Everything made sense now, even the chaos of the body and the cruelty from before. And as Stella arched her back and combed a hand through Veronica's hair, she knew she was asking for forgiveness.

Veronica did not answer with words. She tasted. She licked. She devoured. And then, when she was nearly too tired to keep her eyes open, Stella demanded even more from her. On the bed, an hour later, Veronica's throat was sore from screaming and her lips bruised from desire. Stella turned over, her hand barely gripping Veronica's thighs before she pulled them apart. She took her fill like a crow to carrion, very little effort needed for a resounding reward of her name on Veronica's lips as she came.

"Stella, Stella, I—"

"You can stay for a little while," Stella said as she rolled their bodies together, like little spoon and big spoon, like black key and white ivory, "but please be gone by morning."

Chapter Nine

By 3 a.m., Veronica was out of Stella's room and staring at her fifth-floor door. The bright lights of the hotel hallway seemed even more manufactured when Veronica glimpsed the dark night outside, which was then made that much darker and more bewitching by the woods that flanked the hotel. How could something so dark exist next to bright, as if a travelling carnival worker had swallowed fire? She pressed her ear against the hotel door and held her breath, expecting. She waited and heard a subtle click-click-click on the other side. Soft but persistent. It sounded like a Soviet bug on a phone line during the Cold War—like Jonathan's stilted voice on his answering machine, which now seemed like another world away.

Veronica shifted. She remembered the girlfriend. Was she waiting on the other side, clicking her long acrylic nails against a counter, killing time before confrontation? Or maybe she wasn't angry but eager to meet the person who had bluffed her way inside. Maybe they had something in common, and despite her face drawing a blank in Veronica's mind, they could speak about Jonathan together. Veronica withdrew the key card and slid it in place without fear. She wanted to know this stranger more than anyone else at the conference.

The room was empty.

The bed remained untouched, and her suitcase was in its haphazard position on the floor. The bathroom light was on, and no shadows moved. But the room was freezing, and the temperature hit Veronica the moment she crossed the threshold and almost made her turn around. She held her suit jacket tighter, though it was also damp from sweat. The dampness bore into her bones and sensitive skin. The clicking persisted, louder now, and Veronica wondered if it was her own teeth.

The door slammed behind her, followed by another slam. The clicks became knocks, became thuds and bangs. Had she woken a guest? Was the air conditioning going completely nuts? Another slam, another click. Her reason fell away, especially as the room temperature gauge clearly said it was working. Another bang. *A poltergeist*? She translated in her head. *German for noisy spirit. Noisy ghost.*

Another bang.

"Jonathan?" she called.

Click-click-click. She heard his to-do list in her mind. Click-click-click. This was not a noise in her head anymore. It was in real life. A knock, a drop, a click-click-click through the wall.

Fear laced her body where Stella's teeth and fingers had once been. Her thighs ached from strain. She saw feet dance on the other side of the hotel door, small shadows under the slat of light. She swallowed hard, murmuring his name again in a whisper. "Jonathan?"

The feet stopped. Veronica gripped the handle and opened the door.

The hotel worker from earlier was on the other side, her limbs and arms so gangly, so much like

Jonathan's, that Veronica was convinced it really had been his figure she glimpsed. Without the surreal aura of the hotel's lights, and perhaps inside the plunging darkness of the woods, their bodies could have been twins. The hotel worker's mouth formed an O of surprise as Veronica took a step back, a hand on her chest. The worker's arms held laundry, something of which she dropped and only compounded the noise and nervous energy.

"Jesus Christ." Veronica gasped. "I thought you were a ghost."

"No, no, all flesh and blood here." The hotel worker picked up the laundry basket. "And definitely not Jesus. I'm Bo. I work here. We've met."

"I know. Obviously. But what are you doing?"

"Laundry. Sorry. I should have done it before." Bo's voice dropped an octave. She whispered, the rasp of her baritone that much stronger. "Are you going to rat on me?"

"Rat?" Veronica shook her head. The clicking sounded again, as if it was contained inside her brain. Then she realized the door next to her room lacked numbers and didn't contain a key card slot. The clicking started to sound like spinning. "Wait. Am I right next to the laundry room?"

"Yeah. Sorry. This is why I usually can't do laundry in the middle of the night and why we only rent this room out in desperation. Your boyfriend was one of the last conference-goers to get it. Sort of bad luck but good luck, you know?"

Veronica huffed out a breath of tension. The banging in the room made sense now and so did the temperature shifts. No poltergeists, no bad feelings— just Jonathan's lateness to book a room. From what

Veronica remembered of him, he was always late—but always just in time—handing in Stella's paper five minutes after the deadline and arriving at   a pizza place to celebrate Stella's paper together just before the place filled up to capacity. The memories warmed her temporarily but also made her stomach quake with dread. "No one has come by, have they? Asking about the room?"

"Your boyfriend? No...not even his actual girlfriend, either. You're in the clear."

Veronica looked down. "Are you going to rat on me now?"

Bo shook her head. They stared at each other in the quiet before she spoke again. "He's dead, isn't he?"

"What?"

"The boyfriend. Whether or not he's yours...he's dead. Right?"

"How did you...?"

"A lot of people die in hotels."

"But he didn't die here."

"No, but a lot of people who think about dying often get hotels and then never use them. His room was already paid for in advance. And now he's not here. So he's dead. It's sort of obvious."

"Is it?"

Bo shrugged. "I just know where to look to see things, I guess."

Veronica wanted to nitpick the sentence as if it was a piece of student writing, but she was too exhausted. And Bo was right, anyway. She spoke so frankly, so accurately that it was like she was taking a knife to a gangrened arm. She was hacking away at something she knew nothing about—yet hitting every single note. It reminded Veronica of the one time she'd received actual medical treatment for her eating disorder, and the doctor had known so much about her insides after one glance. *You get a lot of cavities, don't you? You carry around hand lotion for your knuckles and gum, even though chewing it sometimes hurts your teeth. You sometimes get lightheaded and feel as if your chest will burst, especially when you use ipecac rather than your fingers.* She'd stared at him in shock—and then scowled in anger. It simply wasn't fair that he knew so much about her when she needed to keep secrets. What book of knowledge had he read to discover so much—and then use it so callously to project her future? *Bulimia and anorexia are the most deadly mental illnesses. If your mind does not make it unbearable to live, the treatment of your body will eventually end you.*

Bo wasn't a doctor, though. Even her hotel work was subpar, if her midnight laundry was any indication, yet she also seemed to know death so intimately. When that shock faded, Veronica latched on to Bo's knowledge in a way she never did with the eating disorder doctor. Because what she said made sense. Veronica had been avoiding the hotel room because it made Jonathan's suicide tangible, even more than before. Why bother getting a hotel at the conference if you knew you were going to kill yourself? Why workshop the abstract and submit it, then be excited it was accepted? And why invite the girlfriend, too?

The only answer could be that the girlfriend was never real, the abstract submitted was never meant to be a full paper, and that Jonathan had planned to kill himself all along, but in Amherst and not in Canada. So that when he didn't show up on his panel and people became nervous, someone could say they were the girlfriend to get inside to find his body. *And the note?* Maybe that was supposed to be longer, and his apology would have been a full dialogue to answer everyone's questions. Maybe his apology was his paper topic, and his abstract title contained all the answers.

Veronica wished she'd grabbed the conference program along with her nametag earlier in the evening, but she hadn't. Now she'd have to wait until morning to check on all of it for sure. The night seemed so long in front of her, so totalizing and overwhelming. Veronica felt a tear slide down her cheek. Bo noticed under the harsh lights.

"Oh, shit."

"I'm sorry. I—"

"Hey. None needed." Bo dropped the laundry in a pile again. She stepped closer to Veronica, who stepped away. "Don't make this a grief dance. I'm just trying to help."

"I know. But I'm...just so mad."

"Yeah?"

"Yes. He seemed fine. He was excited to come. But now...now it was all fake. All a game he was playing. And...and...I'm in his room. God, why am I in his room?"

"Because you ended up here, too, and let me tell you, none of this is your fault. These things happen sometimes. We try to prevent them, but there is nothing you can do."

"I don't believe you."

"No one ever does," Bo said, sighing slightly. "But trust me. Not as a hotel person who sometimes finds the dead bodies. Because I've never actually found one here—only elsewhere."

"Elsewhere?" Veronica asked. Bo had said it as if it was an actual place name, a location on the map one could visit, rather than speculate upon. She thought of what Oscar Wilde had said—that no map was good enough unless it also contained the no-place of utopia. Maybe Elsewhere was the land of the dead, which was like her own sense of the dead time filling up her university.

"Elsewhere," Bo confirmed. "It doesn't matter where."

"Then who?"

"A friend. And a friend and a friend."

"Three suicides?" Veronica wiped the tear away, suddenly focused on Bo and the shaking disbelief. "You've found three people's suicides?"

"One I found. The others I only heard about through the grapevine. It's viral."

"It's what?"

"Suicide is an idea, and it spreads. When you know someone who's done it, it's like some people realize that it's an option. Like, oh, *of course*, I could blow my brains out or shoot up some air bubble or take a bunch of pills. Why didn't I think of that before? Then they do it, too. It sucks. But it has to stop somewhere, okay? It will stop. Someone will reject the idea, and then the chain ends. I reject it."

Veronica's stomach roiled. She'd never heard of suicide explained as a virus, as something that attacks part of a community. Suicide was always a moral choice or personal dilemma. It was something that Jean-Jacques Rousseau argued for as a testament of will, something you did so you could assert yourself. To kill yourself was to create yourself, and to kill yourself was to have the final word, like Socrates at

Athens. She blinked. She saw the letters forming *I will not apologize* so clearly from Jonathan's letter, though she'd never actually seen them on the page. Whatever would be written for his paper, too, would be another chorus to make Jonathan into Socrates.

But of course, he wasn't alone. He may not have even been the start of the viral idea. Veronica remembered the list of names they'd gathered to raise awareness, the others who had left the school. Not dead, but they were part of that virus, weren't they? Academia's curse, a parasitic bug that would not relent. How could anyone get out alive, if that was the case, and get out for good?

"Hey," Bo said suddenly. "I really have to do this laundry now. So it's gonna be loud. But do you want to have some tea or coffee or something? I'm stuck on the front desk until five, so I have an hour or two to kill."

Bo made a face, as if she realized the weight of the word *kill* in her mouth. Or maybe it was the word *time*. Veronica felt them both like a knife, like Lucretia, Mark Anthony, and the many Roman figures surely felt the sword in their stomach as their last words.

"Hey," Bo said again. She reached out and touched Veronica's arm. "You can reject it, too, you know."

"No. I mean, I know," Veronica said. "But I do think tea would be nice."

Chapter Ten

The backroom of the hotel seemed like another world away. There were no brand names or tiny triangles on worn-down carpets but the smells of dried fruit, flowers, and tea leaves mixed with the faint vanilla scent of old books. The tea was loose and scattered in the bottom of glass mason jars, and a veritable library lined the shelves. The titles ranged from the standard paperback fare one would expect at hotels—a lot of Stephen King, Mary Higgins Clark, and other airport books—but several thick tomes of poetry, philosophy, and even Betty Friedan's *The Feminine Mystique*. While Bo boiled water with an ancient-looking electric kettle, Veronica was fascinated by the second wave masterpiece hidden among the Harlequin Silhouettes. "I can't believe you have this."

"Why wouldn't I have this?" Bo asked. "Other than the shitty politics around Friedan now, this book is a lifeline for hotel workers."

"Um." Veronica was bursting with questions. She went with the easiest first. "How so? You're not exactly a housewife in the hotel. Unless you're married and…?"

"No, not married. Very much single and lesbian. But anyway," Bo said, moving on quickly. "Hotel work is domestic work. I live the Feminine Mystique every damn day when my hands crack from so much laundry detergent and a fat businessman wants his breakfast served in a specific way, exactly like his mommy used to." Bo rolled her eyes but then shrugged away all the malice at which her words seemed to hint. "Sometimes, it feels like I'm living in the 1950s, especially since Friedan and her besties all want trans women to get back in their closets."

"What now?" Veronica asked.

Bo went on to explain how numerous feminists of the second wave moment, like Friedan and especially Germaine Greer, were not exactly happy with the way gender politics were headed now and especially didn't like to hear from trans women since they weren't, according to their criteria, "women born women." "But let's not talk about the shitty politics that sometimes run this country. I much prefer tea and fantasy." Bo ran a finger down one of the red-backed spines of a Harlequin novel. While Veronica laughed at the gesture, the action seemed so forbidden. Not because of the salacious sex hinted between them, but because of the inanity of a book like that. After all, who really read romances? Only people who couldn't really read. Veronica didn't say these thoughts aloud, but she thought them with a neon sign. They seemed obvious, really, because that was what Stella would say.

"Ah. I see we don't like romance." Bo pushed the book back onto the shelf and busied herself with the jars of tea. Though Bo seemed to have completely moved on, Veronica was caught off-guard.

"I...I didn't say that."

"I know. But you had the face that all those academics have out there. The scrunched nose." Bo mimicked it, exaggerated it, to the point where she looked like a rabbit. "They do the same thing when I bring out Stephen King or Dan Brown."

"Oh, well. It's Dan Brown." Veronica couldn't help but laugh. When Dan Brown had been popular, she'd just met Stella. When Veronica had come back from winter break with a copy of the book, given to her by her parents because they'd loved it, Stella had mocked it. At the time, Veronica had wanted to find a reason to disengage with her parents, to leave her family and move on to something else, and rather than looking at her actual past, she focused on Dan Brown. Yeah, she didn't want to read that book. She was better than that. She was just like Stella Flanders, so the book remained in a drawer, and she passed her parents into her memory.

"Dan Brown has made a ton of money," Bo said. "He's nothing if not industrious."

"But it's bad, right?"

"I don't know," Bo said. "I haven't read it. But people tell me it's good, so it's on the shelf for them. Have you read it?"

Veronica chewed her lip before saying. "No. I read something else."

"Well then, neither one of us can attest to its actual value."

Veronica wanted to argue again, to say that surely something this popular couldn't be good, but she shook her head. She needed to change tactics if she was going to get anywhere. "What's wrong with wanting to read philosophy, like Friedan or anyone else from that era? Or poetry for that matter? I worked hard to understand it."

"I did, too." Bo picked up a thick collection of American poetry. She hovered her finger over a passage and read something aloud in perfect diction and breath pattern. Veronica recognized the beginning as a famous poem by Robert Frost, though she didn't know the title. Stella didn't like Frost, mostly because his mediocre work made it harder for female poets to be taken seriously. While Veronica couldn't argue with that—she did find herself enjoying what Bo read aloud.

"That's nice," Veronica said when Bo had finished. "Thanks."

"It is nice. So is Harlequin, Stephen King, Dan Brown…and all that stuff people at these conferences usually turn their nose up at. I get that we should want people to read the classics. I get that Emily Dickinson is good. But why can't we have both, you know? It's why I have this library. I wanted to cater to the snobs and the dumb-dumbs."

"Wow," Veronica said.

"What?" Bo challenged. "You were thinking it. Why can't I say it?"

"I just…I didn't…"

"You wanted me to be nice. Because you probably feel like both a snob and a dumb-dumb."

The kettle hummed to life before Veronica could respond. Bo went to pour tea into mugs. Veronica hoped that would be the end of the discussion, but it wasn't. Bo set up their drinks, but she also picked up more books. As she set out their tea, she also laid out Stephen King's *Christine* next to Thomas Malory's *Le Morte d'Arthur*. "The same book," she said.

"It's not."

"It is, though. King's *Christine* is supposed to be a modern-day rewrite."

Veronica tilted her head and caught a whiff

of the tea. She pressed the mug to her lips, utterly intoxicated by the scent, smell, and taste. Her exhaustion hit her in a wave. She was so tired; she just wanted to relax and not think anymore—yet Bo was presenting barbs and jabs. She went on to explain how King's characters were the exact same from the Arthurian legend, except that they were riding in cars and not horses, and the Fisher King was now a boy with a broken leg from football. "Same story. Same sentiment. Yet one is taught in university, and the other is maligned. It makes no sense. Like Friedan and the other women from the 1970s bitching about trans women."

"I...I don't know enough about that."

"But you know things." Bo sat across from Veronica and sipped her tea. "You know a lot. Yet you, like everyone else at this conference, still feels like a dumb-dumb because you think Dan Brown will rot your brain. Or that you like King. Or that, maybe, you might catch a glimpse of the Hallmark Channel and turn to stone. It's okay, though. You can use your brain and your body. That's the joy of it, really. You get both."

Veronica could only nod. She took another big gulp of her tea, and when Bo suddenly veered into new subject matters, she let her talk and talk and talk. She described her parents' purchase of the hotel, along with their heavy legacy of generation after generation tasked with building the first railroad in America. Now, her parents were no longer immigrants, and they had a new kind of American Dream, one that could completely separate from the past. Veronica noted the ideographic characters sketched onto Post-it notes tacked up on walls, over a calendar, even inside one of the books Bo had set on the table. Then from family history came more cultural history as they exchanged tales about dynasties and ancient texts they were never witness to. Soon enough, their conversation about suicide emerged anew; Bo spoke of Qu Yuan, a Chinese poet who drowned, and then Elliott Smith, a singer who stabbed himself and was then immortalized through songs about twilight. Veronica shared her mourning ritual that was more or less a bust, and Bo reiterated her chain of friendships with sad endings.

"More than anything, after all of that," Bo said, "the one thing that sticks with me is that we need to stay alive for one another because if not, then the idea of death spreads."

"I'm still not sure I buy this as a viral spread entirely, not with Rousseau so close in my mind, but I like thinking that Jonathan's suicide might have had nothing to do with me."

"It has everything to do with you and who you're around. Ideas spread."

"But," Veronica said, "I think I feel better that he may have already had the idea ages ago—hence the hotel room. I couldn't have stopped him. His mind was already made up because he already had the idea."

"True enough. I can't say much beyond that because I never met him," Bo said. "But we still have to take care of one another, no matter who we are, because it all matters. We're all culpable."

Veronica felt a sudden pang in her chest. *We're all culpable.* Brianna wasn't here. She was an Americanist alongside herself and Jonathan and knew enough about Emily Dickinson to complete a decent abstract, but she'd not been accepted. Veronica wanted to belicve it was on personal merit, but she saw how Brianna's illness affected her writing. How could she have concentrated long enough to complete one? It wasn't quite the same as Jonathan's invisible sadness, but Veronica now felt Brianna's absence like a curse, a symptom of what was to come if she let her thoughts think too many bad things.

Veronica needed to message her. But no texts could go in and out of her phone, and the signal for the hotel WiFi seemed to be blocked inside the backroom. When Veronica produced her phone to check this fact, Bo seemed to sense the conversation dying down. She rose and gathered the mugs and put the mason jars back on the shelves. She disappeared into a farther backroom just as Veronica obtained the signal, only to lose it again. She'd seen emails awaiting her. She thought of her laptop in the hotel room and the Word doc on her computer filled with conference notes. This interlude with tea had been nice, a break to make her feel better, but she was feeling the tug of work again.

And the tug of Jonathan's paper topic. Was it possible, she wondered, for Bo to grab her a conference program? Did she have one kicking around? Veronica waited on the edge of her seat for Bo to return from the backroom. When she did, she was holding a pale blue shoebox in her hand and spoke before Veronica could ask her own question.

"This is weird, but I think you'd get this."

"What is it?"

Bo lifted the lid of the shoebox. Inside were several strips of photo booth images, all containing Bo with various hairstyles (short to long, curly to straight, to ponytailed) and with different people. A man, a woman, someone who was indeterminate. Next to the photo booth images were several rolls of undeveloped film, the kind that used to come in cameras from the 1990s and that Veronica hadn't seen since she was twelve or thirteen. Movie tickets, fortune cookie papers, crumpled-up notes. It reminded Veronica of something her therapist, a small woman named Nadine, had told her to make one night. A distraction box? A memory box? *Keep all your happy things together, so that when you are sad, you have a place to retrieve your happy objects and retreat to.* Veronica thought it was a stupid idea—but maybe there was something to it, and Bo had read her with the clear precision of a surgeon once again.

Veronica reached into the box. She smiled at some of the photos, especially the goofy ones. She dug deeper and found the frayed edges of friendship bracelets. Of trinkets and toys from Christmas crackers. Then she found licenses and other government documentation. An ID card with a mismatched sex marker and photograph that looked similar to the woman in one of the photo booth images, but also not quite. The nose was different, smaller—possibly rebuilt. The more Veronica dug, the more she found licenses for strangers, people with different last names, different age categories, all distinct, yet so similar and strange.

"What is this?" Veronica asked. The box felt sinister all of a sudden. "What are you showing me?"

"My viral box. I try to keep the ideas together, so they don't spread."

"What?"

Bo sighed. A flicker of fear crossed her face, as if she'd realized Veronica's discomfort. She'd read her wrong. She now wanted to retreat. In that split second, Veronica understood. "All these people have died? In this hotel?"

"Not all in the hotel. My three friends were first. Natasha, Morty, and Dani. I found them, then I contained them, and then...there were more deaths in the hotel. On the street corner. At my old apartment building. It was as if when I found one death, more cascaded. Not all of them are suicides, but some were hit-and-runs. Random illness, sickness. I figured if I kept them all together, they could be contained no matter what it was. No matter who they were. It's—"

"*Why?*"

"Protection, maybe. Superstition, most likely. It's stupid. It's..."

"You stole their IDs."

"They left them behind."

"So?"

"So," Bo said, her voice getting louder, "I doubt they need them where they're going. It's just like the books. Most of these were leftover, already read. Why waste them? Someone else can read."

Veronica looked down at the King book she'd been fiddling with. Her fingers leapt back as if she'd touched fire. She stood, backed away. The smell of the room, once so sweet and enchanting, now turned her stomach. Chloroform, cherry-scented alcohol, death from insulin resistance. It was all too sweet, all too sickly. She needed to leave, to go back to her ghost room that was too cold, but at least smelled like nothing at all.

"I should go. I need some sleep before I work on my paper."

Bo nodded. She shut the box with a defeated sigh. Veronica wanted to ask about the conference program but knew that once she uttered it aloud, it would end up in that box. Maybe that wasn't such a bad thing. She understood what Bo was trying to do, and it was almost cute, quaint. Keep all the bad things together, so they won't spread. What a childlike innocent thought, magical thinking at its finest. Maybe whatever Jonathan had written down and refused to apologize for needed to be contained. *Maybe, maybe, maybe.* Apologies were making her sick, and these objects looked like the talismans of death rather than a folk remedy to ward death away.

When Veronica realized the two of them were waiting for the other to say goodbye, she merely left in silence. She had no idea how or why she'd wandered this far away from her course; she felt meandered, an arm sticking out of a grave. The image of the arm, and the wilful child, was the last she had in the haze of half-dawn light before she finally fell asleep in a ghost's bed.

Chapter Eleven

Veronica should not have been surprised to dream about him, and really, she wasn't. She'd been thinking about him endlessly, a dull throb at the base of her neck. But the *how* of the dream, the dotted colours of the landscape, and the swirls and textures of the experience—like living in a van Gogh painting, like a Richard Linklater film about philosophy—made her want to stay in bed. Veronica began to understand, beyond sadness and infinite melancholia, why someone would want to stay asleep forever if their dreams were this beautiful.

It started out with Bo. The two of them at the table in the backroom of the hotel were in stark, familiar colours, like an extended memory. They drank and talked without the heaviness from before. Then the edges blurred, a film lens changing. Bo's nearly six-foot height became even larger as her knees pressed against the hotel table. The wood snapped and rounded and elevated, like the ledge she and Jonathan had sat at when they'd celebrated Stella's paper success. With one sip of her tea, Bo's black hair morphed into Jonathan's red strands, flatted against his forehead from bedhead. Bo's Asian features melted away and into the gangly man who was now dead.

Veronica was not afraid in her dream because it was all so, so beautiful. Jonathan looked like a self-portrait done by Vincent van Gogh, all bright reds and blues. The edges of the tables and chairs in the coffeehouse were painted in large swirls like van Gogh's other work. Outside, the night sky was starry, swirled. A jazz song played, and Veronica realized it wasn't from speakers like it had been in reality, but a band that moved in jerky gestures, all painted in midnight blue. She thought of Wallace Stevens' poems and Jack Kerouac's words on Charlie Parker, but they were passing thoughts.

Jonathan was talking. "You notice anything?"

"It's so beautiful."

"Don't romanticize it. Do you notice anything?"

She furrowed her brows, unsure. "What am I supposed to see, other than how beautiful this all is?"

Jonathan gestured to the table. The tea was now coffee. The shoebox—which had been present when Bo was in the dream—had flattened into paper. The paper they'd been working on. He touched the sheet and pointed to the jazz band, the bartender, the other patrons. None of them had been in the original memory, yet they all looked familiar.

"Do you see it yet?" he asked. "Do you recognize them?"

Jonathan's voice was desperate, but his tone sounded like part of the music, part of the overall song. Crooning sadness, a wailing that was all vowels. It was hard to be afraid, even as his eyes seemed painted with fear. Veronica was sure she could stay the entire night here. She drank some of her coffee and tasted it in the dream. It was hot and muggy, something rotted. She looked down, saw the back of a beetle floating on the surface, and looked up again.

The song had stopped playing. In the centre of the band was Emily Dickinson. She tried to walk forward, but she had no legs. They had been replaced by bottles of ipecac, which then shattered as she moved.

Veronica vaulted awake. She ran to the bathroom and dry heaved for several minutes. The dream had become so horrifying in a matter of seconds, and then her own bodily needs took over, so it was a while before she could relax and revisit the better parts. She knew Freudian analysis was bunk, like the horoscopes Stella hated and the tarot cards Veronica still kept under her bed, but she wanted to go back and examine her subconscious for messages. Take apart every scene of her dream and frame it in the art gallery of her mind. Even Jonathan, in his Vincent van Gogh portrait, she wanted to keep, though his parallel to the painter made her sad. Perhaps he wasn't Socrates dying for a cause anymore, but van Gogh being devoured by unrelenting sadness caused by his failure.

Do you see it yet? Do you recognize them?

Veronica rolled over his words in her mind. She Googled them, thinking they were song lyrics, but came away with a blank. She tried to close her eyes so she could conjure the band, the bartender, and the patrons again. Their faces were swirls, distorted pixels. She gave up.

She was halfway through brushing her teeth before it dawned on her. She may not have known the faces, but she was sure that the people in the coffeehouse were the same names from the mourning ritual. From history, the ones that she and Bo had bandied about. Every single person in the dream had committed suicide. Every single one.

"And me?" she asked aloud.

She waited in her room, hoping for an answer but knowing there would be none.

Chapter Twelve

Veronica's phone finally connected to the WiFi when she stepped into the hotel community room. Trays of steaming breakfast foods tempted her until the ping made her examine her school inbox with a critical gaze. She became so obsessed with the formal messages that she didn't even notice Stella emerge from the elevator and take a seat at a table by the front door. When she did, Veronica could do nothing but fall into the empty seat across from her.

"Good morning, Veronica. How is your paper going?"

"Fine."

"Are you willing to share?" Stella held cutlery and cut at one of the waffles on her plate. She gestured to Veronica's phone with a tilt of her head. "I'd like to be included."

"Oh, this isn't the paper."

Stella waited. Veronica realized her hand was shaking. She set her phone down. In a rush, she summarized what she'd just found out from her student inbox. "The dean of the English Department emailed me this morning. A student is contesting his grade. Two students actually, but one of them I know why. They're both from my Intro to Literary Studies class. I'm...I'm not sure what to do."

Light came in from the dining hall window,

causing Stella to seem as if she had a halo around her blond hair. She reminded Veronica of the woman from the *American Gothic* painting, staid and serious. Veronica turned away, not wanting to think in art after her dream. She was then met with the continental breakfast and soon turned away from that, too, her nausea too present. She didn't want to eat ever again. Her tongue felt like shag carpeting that she remembered her parents having in the basement until she was twelve, when they tore it up for the piano since it muffled the sound. Her fingers shook. Her limbs ached. Even coffee seemed too acidic for her stomach, already depleted.

Besides, she needed to deal with this new problem before she could eat again. Forget dreams and nightmares. The two students who were contesting her grades and the school that now wanted her to answer for her actions were far scarier than anything her unconscious mind could dig up. Veronica leaned forward, closer to Stella, without giving away their intimacy or her incipient hunger. "What should I do?"

"Is it worthwhile?" Stella asked.

"What do you mean?"

"The grade. Is it a worthy protest? Either one of them?"

Veronica shrugged. Stella tapped her fingers against the table, as if to say, *use your words*. Veronica remained silent.

"You said you understood one of the students. Which one? How come?"

"He failed. Don't most students protest when they fail?"

"Most are too filled with shame. They often know why they failed. And if his fail is worthy, then you have nothing to worry about in order to justify it. The other student?"

"I...I don't remember the other student. Their name...is a blank." She knew that was a lie. Their name was in the email, Jiang Zhang, someone she had never met in person all semester, to the point where she didn't even know their true gender. That wasn't uncommon, though; some students enrolled and never came but never dropped out, most likely so they could still qualify for student loans. *Ah, my ghost students*, Brianna had once told Veronica when they'd talked about a similar attendance issue, long before the word ghost itself had become so loaded. Ghost students, invisible students, or just random names you never met were common; them contesting their failing grade was not.

When Veronica explained the lack of appearance in class, Stella sighed. "So it's easy. No grades for no presentation. What's the problem?"

Veronica stuttered and shifted again. How could she explain that she hated to think of this student most of all because their name made no sense? Not only could she not produce a face for it, but she had no idea how to pronounce it, whether they were male or female, whether or not they may have actually been there, but she'd not registered this fact, and so, she might have left them behind and not noticed them for an entire semester. What if she had been wrong about Jiang Zhang, and they had shown up, but she never saw?

"I can't get the grades here," she said instead. "I don't have anything that proves they didn't come."

"Attendance. Missing assignments. You're the authority."

"Yes...For the other student contesting, I have some of his grades but not others. I might have even thrown out what I used for attendance, with the semester over and all. Spring cleaning."

"You threw it out?"

"Yes," Veronica said. She wanted to repeat spring cleaning, but it was clear Stella was annoyed.

"Everything?"

"Everything. After I handed in the final grade, I thought I was done."

"That was not a smart thing to do."

"I didn't know. No one told me."

"No one tells you because it's obvious. You should have kept it. You should have expected an audit. You get at least one student who needs the English credit to get a science degree or who is just a plain asshole. You seem to be lucky this time around and have gotten both. You really shouldn't have done this, Veronica. We even have to keep our tax records for seven years. Surely, you could have kept this for seven days, maybe even seven weeks."

Veronica balled her firsts. "I know. I should have. But it's like...the longer I'm here, in the U.S., the more it feels as if home doesn't exist anymore. Even if I had kept the attendance sheets, what would it matter?"

"You're being dramatic. It's a grade. It's not personal."

"How can it not be personal when my name is on it?"

"That's by accident, by chance. It has nothing to do with you as a teacher and everything to do with a scholarship. Or parents. Or English requirements in a science degree they must take and receive a certain grade in. Maybe you gave the student a grade ending in a nine, and he wants to know the decimal points. There are a million different reasons to contest and a million different justifications and apologias that you could use to go with it. This is not a problem."

"What do you mean? Should I apologize?"

"No." Stella's voice was thin, persistent. "That's not what *apologia* means. Apologia is a defense, intellectual and unemotional. It's a defense of your stance as a teacher, for assigning the grade in the first place. That is all that is required from you. Not your identity, not your emotion. Just because we're living in an age where confession gets you capital doesn't mean you have to smile through your own exploitation. Just defend your grades. Your actions. Your logic and reason. Start thinking of apologias, and you will always be fine."

Veronica drew quiet. Nothing like this had ever happened before. She'd been a TA for years and always deferred to the professor when any issues—like plagiarism, excessive absences—came up in her small student body. But the university now thought she was ready to handle a class of her own. Brianna also had one. So did Jonathan. It was a milestone one had to reach, like the exams and the eventual blank page of a dissertation. Veronica thought she'd been doing fine, though she spent weeks agonizing over her syllabus, and then been shocked at how much conducting her own class was like running a one-woman show. If the students seemed bored, she felt bad—after all, she'd been the one to select the readings. Yet when their pens scraped against the page with every last word she said, she felt powerful. Because, once again, she'd been the one to come up with all the material. It was a constant oscillation of I am the best teacher and I am the worst, I am the smartest and I am the most boring, nothing I know is useful and I know absolutely everything.

She'd been assigned a class that was theory-based, and because of that, it dealt a lot with writing. This seemed to make the entire predicament worse. How could someone teach theory without a core text? How could you teach writing to anyone, really? Especially to a group of students in their late teens who, presumably, already knew how to read and write? It was a process of pulling bad teeth out of a jaw and hoping something new was there underneath, a freak of nature who had another set, like the people who grew up in Love Canal. You could only do so much to break bad habits already engrained in a psyche, and only so much you could do to make theory accessible before you just ran out of examples. Because of this, she assigned a lot of bad grades. She taught her own methods of writing, her own methods of understanding, because she'd been able to get this far, so she must have known something, but it was like teaching in a vacuum. You needed a *text* to fill the void of a writing class. You couldn't just teach nonsense words. And since she couldn't be the text and was so sick of being an entertainer, she'd assigned what she knew. The books and articles and essays she assigned were all on nature, on poetry, on the history of books, on fairy tales and wilful arms. They were things she liked. Some students responded. Others gritted their teeth and got through it.

And others failed or didn't show up at all and then contested their grades. The email she received gave very little detail other than their names and student numbers and a potential date in the near future so she could produce their grades and everyone could go over her records. The date made her skin feel hot, like a doctor peeking inside an examination room before you were ready. Her gown had a slit in the back; the emperor had no clothing. She had a spreadsheet full of grades, sure; she'd handed it in on the last day possible to hand it in, thinking that was it.

But she'd thrown away the rest. That was the benefit of April being for the dead. It gave you the freedom to grieve and move on.

"They're asking for a body I don't have," she said. When Stella narrowed her eyes, she went on. "I know I shouldn't have done this. I get it, please stop telling me that. I...I just need to know what to do now. What do I do?"

Stella sighed. She withdrew her phone from her briefcase and unlocked the code. She seemed to struggle, as if she couldn't hook up to the hotel's WiFi. Veronica wanted to apologize—she opened her mouth to do just that—but then she pulled away. She knew it was not what Stella wanted to hear, and most likely, it wasn't what the student wanted to hear, either. *Whoops, sorry, your grades are in the trash. Or whoops, sorry, I don't even know how to pronounce your name.* Veronica bit her lip, wondering if she could ask Bo for help. She pushed the thought away the moment it occurred. What would it help with, anyway? What good would the correct pronunciation of a name mean if there was no face to put to it?

Veronica produced the email on her phone for Stella, and the two of them drew closer at the table, their Danishes and other sweet treats forgotten. Stella took out reading glasses and placed them on the bridge of her nose. Having her so close made Veronica shudder; she wanted to slip away and do something else, but the stress made her nerves stand up and pay attention.

"You lie."

"What?"

"That's your option at this point. Find a justification for the grades. Make up the attendance sheet and mark the student as away. That's it."

"And if someone calls the bluff?"

"The department is going to be on your side. You're the mask they need to wear. They will take your side, even if they see through this entire act. After the meeting is over, though," Stella said, swinging her chair back to her proper seat at the table, "they may chastise you."

"May?"

"May. It's more likely that this whole incident is a blip on their radar. Don't internalize it. But also do better next time. You're the authority. Never forget that."

Veronica nodded. The solution was so simple. So clean and pristine. Of course she had power because she was an extension of the school. She even started to feel better about the entire event and rose from the table to get her own plate of waffles, Danishes, and other sweet treats.

Then she remembered the protest from outside the other school, the one about the graduate student named Melanie Knight. In between the messages from the school, Brianna had emailed her more information on it, especially since she also seemed confused about what side of the argument to fall on. *The incendiary material she gave the class,* Brianna went on, *was a video. It was taken from a public talk show. How could that be bad?* Brianna's question had been rhetorical, but Veronica still felt compelled to answer—yet came up with nothing, even as Brianna sent her the video and it seemed utterly banal.

This was the difficulty in being a grad student though, Veronica now understood. While you were faculty, meaning that you had a mailbox and keys to get into buildings, it was so obviously clear that you did not have any true authority. The higher-ups could strip it from you in a matter of seconds during a damning meeting, all because you were also a student and paid tuition as such. It never made sense. It always felt strange, as strange as the first time Veronica showed up to lead a seminar at barely twenty-two in her MA and she realized no one had really prepped her. They insisted she knew enough to lead. And of course, she did, she could always fake her way through a 100-level English course since she was a fiend and read, read, read everything in her youth— but the dawning realization that she, a barely there scholar, was in charge of a classroom pulled back the veil on all her past classes. When she was eighteen, in her undergrad, the guy in a sweater who had said her introduction was bad on that first paper had been just like she was now. She'd thought he was so smart, so much better than she—but he had most likely struggled with his grad school readings while wearing only underwear and eating dry cereal. Academia was full of cloak and dagger assumptions, but once you got past the curtain, Veronica was sure she could survive.

Except that Jonathan had died. So had a bunch of other students. And Melanie Knight's survival left her beyond confused because she wasn't sure who won here. Who teaches the teachers? Not anyone in graduate school, from what she could see. No one really knew anything. But people did have power. That was the real issue here. That man in a sweater said her intro was bad, and he may have been wrong or right, but he still gave her a shitty grade. Melanie Knight might have gotten a raw deal, or she may have gotten what she deserved, but the ending was still the same: her power stripped back.

Recording what had gone on was the only way to—not get the power back—but to let people know what was happening. *Do you see it yet?* Veronica heard the distant voice from her dream. She swallowed. Then she remembered the real voice of Jonathan and that he'd wanted to tell her something.

Had Jonathan done what Melanie Knight had? His *I will not apologize* could be a statement of power, even in the midst of utter powerlessness. His answering machine message could have been one of many he left behind. I will not apologize, Veronica thought, but maybe, just maybe, I might explain. And in doing so, all the secrets of the academia, spilled forth from Pandora's Box.

"What about Melanie Knight?" Veronica asked. Saying the name of the grad student out loud had a magical effect on Stella, almost turning her to stone once again.

"You are not Melanie Knight. And she should not have taped that meeting. Do not tape that meeting you go to."

"But what if this is fundamentally unfair? You told me not to apologize."

"That's true. I also told you not to internalize this. You can never internalize this nonsensical bureaucracy without turning into Kafka's Josef K.

or Gregor Samsa. The service they make you do in this job is not service, it's grunt work that slows you down. But you have to do it. You have to show up. The moment you start to tape it, you start to wear it. You start to smile during your exploitation. You forget it's a mask, and suddenly, it's your own wound. Suddenly, you want to stay a bug. So don't tape the meeting. Don't become the meeting. Don't apologize."

"But..." Veronica did not finish the sentiment. She took a bite of her food, as if to quiet her tongue. Each bite felt too buttery, too sweet, like cotton candy in her mouth. She thought of the cotton candy professor, lambasting the same grad student who had opened Pandora's Box. No one seemed to care that the video she showed in class was not forbidden at all. No knowledge was forbidden. They only seemed to care about who got to speak, who got to be named, who got to have power. Veronica suddenly felt exhausted trying to trace all these influences, all the correct and incorrect ways of going about work that had once given her such hope.

"You know, sometimes I think Brianna is right," Veronica said. "We should just get a union. Then we don't need to worry about this."

Stella smiled. "It is not that simple. It never is."

"Workers of the world..."

"Unite. I know. But this is a job about intellectual pursuit, survival of the fittest. I do not mean that in a biological sense, but in its intended financial realm. After all, nowhere in *On the Origin of Species* does Charles Darwin talk about survival of the fittest—that is all pure Adam Smith, pure capitalism, and quite frankly, that is what academia has become. This is why you do not do contract work. This is why you do not bother with the nonsense and the chatter at the grad school level. It does not matter. It slows you down. Don't internalize it or you will never leave."

Veronica heard the other request in the background: *Do not talk to Brianna.* They both shared Stella as a supervisor, but Brianna was...being slowed down. Her illness, whatever it ended up being, caused her to take a leave from the school. Then she was part time, still struggling through exams and paying tuition. She was picking up contract work on the side, but Brianna was stuck in the muck of this form of life and was always going to be because, as Stella put it, she'd fallen too far behind. Survival of the fittest, in the economic sense. Whoever could survive this kind of abject poverty got to move on to something better, especially if they did not internalize it, and not everyone got to move on.

Veronica could understand that. It was harsh. It was mean. But Stella was speaking the truth. She just didn't understand how hungry Veronica got sometimes. Not the disorder, but the hunger for something more, something beyond this. Students contesting a grade reminded her of her power while also robbing her of it. A trigger, in the purest sense, because it could trigger her to survive or to freeze and fall apart.

She shoved the last bite of the Danish in her mouth. It tasted thick. It tasted good. *My God, I am starving. I am starving myself. I have been starving myself for years, ever since I stepped through that door.* She rose from their table to get coffee, she said, but she got more bacon and eggs. The hotel staff was already cleaning up the display, the breakfast hour almost over. She took all she could find, all that had not yet been touched by hotel hands, and felt like a scavenger.

When she arrived back at the table, Stella was consumed by her phone. She set it on the tablecloth with an icy stare.

"Are you okay?" Veronica asked.

"I just received a call from Officer Neilson. About the man we hit."

Charles Baudelaire. Veronica had named him after a line of *Les Fleurs du mal* about the bloat of a belly. A joke, even if she could not share it with Stella. Her attention was raised. "What about him?"

"He was a pedophile. There was a warrant out for his arrest. They are ruling his death a suicide or an accidental overdose, long before I arrived. Either way, I'm cleared."

"That's good then. Right? It's what we figured."

Stella's gaze was icy as it met Veronica. It struck fear into her. "I cannot believe I wasted my emotion on him."

"What?"

"Last night. I was rude. I was cruel. And all because I thought I had hit a person. All because I thought I had hit a human being, rather than a pedophile. I can't believe I did that. This...this is why I tell you not to internalize this nonsensical chatter. Because it ruins you from the inside, a corroding cancer."

Veronica blinked several times as Stella stood. She slipped her phone back into her briefcase and combed her hair behind her ears. Veronica could still hear the icy sharpness of the words. Wasted her emotion. Wasted her fear and guilt. She was so angry, angrier than Veronica had ever seen—and all at herself, at the random man on the phone. At first,

Stella's tone had been so strained that Veronica had heard petal-phile, a lover of flowers. But now he really was Charles Baudelaire, and those flowers were evil.

"I'm sorry, I—"

"No." Stella raised a hand. "None of that. Forget everything that occurred."

Veronica was silent, but she could not forget.

"I'm going to go work on my keynote speech. I've wasted enough time. You should do the same, you know. Get off the internet. Forget about the university. About that graduate student. Unions. Try to focus your energy on surviving instead."

Veronica stared at Stella's back until she disappeared in the hotel hallway. She tried to swallow, but her throat felt swollen. Her food seemed to rot in front of her, stinking and too much, as if it had grown in volume. Her paper was barely started. She wanted to hear some of the papers today, maybe even figure out Jonathan's missing panel, but all of that faded. She thought of how callously, how cruelly, and how quickly Stella had changed.

And she wanted to know more about the man. What about his backpack? They had hit *something*. What if it was a murder, not a suicide or overdose, and Stella wasn't responsible—but someone else was? Or what if his suicide was an apology for all his past behaviour? She wanted to know so desperately. So silly and useless. Internalizing.

But her insides were already corroded. Her knuckles red from the familiar scrape. She set down her food and headed out the door.

Chapter Thirteen

The more Veronica walked, the more she felt as if she was stepping backward in time. On either side of the hotel were woods but woods that only lasted a few kilometres before they became buildings, loud and neon, landmarks of late capitalism, familiar and yet indistinguishable from anything else. Veronica's sneakers pounded the sidewalk with cigarettes from packages free of French warning labels. As she walked, Dunkin' Donuts replaced Tim Hortons along the street, followed by the familiar-as-ever Golden Arches of McDonald's.

Soon the sidewalk ended. It became a road. Road and dirt and then grass and grass and grass as the pastoral Amherst wilderness swallowed Veronica whole once again. She thought of the Emily Dickinson poetry as she waltzed through the mud, only to realize that Dickinson must have seen Amherst through a window and in snippets of letters. What she had written about had been her own Eden, not the Eden of the perceived pastoral Americana that everyone else spoke about to one another or referenced in poetry. Knowledge from Stella's class, coupled with her own intensive academic study came back to Veronica, and all her thoughts felt like what a former biology student must feel when they go to the zoo. America in cages: passages from *Walden* by Thoreau, *Self-Reliance* by Emerson, and *Leaves of Grass* by Whitman emerged in front of her, verdant green and golden. They were highlighted in the page of her mind, marked off and pristine—but now out in the open for her to sink her hands and teeth into. Her fear and worry faded. She smiled more as she hiked, as if she wasn't searching for a dead man's backpack and was actually searching for a Virgin Land, like Henry Nash Smith had written about and then Leo Marx solidified in his own writings on America. Then Veronica started to feel as if she was in a solo *Stand by Me* movie; together, she was a bunch of young boys, nostalgically looking for a dead body and finding themselves.

Ah, America. She could not tell if she was being sarcastic or sentimental. The curves of the dirt road led her toward a wooded area that started to seem familiar. She lost track of how much time she'd been there, but she couldn't already be at the place where they'd had the near crash. She walked through long grass and paused at the edge of the woods. The hum of nature, buzzing and inchoate, filled her body as if she was a balloon. She floated between the leaves, the trees, the dead animals rotten and stinking nearby.

She saw someone.

A lean body, tall, eclipsed the trees and was only given away by the neon pink of a hoodie. Hard to miss and so starkly out of place. She thought of the train whistle at Concord, the steamboat destroying Huck Finn's raft. A machine in her garden. A stranger in Eden. She was about to call out when the person turned around.

"Bo?"

Bo froze. Veronica was just far enough away, and wearing enough dark colours, that she probably seemed as if she belonged in this pastoral landscape, rather than out of place in paradise.

"What the fuck?"

"Hey," she said, stumbling forward. "It's Veronica. From…last night. I…What are you doing here?"

Bo let out a long sigh that became a laugh. She stepped closer to Veronica, her face now alight with expression. She held a white bowl, flat and wide as if used for a large salad. It was filled to the near top with spidery-like leaves and other green matter and several petals of flowers Veronica could not name.

"You know, out of all the people who have yelled at me in the past twenty-four hours, I'm so glad it's you I meet alone in the woods. Damn, man. Like a horror film right now."

"I…I…" Veronica's face was flushed red, no longer just from the sun. Images from Bo's box and her dream came back to her. She wanted to apologize—no, she thought. Not apologize. She wanted to explain *why* in an apologia that the box and its contents had made her so upset. Her stutters overwhelmed her, though, and soon Bo was waving a hand.

"It's okay. Don't worry so much. You had a right to be a little creeped out. I mean, it's a little weird to keep a dead people box. I get it. I should get it. I was also talking some heavy smack about your exact crowd. I shouldn't have said anything about snobbery or dumb-dumbs. My bad."

Bo looked down, seemingly cowed. When she remained quiet, Veronica realized she was supposed to say something. But what?

"Is…is that an apology?"

"No. I apologize better than that. I don't think I did anything wrong, per se, but…I just wanted to say hi again. Like, can we start again? If we could, I know I'd keep my mouth shut about my book tastes. And maybe—"

"No," Veronica said. "I didn't mind. Really. I mean, when else was I going to learn anything about King? Or Dan Brown, for that matter. I should have given him a chance in my youth."

"Oh, don't talk to me about youth. It all feels like another life." Bo smiled, but it was gone as soon as it flickered. "Anyway, I should have been more in tune with the vibes. You're here at a conference on Emily Dickinson, and I should be kinder to her work. Because I do like it. You know that poem about Eden?"

"Come slowly," Veronica said. It was a trained response, so much like breathing.

"Yeah. That one. I like it. I think it's called something like *Slow Eden*?" When Veronica nodded, Bo smiled. "Either way, I like it. Sort of reminds me of O'Keeffe, too."

"You like O'Keeffe?"

"Yes. Well, I should say I like what Rebecca Solnit has to say about her work." When Veronica didn't respond, Bo brushed a hand away. "You don't want to hear me talk about books again."

"I might," Veronica said.

For a while, it was quiet between them. The hush of the wind against the grass and the humming of bugs made Veronica feel as if she was truly in an Eden.

"Anyway," Bo said, breaking up the feeling. "It's just a line of O'Keeffe's I really like. Apparently, after she moved to Mexico and was away from all her New York City friends, she used to sign her letters with *From the Faraway Nearby*. I kind of like that. Even when she was across the country and everything was so slowed down by the post office or long-distance phone calls, she didn't sugarcoat the distance as nothing much, but she didn't dwell on it, either. She just signed her name. Bam. *From the Faraway Nearby*…sort of like those postcards that say *Wish You Were Here.* You know those, yeah? They have them in Canada?"

"Of course," Veronica said, almost aghast to think that they wouldn't. "Those are so common."

"Good then. The expression is common but no less powerful. O'Keeffe made it her own, but what she says is universal. She even named a painting after that, though I don't know what one. I suppose…" Bo paused, suddenly overcome. Her grandiose explanation now became a softer register. "I thought of the box I showed you last night in that way. It was my Faraway Nearby, my Wish You Were Here. These were my friends' sign-offs, emblems from another time, strangers I'd wish I'd known better…but it's not quite as endearing as a postcard. I should keep that box hidden. Contained. Even postcards are meant to go to a specific someone. So the box is my thing, and that's cool, but I really should be more careful about who I show it to."

"Maybe," Veronica said slowly. "But we got O'Keeffe's letters. Someone recorded her personal words. The personal has to matter."

"The personal is political," Bo said, then laughed lightly. "But that's second wave, anyway."

Veronica nodded. She didn't add anything right away; she was still trying to recall her own limited knowledge of O'Keeffe—solely from that first-year class—to remember the painting. She eventually shrugged. "I still think I'm a little rattled. From Jonathan. It's still—"

"Fresh. I know. No need to explain."

Veronica nodded. She gestured to the bowl in Bo's hands. "So is this...more dead things for the collection? Even if it's a private one now?"

"No, no," Bo said quickly. She held the bowl higher. "These are very much alive. You don't know fiddleheads?"

When Veronica made no claim, Bo grabbed one of the fiddleheads from the bowl before setting it on the forest floor. When Bo held it up to the light, it looked like a sea spiral, the kind of seashell that her piano teacher had kept as a make-case, like the Fibonacci spiral used to deduce art's inherent symmetry. Bo pulled out the frond and revealed its fern-like structure from the inside.

"Is it for tea?" Veronica asked.

"No, but good guess. Too bitter for tea. It's sort of like an edible fern, tasting more like Brussels sprouts' and broccoli's little brother who moved into the woods and decided that civilization was much too harsh for its delicate soul."

Veronica laughed.

"Yeah, see? There you go. You get it. These little ferns taste really good if you know how to cook them. Pretty sure they're considered a delicacy in Montreal, too—or so I've heard. I've never gone. Want to one day, though."

"Why? Do you speak French?"

"*Un petit peu*," Bo said all the letters, even the silent ones. "Am I saying it right?"

"Not even close."

"Well, you're the expert then. I should use you as my travel consultant."

"I've never been to Montreal, either."

"But you still know more than me." A quick

smile passed between them before Bo added the spiral frond to her bowl. She gestured to a patch of land that seemed to be a mess of green a few feet ahead of them. Only when Veronica focused her gaze did she see a dozen more spirals laid out between grass blades. An ebullient feeling rose inside of her, spirals, a sign of infinite life, even more than the infinity symbol. She loved them. They were so small and compact, and part of her was desperate to taste.

"Want to help me look, or are you on another mission in the woods?"

"I'm...um..." Veronica wondered if she could enlist Bo's help with the backpack. Maybe she knew the dead man or maybe she had saved what she'd seen of the dead man's things so she could add it to her box later. For a second, she saw Bo in the light as a painter would have seen her, a new version of Andrew Wyeth's *Christina's World*, reaching out not for a house on the plain but the secrets that the dead held.

Veronica nodded and decided she wanted to risk her own secrets.

Bo did not flinch during the entire explanation. She tilted her head, responding at the right time with the right words, and when the story seemed to go on too long, she busied herself in the fiddlehead patch. Veronica got down on her knees with Bo and continued to explain her curiosity of the stranger she'd named Charles Baudelaire, then her frustrations about her student situation. Then she even explained the differences between apologia and apologies, her own paper topic, and Jonathan's final abstract, and the answers it could have, as well.

"I've been talking for so long," Veronica said. The sun hung low in the sky, sweat tickled her brow.

"I'm so thirsty."

"Figured you would tire yourself out eventually. I have water around the corner."

"There's a well here?"

"No, but there's a bed and breakfast my parents also run. It's not the best place, but it's empty right now. And there's food. We could get these all washed up and try them out."

Veronica liked the sound of that a lot. She rose to her feet with Bo's hand and followed her gesture toward the parting trees. A well-worn path emerged. Up ahead, she saw the wooden slats of an old farmhouse, red-roofed and rounded. Walden-esque, a place in the middle of nowhere if she'd ever seen one, something to write about and to write inside.

"Ah, *From the Faraway Nearby*," Veronica said. "I remember that painting now."

"Oh, yeah? You'll have to tell me all about it. And then," Bo added, "if you still want to search for the backpack, I'll go with you. But I honestly think the police probably found it."

"You know, you're probably right." Veronica nodded, letting go of one mission and gradually switching to the next. "In '*The Faraway Nearby*', O'Keeffe paints a cow skull, like most of her work, but now it hangs in the middle of a blue and pink skyline. There is nothing to hold it up, but it's strong. It's a horizon piece. Like those postcards."

"Wish You Were Here," Bo said.

"I am here," Veronica said softly, surprising herself.

"I know." Bo smiled. A flicker of something more passed between them before Bo turned toward the cabin. "So let's do something about that."

Chapter Fourteen

Fiddleheads need to be unfurled to be cleaned," Bo explained as she set Veronica up in the kitchen at the steel sink below red curtains. "The water can only touch them for a few moments, though, before they start to wilt. It's a bit tricky, but you're smart. You'll get the hang of it."

Bo winked playfully before she demonstrated with the first fiddlehead. She unfurled the spiral with the edge of her thumb and set it aside in another bowl. "Now you go."

The water was cool and clean; after relieving her parched throat, Veronica flicked the water against the green fronds and did her best to keep them intact. Soon her fingers and the sink were dotted with green freckles, and her nails contained a brown ring from dirt. Even when bugs jumped from the dish, it didn't startle her. It was the most natural thing she could think of, the most alive she'd ever felt and most like she'd been torn from the pages of a novel. It was a strange sensation, one she found herself spiralling into as she continued to clean while Bo did the cooking.

"Fiddleheads are best served with loads of butter," Bo said. "Sometimes a hint of lemon. You like lemon?"

Veronica nodded.

"Good."

From her peripheral vision, Veronica watched

as a huge hunk of butter splattered in a frying pan. It would have normally made her skin tense—what to do with all that butter, where did it go on the body, how would she get rid of it later?—but she was calm. She wanted to taste it. She wanted it to be part of her body because it felt like she'd been rejecting too much.

No thoughts or concerns of pesticides or piss from animals in that part of the woods rose to her consciousness. Only as Bo warned her that sometimes fiddleheads could be poisonous—or even cancerous— did she feel fear. Bo insisted that she'd done this before, picked from that area, and that these were fine. She set a place for herself at the table and demonstrated that she would be eating alongside her, so if they got sick, they got sick together.

"But I assure you," Bo said, "this is perfectly safe."

Safety seemed like an illusion, yet another photograph framed so that certain people were cut out of the corners, but Veronica believed in it. Once she was done washing, she set to work making tea from the petals remaining in the white bowl. An hour after getting inside, they sat at the table with a heap of green, buttery weeds and the tea that smelled like hickory and wood smoke. The meal was small—that many fiddleheads did not amount to much—but it was splattered in rib-sticking butter. The first taste on Veronica's tongue was astringent from the greenery but then undercut by the fat and citric acid in the lemons. It was good, one of the best things she'd eaten in a long, long time, and she made sure to tell Bo as much.

Bo pulled her arm back in a cheer. "Yes. Thank goodness. I can tell my mother now that I'm not disappointing her. At least, not entirely."

Conversation flitted from topic to topic; Veronica found herself explaining the references that had been going through her head all afternoon, elucidating on her Emily Dickinson love and the neo-pastoral landscape she felt consumed by through citations. Bo knew Dickinson, obviously, but this time, she surprised Veronica with additional knowledge of Dickinson's legacy amongst the handful of lesbian novels she'd read where the protagonists liked to quote her words. It was a total trope, almost a cliché at this point, Bo insisted, but it seemed to make up the foundation of "dyke lit." Bo listed off the titles when Veronica had been in disbelief. Then she merely felt bereft of knowledge. How could she not know about lesbian novels as a lesbian, and how could she not know about this use of Dickinson's words as a scholar? She wondered, almost frantically, how it could fall into her own paper and turned to Bo for assistance.

"I'm not too sure about your topic, honestly," Bo said. "But I can leave you the books to borrow. Does that help?"

"Very much." Veronica thanked her again and again but knew that her time was running out to revise her planned paper trajectory. She watched as the sun sank lower and lower behind them in the horizon, the red drapes turning purple under the darker light. Soon enough, she'd need to go back, and she wasn't sure how long that would take.

But she didn't press the matter. Instead, she listened as Bo explained more of her parents' inheritance and their plans for her in terms of the chain hotel, the bed and breakfast, and all that other "hospitality nonsense" that Bo was not into.

"So what are you into?" Veronica asked. "Other

than fiddleheads and dead things? Why do you want to go to Montreal?"

"Oh, that is a pet project. Some of the best surgeons are there."

"In Montreal? What kind of surgery?"

Bo tilted her head, her expression suddenly confused, then troubled. "You haven't made that jump yet, have you?"

"What jump?"

"I'm a transgender woman."

Bo waited with the patience of a kindergarten teacher as realization dawned on Veronica. She knew the word—everyone did now, especially in academia—but she had not really considered it beyond that academic interest. There were standards you had to uphold in the classroom, things you could and couldn't say in class, a code of conduct. But transgender as a reality was still removed from her own daily life. Even when Bo spoke about the second wave feminists and their disregard of trans women, Veronica had still failed to see that connection beyond a mere conversation, a point of interest. With new clarity now, Veronica remembered the IDs in the death shoebox and how many were mismatched. A wave of suicide among friends. And the desperation that sometimes crossed Bo's face as she talked about her parents and her legacy.

"What...is Bo your real name?"

Bo sighed. Veronica knew she'd asked the wrong question. She apologized and watched as Bo's back straightened out again.

"It's what people call me, so yes, it's my name. That's all names really are. Anyway," Bo said, her back and voice stiffening once again. "I'm a trans woman, and Montreal has some of the best surgeons who specialize in the care I'll need. Or so I've heard. Many people talk about Canada in the trans community like it's some magical land. *Oh, Canada*, and its kooky ways with bagged milk and Mr. Tim Horton and surgery practices that can be funded by the government. Insane. Unreal. Something I think I could want, even if I end up needing to use bagged milk for my coffee in the morning after."

"Oh. Okay. Well, I can attest to Tim Hortons and bagged milk, but I don't know everything else."

"You know more than you give yourself credit for."

"I will take that as a compliment then."

Quiet descended over their shared table, like another negative space that took over Veronica's mind. What was once easy between them now seemed to be a shadow of an era that had once passed. Bo rose to take the dishes away, and Veronica tried to fill the void with niceties, comments about the bed and breakfast décor, but the tension persisted. She knew she was the one making it worse; all her words seemed foolish now. She repeated and replayed all their conversation to be sure she hadn't said something silly or offensive. But that wasn't the point. The point was that she was silent now in the fear of offense. She needed to eradicate this knowledge from her mind to proceed, but she couldn't stop thinking about it. All knowledge was good, she knew. She needed to keep this present, but she needed to not be afraid of her own ignorance.

Veronica rose from her chair, determined to talk about Montreal. *You didn't need to speak French there to survive; lots of people speak English and don't mind doing so, they even passed a law where shopkeepers have to greet in English first; I hear the old city is beautiful and the universities, too*—but all of her trivia came to a halt when she saw the piano. It was like a second sense, a scent in the air that she could follow with enough clues. Next to the kitchen was a living room that looked down into a rec room or basement den. From one angle, she could see into its subterranean living space, where the edge of a piano, top closed, sat. A beautiful one, old and ornate. She flexed her fingers as if she was about to play. She felt her shoulder, where a phantom bruise always appeared, like a song that became stuck in her head after the first bars. She let go of herself and her memories and only thought of music.

"You have a piano here."

"Oh? Yeah, we do." Bo glanced over her shoulder as she washed dishes. Boredom turned to intrigue. "You play?"

"Yes. Not in a long time, but I did. I do."

As Veronica walked toward the piano, her limbs felt like jelly. Her hands shook. She thought of the first time she climbed into her mother's lap to play. She put her tiny hands over her mother's hands and played a song. Like a player piano, she was not the one controlling the music but only the movements. That had been how she'd learned up until she surpassed her mother's hands—and height at four feet eleven—and her skill level. Then Adele had come in. Then everything had changed.

She was thinking of Adele's hands on her shoulder, watching and directing her in a much more formal way than the lap lessons with her mother, when she realized her memories were too present. They played against the back of her eyelids like a movie screen. They walked out of the screen like living hallucinations, like demigods come back to take over the world. The memories and fantasies were blurred; they happened in real time, and Veronica was no longer part of this show.

A hand on her shoulder turned to a hand on her thigh. Adele's lips over her ear, whispering instructions, then commands and then silencing Veronica with a tongue. Adele's fingers taking off her clothing and guiding her inside. Piano keys smelling like sex; ivory and ebony skin, just like the keys, beautiful just like the music. Such beautiful music. *Marche Funèbre. Clair de Lune. Moonlight Sonata.* Even if the desire was then torn open and apart and her mother's harsh words cut like piano wire, being with Adele had always been beautiful. Veronica had learned how to play. She'd become an adult. At fourteen, she'd felt and tasted desire, and then at fifteen, when she refused to eat anything at all and her clothing hung off her like a ragged skeleton and the words and tongues and everything came back up in vomit, she still knew that the music was beautiful.

The music was all she heard now. As her feet fell out from under her and the floor rushed to meet her, Veronica felt like she was coming home.

Chapter Fifteen

Veronica felt like she was in Eden. Her Eden. Rolling grass hills flanked her, the deep green colour so thick and lush she swore she could smell the first hint of summer rain. A stream was by her left side, the water the crystal-clear blue of her favourite nail polish as a child. Frogs, tadpoles, tiny fishes made the water move in a cascade of light. Out ahead, dotting the hills with brown and burnt ember, were deer and foxes. A forest paradise. She felt like she was in Walden Pond, only this was her Walden Pond. One where she, like Eve, did not need to wear clothing as she walked around because there was absolutely no need to feel shame.

She bent down by the water and pressed some to her mouth. It tasted salty. After she'd stayed in the hospital one time and they'd only given her liquid meals, everything for a week afterward tasted like that. Everything had so much salt, even tea, even herbal tea. Veronica didn't like the memory that had gotten its hook into her skin. She stood from the pond and looked at the sky, the trees, her rolling Eden. She felt safe here. Better here. This was not the biblical kind of Eden since that one professor who always showed the paintings in her lecture made a point to note that Eden was most likely an arid desert or jungle, given where the Bible was likely written. That professor also liked to point out that the forbidden fruit in that garden was never actually named an apple. It was just forbidden fruit. Most likely, given the climate, she mentioned over and over, that fruit was a pomegranate. Maybe even a banana. *We don't know. But it's fun guessing.*

Veronica wanted to remember that professor's name. She could see her face with its ruddy cheeks—that professor was so unlike Stella in that she always blushed every time she stepped on the large teaching stage. Veronica remembered she had tattoos that poked out from her T-shirts and onto her forearms. She'd shorn her hair off, right down to a pixie cut, halfway through the term, and it had changed its colour from blond to dark brown in the process. The professor was beautiful, yet tender. Strong, yet soft. She kind of reminded Veronica of Bo. The comparison made her feel funny, almost like the taste of the salt in the pond, so Veronica moved on.

She turned from the hills to see an orange frog cut across her pathway. It looked up at her and opened its mouth to ribbit. A fiddlehead leaf unfurled on its tongue. Veronica smiled. She wondered if there were fiddleheads here, too, and if that was what the forbidden fruit was. She was about to walk away from the frog, in search of a new mission, when she heard the words mixed in with the ribbits, almost like a DJ sampling from another track.

Ribbit. Ribbit. Do you see it yet? Ribbit.

Veronica turned back to the frog. It was bigger now, as if growing to a full human size. The orange of the frog became the burnt fire of Jonathan's hair. His ruddy cheeks, so much like that professor's and so much like the gender ambiguity she saw in Bo's body now that she knew where to look. Veronica knew—even in her dreams—that she should not be comparing the male body to the female body. Bo was, and always has been, a woman. Her professor, too, if her professor had gone on to transition and become a man at the front of the teaching stage, then he would have always been a he, too. There was something oh so forbidden in mixing all these identities up in the blender of her consciousness and then consuming it. *Identity*, she realized. *In my dreams, identity is the forbidden fruit.*

Do you see it yet? Do you recognize them?

The frog—Jonathan—continued to speak. He listed the to-dos from the machine message. He spoke in a computer-generated voice that the memory was out of space. When his mouth opened again, the fiddlehead tongue became a cellphone, a thick one, as if from another period. As if it was a burner phone for drug deals. The phone was gone in a blink, then his tongue became a set of keys. Office keys. The same damn office keys that fit into the entire bank of rooms. No privacy. Always recording.

Veronica's anger twisted in her guts. She wanted to kick the frog. She stepped closer to him, and he shrank back down to normal size. He became unlike Jonathan. Now green, now with two sets of legs, a double Siamese frog. Then he was an apple. Just an apple, green, and sitting on the rock by the pond.

Veronica figured there was no harm in trying to eat him now. She picked it up, bit inside, and watched as the blue sky and green grass—her Eden—became a pool of utter darkness. Nothing surrounded her. She felt like she was free falling, the fall from Eden, from the garden. All she heard was her name. It was the only thing she could grasp on to and hope for some kind of resolution.

Veronica. Veronica.

Yes?

Wake up.

She tried. She really did. Her entire body seemed to turn itself inside out—and then, and then—disappeared entirely, into a faraway place she was never sure she could return from.

Chapter Sixteen

Veronica."

"Yes?"

"Wake up."

Veronica opened her eyes. She was awake. Alive. "What...what happened?" She blinked and blinked again. The cabin was dark but swelled with artificial light that hurt her eyes. Wood grains pressed against her back. Her head throbbed. Bo appeared by her side, a hand on her chest.

"Jesus Christ. You had a seizure. Or maybe you fainted. I don't know."

"I...what?" Veronica blinked again. She heard music. Swore she tasted Adele, but it turned out to be vomit at the side of her mouth. There was spit-up—her spit-up—against the carpet. Veronica couldn't help but think it was shaped like a frog. Bo had been in the middle of cleaning up her mess when she came to. "I'm so sorry," Veronica said. "How long was I out?"

"Not long, honestly. But I freaked out. Ambulance should be here soon."

"What?"

Veronica scrambled up from the floor. Dizziness struck her and made her humble. She grasped the couch with a floral pattern on its side, a pattern she swore she recognized from her childhood. Her nails scraped and let go; Bo held her instead. Bo mumbled "easy, easy" under her breath and guided her to the couch seats. Veronica wanted to throw up again. She remembered the taste of the apple in her dream: metal, like blood, metal like the keys. It was disgusting, yet she was so utterly convinced it was trying to tell her something. The secrets of the world were in that dream, she was sure of it. And if not the secrets of the world, then just the shitty situation she found herself in. Maybe some final words from Jonathan, something beyond the cryptic lines, so Veronica could move on.

She turned to grasp Bo's forearm to tell her all this, but she was already there. Bo stared at Veronica so harshly it felt as if it went through her. That was the point, though, Veronica soon realized. Bo was checking her pupils.

"My aunt is a nurse. She taught me a lot. But… this is out of my depth."

"It's just low electrolytes. It's nothing."

"I don't know about that. I saw you go down and then flop and vomit. I'm pretty sure those are three things that shouldn't happen in a row."

"But I'm fine now. I'm talking. I'm walking."

"Barely."

"Just…trust me," Veronica mumbled after a moment. "I'm fine."

Bo's gaze this time was fixated on her. "This has happened before."

Bo asked a question that wasn't a question, yet Veronica felt compelled to answer. "Not precisely, but I know what caused it."

"Not the fiddleheads?"

Veronica shook her head. It felt like her brain was rattling around. She wanted to vomit again, but she held off. She was fine. She was stupid, but she was fine. She pressed her palm to her forehead, as if to keep her third eye from spilling out onto the floor. She thought of Adele. She always thought of Adele, in that way in which something so profound affects you all the damn time, so you always think about it without thinking about it. Adele was the void she always returned to, the bruise that was always there. But this time—this time she'd actually *conjured* Adele. Then Adele, just before Veronica had come to, had become Bo in her visions, then Jonathan, and now she was back to Bo again. And Veronica had wanted to kiss Bo so strongly at that moment. She held back, though. Not because she was trans—Veronica told herself that over and over again—but because she wasn't sure what timeline she was in right now.

The whirring of the sirens broke her reverie. Bo rose and went to the door. She peeked out the red curtains before she turned to Veronica again. "I think they should check you out."

"I have no insurance in this state."

"Oh. Shit. I didn't..." Bo went to a drawer in the kitchen. She desperately dug through them until she pulled out an ID. She tossed it at Veronica. "Not the best, but it's close."

A woman named Julie Tillman stared back at her with green eyes and brown hair flecked with blond. At least three inches taller, according to the license, and with round cheeks that would make her at least twenty pounds heavier. A bust size that was bigger, too, no doubt. Not the best match indeed, but something, Bo quickly explained before the paramedics came inside, that could be used to throw them off and divert any or all billing. Veronica eventually relented but insisted she was not going to the hospital.

The paramedics surrounded her in a haze.

One took the ID and wrote the information down. Another checked her pupils. He seemed to find no more information than Bo had. Veronica gave a vague medical history. When they started to interrogate Bo, asking for her ID, as well, Veronica found herself getting defensive. She was no longer polite to the medical staff. She refused any treatment.

"If you've had a seizure, ma'am," the one paramedic said to her, "we highly suggest you get checked out."

"You're checking me out now. I'm fine."

"You need to go to the hospital."

"No."

He huffed. Veronica wondered if it was the same older man paramedic from before, but she was sure these two were strangers. "Let me take your blood then."

She relented and presented her arm. They tapped her skin, trying to find a vein in desperation. When they did, they said she didn't drink enough and was most likely dehydrated. "Your blood is like sludge," one of them commented, thin chastisement in his voice. "That's probably the cause of all this."

"I *know*," she said, obstinate.

When the paramedic took her hand and flipped it over to see the marks on her knuckles, she withdrew in a tight motion. He gave a look she understood to be even worse than the chastisement in his prior tone. *Disgust. Loathing.* The same thing doctors always gave her before they stopped understanding anything else that came from her mouth.

"I'm fine," she insisted, holding herself in a hug. She stared at the floorboards, toward the staircase that led to a piano. "Just please leave me alone."

The crew left. It was pitch black in the cabin, soon marked by the red and blue of their lights. Veronica rose from her feet. She swayed. Bo grabbed a glass of water, and Veronica downed it. Each action silent, each one so finely choreographed between them, as if they were in time with each other. When Veronica handed back the empty glass, she touched Bo's hand. Concern etched in her stare, which quickly turned to something else more familiar.

"You okay?"

"I...I will be. I just should go back."

They stared. It lingered. Veronica felt it like her memories. She wondered if the kiss hadn't been triggered by her own desire, but by the reality of Bo giving her mouth to mouth. She wanted to ask, but she pushed it away. She focused on her paper. She'd have to present in less than twelve hours, and she could not fumble like this.

"Let me give you a ride back," Bo insisted. She grabbed her keys before an answer came, but the answer was, as always, like it had been with Adele in spite of what everyone said, "Yes, of course."

Chapter Seventeen

Bo's hand on her shoulder made Veronica wince. It wasn't that the touch wasn't nice—or necessary, especially since Veronica was still feeling woozy. Seasick, really, even though that made no sense. The drive back had been harrowing, and she'd kept her eyes closed the entire time. Moving from sitting to standing and then walking into the front of the hotel left her feeling as if she was the captain of a ship and the only one left alive.

Bo's hand negated that feeling. Bo was there. She was with her, helping her, and asking a dozen times over if she could get her tea. "I know I have some for nausea. Fennel seeds. Like magic, I promise you. Also, licorice root, valerian..."

"No, thank you." Veronica winced again. Her words sounded underwater. "I think I'm just going to bed."

"I have tea for that, too." Bo's eyes beamed. She seemed genuinely excited she could help before she then seemed to realize that helping meant something was wrong. "I have tea for lots of things, really. 'Cept for, you know, the bigger kind of transformations."

"Like becoming an adult?"

Bo laughed. It was uproarious. It acted like a balm to some of her nerves. Veronica was so used to her sickness, any kind at all, being the gigantic problem in the room. Ever since her parents asked her to take off her jacket in the summer, and she revealed arms like twigs, Veronica felt like her body was the problem, rather than what had been done with her body. But Bo didn't give her that feeling, no, not even close. She knew what it was like to have a body that was a problem and then treated as such. She knew what it felt like to be poked and prodded. Veronica's heart swelled. She was giving her tea, not to make her feel like she had to be fixed, but because Bo just liked tea.

"Are you sure?" Bo asked.

"You know," Veronica said. "I might take one for the road."

Bo let out a low yes sound and disappeared into the back. Veronica set her arm on the hotel front desk to keep herself steady. Her stomach was better. Her head was better. She knew she'd need to eat something very soon, but that was okay. She counted the triangles on the carpet and pretended she wasn't counting calories in her mind. Bo had just returned from the backroom with a single-serving pouch of tea when Veronica felt that now familiar feeling of goose bumps on her neck. Like she was being watched. She turned behind her and saw no one in the front hotel foyer. A few people lingered in the conference area, but it was mostly done for the day. There was a social event planned in the city proper, something that Veronica never wanted to go to anyway. No one was watching her. The elevator doors pinged close by, but no one got off or on. If there had been anyone, they were now long gone.

"Here you go." Bo tilted her head to the side. "You sure you don't need anything else?"

"I'm fine. Really. Just looking forward to a bed

and some food where I can then work on my paper."

"Exciting."

"It's at nine in the morning." Veronica sighed. "I suspect I might be asleep."

"I can give you a wake-up call. That's something I love doing, actually."

"Really? I thought you hated all that hospitality nonsense."

"I do…well, I do when I'm getting bitched at for not doing laundry. Or when someone's bickering over something pointless or petty, like the way we fold the corners of the bed or the fact that they don't like that they have to pay for parking. That stuff sucks. But I like the small things, the things like giving someone a toothbrush because they left theirs at home and them being so grateful to have it because they want to look their best. I don't know." Bo blushed slightly. "Just small things. Nice things."

"Like a wake-up call?"

"Oh, yeah. For a while, I loved it because it was voice practice since it's notoriously hard to pass as a woman on the phone. So hard. Testosterone's a hell of a hormone, and those vocal cords are never going backward. But alas, I love being that voice for someone as they wake up. It's…nice, you know? I don't want to get too Freudian and say I'm fulfilling a mommy complex, but you know, I'm the first person they hear for the day. I want it to be a good memory."

Veronica could only nod. Too much emotion welled inside of her. So she just said thank you once again, held up the teabag, and got on the elevator.

Stella was waiting by her hotel door when she arrived. Veronica paused at the edge of the hall corner, just as she'd turned, thinking she'd seen another apparition. Stella was wearing white jeans and an off-white top, too, making her look more like a resurrected version of Emily Dickinson herself. When Stella spotted Veronica, she gave a small wave. Her face was impassive, no smile or any expression.

Veronica felt as if she was in trouble. She knew that look, right? She was suddenly reminded of a Toni Morrison interview she'd seen when she'd talked about her children. Morrison realized she was criticizing them as they walked into the room—dirty shoes, untucked shirt—so her face was always frowning. She wanted her face to light up when she saw her children, so she deliberately changed her motions. Veronica tried to remember it for her students, for those anxious first days of classes.

But Stella's face did not light up. Veronica had never noticed this as clearly as she had now. Bo's does, she thought. Bo's seemed to always light up, no matter what. *That's why she likes wake-up calls. A good note to the morning.* She suddenly wished she'd said yes to the call. She wanted to wake up to the light and not... this anymore.

"Veronica," Stella said. "I've been looking for you."

"I'm here."

"I see that. But have you been in your room all day? In spite of the conference?"

"I. Uh...I thought your paper was tomorrow."

Stella folded her arms. She breathed slowly through her nose. "It is. But do you not care about the conference itself? The scholarship?"

"I...I thought you said most of these papers were fads. Perfect on the surface, you know?"

"Your friend Samantha's might be. But even if

it is as vacuous as it sounds at first, you should still show up. They need to see your face. They need to see you participating."

Veronica didn't want to ask who "they" were. Professors? Colleagues? Potential job offers? She thought she'd done the glad-handing at the opening dinner. She truly thought that she was there for scholarship, her own work, and then Stella's. She thought she had time, but apparently, she'd been wasting it.

Stella let out a small tsk-tsk. "I certainly hope this incident with your student hasn't dampened your experience of the conference."

"What? Oh. No. But it is upsetting."

"You cannot let incidents like that take on too much importance."

"That's not why I missed today. I just...I didn't feel well. And I had to work on my paper, so I was talking to Bo."

"Who is Bo?"

"The hotel worker. She gave me..." Veronica held up the teabag. She thought Stella would approve. Wouldn't it be something Dickinson would have done, like Stella's baking of her old muffin recipe? But she seemed derisive. The teabag now felt like a witch's potion, something fanciful and magical. A tea for transformation. Veronica sighed. She felt woozy. "Can we go inside? I don't feel so great."

Stella gestured toward Veronica's door, demanding a key card access with the tilt of her wrist. Veronica opened it, and Stella held it for them. She seemed to inspect the way Veronica had set up her laptop in one corner and notebook on the bedside table. She'd not made the bed and put up a *Do Not*

Disturb sign on the door so no one made it. Stella seemed to criticize everything in her mind, from a wrapper in the garbage to the sheets unmade to her black dress hanging in a closet. Veronica placed the tea next to the kettle in the room, but she didn't plug it in.

"You were not kidding." Stella was in front of the laptop screen. She'd known Veronica's password to get inside, so she was now looking at the paper. "It's not done."

"I said I was working on it."

"All day, and this is what you have?"

"No. Well, I felt sick. I was going to do it tonight."

Stella seemed disappointed. She *was* disappointed. She didn't need to say anything at all for that to show. Normally, Veronica would have crumbled. She would have fallen by Stella's feet and begged for some kind of forgiveness. Maybe even helped with her structure, her arguments.

But she was so tired.

"Look," Veronica said. "I feel like shit. I'd like to get some food."

"What an excellent idea." Stella sat on the bed, tucking one of the corners before she did. She gave Veronica a look of desire rather than derision. "I think that will go a long way to making us both comfortable."

Veronica swallowed hard. This was exactly what she'd wanted yesterday. Stella, delivered on her bed. Stella's talents—all of them—at her disposal. Her stomach fluttered. Stella ordered the food, and as she hung up the phone, Stella patted the space by her on the bed. Veronica's stomach tightened. She was tired. She was weak. She sat next to Stella and let their mouths meet, over and over again. Stella tasted so, so sweet. It was like a dream, a good dream this time.

By the time the room service meal arrived, Veronica had come once. Stella had slipped her fingers into her pants and run along Veronica's folds in all the right ways. One breast was out of her bra, and she had to slip her shirt around and do up her pants before she answered the door. Her cheeks felt red, her prior actions utterly transparent. She didn't care. As she answered the door, she caught sight of Stella in the corner licking her index finger to remove the remnants of Veronica from it.

"Hello again," Bo said. "Here is your immaculate dinner. I am so happy your appetite is back."

Veronica's face fell. She tried to smile, but it was hard. "Yep. A little better. Thank you."

"So can I wheel this in, or did you plan on eating in the hallway?"

"Oh. Thanks. Sure." As Veronica opened the door, she felt torn in two. Bo's smile turned to a mute professional stance as she wheeled the cart in and saw Stella on the bed. There was no reason to think that they'd done anything. They were both clothed. The bed had been made. But Stella's smirk, that downright boastful glare she got sometimes when she could make Veronica come so easily, was on her face. The room, too, probably smelled like sex. Bo could sense that. Bo had worked in the hotel industry long enough to sense that.

Veronica couldn't hide a damn thing.

But what was there to hide? She couldn't tell anymore if she was protecting Stella from the fallout of her job or if she was protecting herself from the disappointment of not knowing who she really, truly wanted to be with tonight. For a moment, Veronica thought of the philosopher Sara Ahmed, the scholar she was supposed to be citing on her paper for tomorrow, and realized that she must become the other woman tonight. It was the only safe choice; Veronica had to spend the night with work, and only work, and hope the rest sorted itself out later.

"Thank you." Stella rose from the bed and grabbed her bag. She took out several bills and put them in Bo's hand. Then she turned away, toward Veronica, and gestured to their meal. "Let's go. We have a lot of work to do."

Veronica nodded. She thanked Bo once again, but she was already heading out, down the hall, and a long way from the room itself.

❧ ❧ ❧ ❧

"That was interesting," Stella said.

"It was. Pretty good for room service." Veronica wiped her hands on a napkin that came with their meal of chicken salad sandwiches and roasted potatoes. She would have normally not eaten something like this, with so much mayonnaise, unless she could eat Cheetos or licorice beforehand. That way, bright colours of the first food always made it easier to know when the meal was done, when the purging was complete. A colour-coded finish line. She realized Stella was still talking, and she eagerly pushed aside the thoughts of vomiting. She really, really did not want to do this tonight.

"When I spoke on the phone and when I ordered the meal, I thought I was talking to a man. But that was a woman. So I think I might be losing my hearing.

Perhaps I'll need a hearing aid. Maybe I will be an old relic in the department sooner than I thought."

"Bo's trans," Veronica said right away. She bit her lip. She wasn't sure if that information was hers to tell. Bo seemed to be open about who she was, but revealing someone as trans, she knew from her own experiences with her own sexuality, could be dangerous. Sharing identities was always contentious. Yet it didn't seem to matter, as long as she protected Stella. She was not old. She was beautiful, stunning.

"Ah. There it is." Stella nodded. Veronica met her gaze and realized with sudden clarity that she'd been played. Stella knew something was amiss with Bo, and especially Bo's expressions and mannerisms toward Veronica, but now she knew for sure. She just had to poke long enough, and something, something always came up. "How did you know that? Were you swapping confessional stories in another mourning ritual?"

"No. She's very nice. She helped me."

"She's in the service industry. All help is expected and paid for. It is precisely her job to be nice."

"So?"

"So," Stella said, "do not believe that because you know some sordid details about her that you are best friends now. She's a hotel worker. She's supposed to bring us food. It's why I gave her money."

"She gave me tea, too."

"That comes in the rooms."

Veronica bit her lip. Why couldn't she just tell Stella that they'd also gone to the woods together? It hadn't been planned, but it had happened. And when she'd passed out, Bo was there. Bo cared. That was not a *quid pro quo* arrangement based on the hotel's star rating; that was not emotional capitalism at work, a trade of "I'll show you my pain if you'll show me yours." "It wasn't like that. Not in the least."

"So what was it like?" Stella ran a hand through Veronica's dark hair. "Don't tell me you want to ruin your good looks."

"What?"

"Transitioning. Surgery. It's a horrible way to treat a body, especially when so many other things can happen to you."

"What?" Veronica swallowed hard. When Stella only stared, Veronica pressed further. "And what if I did?"

"Veronica, you're clearly a woman."

"I'm not saying I want to transition. But people do transition. It's not horrible to them. It rather seems like a relief."

"A waste."

"I don't agree," Veronica said. The words felt awful, like the rug had been pulled out from under her. "And so what if it was a waste? Who says a body must be productive? That even gender must be? Let's waste it. Why not?"

Stella let a beat pass between them. She took her hand away from Veronica's shoulder. "You know I fully believe that people can do whatever they want with their own bodies. I would be a hypocrite if I didn't believe that."

"Right. Exactly." Veronica let out a breath. Perhaps she was acting too hastily, reacting too strongly. "You know I'm the same way. I don't want to be a man, and I know I'm cis."

"Cis?"

"Cisgender." Veronica had to fight back laughter.

Was there really a word that Stella didn't know but Veronica did? "Cis means on the same side. Trans means across or beyond. So if someone is cisgender they are on the same side as their birth gender."

"I know what cis means. I was a scientist. They use those terms in chain reactions, chemical compounds. Hence trans fatty acids."

"Oh. Right." Veronica decided she was still going to count that as a win. Stella may have been a scientist at some point, but she still didn't know gender like Veronica did. "So yeah, I'm cis, but obviously, trans people exist and need to do some things. They should be allowed to. It's not that big of a deal or a revelation. And it's never a waste."

"No, I suppose not in this culture."

"What do you mean 'this culture'?"

"Confessional. A wound for a wound for a wound. We exchange stories, and we think that everything is hunky dory and that it all makes sense now."

"I...I still don't get it."

Stella nodded. She leaned forward on her knees, the same way she'd done in her reading classes. "Bo may believe she's a woman. She may tell the story enough times. But all stories are fabrications of real-life events. We all know this, some of us even embrace it, but Bo is one of the grander narrators."

"So she's lying?"

"No. But I am saying that she thinks she can steal femininity from an outside source, slap it onto her nails in bright red polish, and that's it. Ta-da, womanhood."

Veronica's stomach turned. She wanted to be sick again. She didn't like the way this was going, yet she knew she was going to keep asking. "So you're saying...what?"

"I'm saying what everyone else has been saying for centuries, all the way back to Plato in *The Symposium*. We think we're searching for our other half, but we're really just searching for a nice story about ourselves. We're far, far more like Narcissus in the pool of water than we care to believe."

Veronica sighed. "He drowns in that story."

"He does. That's what happens when you're too in love with your own story, rather than your own survival. Now." Stella rose from the bed. She flicked on Veronica's computer. As the machine warmed up, she wheeled the food tray into the hallway. She added several other bits of garbage from Veronica's counter. When she picked up the teabag, Veronica wanted to tell her it was not yet used. It was hers. It was the last gift she had from someone that felt genuine.

But she was quiet. She imagined herself falling into the water of her dream. She had wasted too much time.

Now it was time to work.

⁂

Stella left at two in the morning. They'd had sex once after finishing a dry run of Veronica's paper, and Stella made Veronica come once again as she read it through the last time. Veronica still shuddered at every last touch Stella gave her, but it felt purely mechanical now. It was the rote, biological functions. No romance, no love—if it had ever been there. Stella seemed to like it that way the most. She seemed to have been prepared for that the most, even bringing her own hand cream and using it to get Veronica wetter and wetter the second and third times around. Then as soon as two in the morning displayed on the clock, Stella wished her good luck for the morning, planted another kiss on her mouth, and disappeared down the hallway.

Veronica knew that she would not see her until later. Stella would not attend her paper. She would practice her own, hone her own speech and mannerisms, and network for herself. Veronica was relieved. All the failure that she'd felt clinging to her as Stella nitpicked every word melted away. What did it all matter, anyway? Stella would not see.

She could literally do whatever she wanted tomorrow.

Anything. There was no one to witness, after all.

The thought was both intoxicating and sickening. She wanted to throw up again. And despite desperately not wanting to, the actions were so familiar. She was in the bathroom in no time, vomiting and then searching for cold water. All the ice from her room was gone, so she went hunting in the hallway in her short-shorts and a tank top.

The ice machine seemed to hiss and growl. It was so loud. When she heard the clanging of doors behind her, Veronica expected one of the guests was going to complain at her late-night trip.

Instead, it was Bo.

"Oh." Veronica glanced down at her outfit. She wore no bra, but her breasts were small and barely visible under the fabric. Her legs were bare in the shorts, but it wasn't anything shorter than some of the outfits she'd seen on her students this year. She was decent, really. Even the marks on her neck from

Stella were fading.

But she was still embarrassed. She was still see-through.

"Hello," Bo said. "How are you feeling?"

"Fine. Yes. Better."

"That's good."

"I...I didn't use the tea, though. I'm sorry."

Bo brushed it away. She looked around and then stepped closer. Veronica wondered if she was looking for Stella, too. Bo dipped into her pockets and pulled out a teabag. The same one. Bo's grin confirmed it. "I took the dishes about an hour ago. It seemed like it was not used, and I figured, oh, why not? I hate waste. But here. Use it. I also have some more books from the front library, if you're interested."

Veronica no longer felt the slight horror toward the ideas of books from dead—or gone—patrons. Now it sounded perfect.

❧❧❧❧

For the next hour, she and Bo glimpsed through the cracked spines in the hotel back office. Everything seemed new again, as if she'd never truly seen these works before. *The Corrections* was beside *The Great American Novel* by Philip Roth; *The Witches of Eastwick* by John Updike was on the next shelf, along with at least a dozen more by him. Updike and Joyce Carol Oates, Veronica remembered, seemed to write like there was no tomorrow. So much like King and his near constant output, but somehow taken more seriously. When Veronica cracked open a page from Updike's famous Rabbit series, she was shocked at how poor the prose was. She tried to find another page, then another book, but she returned to the same stilted words. She opened one of the numerous Stephen King books there and became even more shocked. She liked his work more. Updike, who had a Pulitzer, was worse than King. No, she rephrased it in her mind. Stephen King was better than John Updike. A shock, she thought, but then maybe not at all.

When she voiced her discoveries to Bo, she merely shrugged. "Give the people what they like."

"I guess." Veronica sighed. "Where are all those other books you mentioned?"

"The lesbian romances?" When Veronica nodded, Bo went on. "Ah, they're my Kindle reading. Secret reading." Bo winked. When Veronica's face fell, she quickly added, "But I will see if I can find some print versions of them. I know you're kind of old school."

"Thank you." Veronica wanted to say something more, but what was there left to say? Nothing, Veronica knew. Only a kiss, a kiss, a kiss.

Veronica saw the red and white cover of a Harlequin romance and the protagonists meeting on the cover for a romantic kiss, a flyaway kiss, an engulfing kiss. Oh, Veronica wanted to kiss Bo. That was all it was. That was what this feeling was, so close to the sensation she felt in summer camp, a latent desire but without a seeming cause.

Bo opened her mouth. She shut it.

Veronica did the same. She yawned.

"It's late," Bo said. "Or early. Whatever your perspective is."

"I need to go to bed," Veronica said. "I have to get up in a couple hours. Oh, man."

"I'll walk you back to your room," Bo said. "And

I'll give you a call later."

Veronica nodded. She allowed herself to be led through the backroom and up the backstairs, all the while casually talking. She was exhausted. She'd get sleep. But she was also afraid of going to sleep in case this moment would pass, and she'd never get it again. Outside her hotel door, she examined Bo. Bo examined her.

"So."

"So."

They both stared. They both yawned. The moment was gone with laughter and then a casual "good night."

"Good night," Veronica mirrored. She stepped into her hotel room. The moment was gone. Passed. She wished she'd kissed her. She wondered what it would have been like. She was still thinking of that moment as she fell asleep. She even thought she was still dreaming when the phone call came, and it was Bo again. To her surprise, it felt as if she'd slept for years. Except unlike Rip Van Winkle and everything changing, everything good was still the same.

"Good morning," Bo said. "And good luck."

Chapter Eighteen

Veronica was exhilarated. There was no one at her paper.

When she'd shown up ten minutes early to an empty room, she was convinced she had the wrong conference room number. She pulled out the pamphlet from her blazer jacket and checked it three times. It was the right room. The right time. The right day. She was ten minutes early, but no one was here.

Instead of despair, a smile spread across her face. She'd done the best she could. She stayed up all night with Stella to get this right. She quoted the right people in the right way. Her abstract had been accepted. She got herself here...yet no one had shown up.

So this was not her fault. How could it be? If she'd done everything right, but still it had not gone well, she would have nitpicked her performance. She would have found something that she could do better on next time. Then next time, then the next... But now she'd tried. Something hadn't gone right, but at least, for once, she did not have to nitpick herself to death.

Unlike her eating disorder, unlike Adele, this was a hundred percent not her fault.

Even though numerous counsellors and some doctors had tried to tell her that anorexia and Adele were not her fault, either, Veronica had a hard time listening. After all, she'd still been in love with women, she still wanted to be with Adele, so she had a hard time envisioning herself as wholly innocent in their affair together. And sure, maybe her anorexia was not her fault, either; maybe it really was like an illness, and it was never the patient's fault for getting sick. Especially since she was a teenager for both of these things, and being a teenager was already hard. Sure, maybe, in her better moments, she could believe the counsellors.

But her bulimia was definitely her fault. She ate the food. She threw it up. It was the ultimate expression of her willpower. The ultimate examination of her agency and control. It was her wilful arm sticking out of a grave. It was her only chance at redemption.

But this? This was a stupid conference, and it was out of her control. Someone else had fucked it up. And that fact flooded her with relief. Now that it was out of her hands, she could do whatever she wanted.

To her surprise, she wanted to see Bo.

She turned around to leave the room and almost ran into Samantha. "There you are!"

For a split second, Veronica frowned. She'd been so close to freedom—but now she was facing her old friend, her old colleague, and she was informing her in quick movements that the conference room got changed this morning. "It's just down the hall now. We were worried about you!"

Veronica sighed. She nodded. She knew the worry was not genuine worry, but more like professional courtesy. Even if Samantha's smile warmed some ancient part of Veronica, she pushed it aside.

Now she had a paper to give.

She sat in the middle of a panel of three. The table was long, the kind that would have been used for a wedding or display centre at an automotive show. It was nothing special, like the chairs weren't anything special, either. The same set at every hotel. The same thing used over and over, utterly banal. The words that came out of her mouth were the same; she was no longer special as Ahmed might seem on the page. None of the readers on the panel seemed enthused or excited, either; they all sat as they gave their papers, not even bothering to stand or use a microphone. When it was over, some members of the audience stood as they asked their questions, but most of them sat, as well. And their questions, as ever, were not really questions. Though a woman with grey hair picked up on her argument about Sara Ahmed and the wilful child, extending it slightly to another German folktale, Veronica couldn't care less. She was polite, of course. She smiled and thanked them. She moved on and answered another question and even retained enough concentration to ask one of her fellow panel members about their work, but it wasn't genuine. A year ago, it would have been exhilarating. It would have been validation. It would have given her hope for the future.

Now she didn't want that future, so she didn't care about success or failure. She just wanted to get away from the table. She kept thinking, *I will not apologize* as the emcee finished up their panel and dismissed everyone to the coffee bar. As much as she wanted to run away, coffee sounded appealing. Only coffee, though. Maybe a Danish, Veronica reconsidered after another moment, but it was a transient thought, almost too brave to consider fully just yet.

While she was getting that coffee and debating on whether or not to add two or three creams—seventy or one hundred five calories—Samantha stepped up beside her. She wore a burgundy pantsuit that somehow made her look younger. Her hair was tied back in a floral headband. She wore more rings than the last time she saw her, as if she was accumulating one for each day of service at the conference. "That was fantastic," Samantha said. "I've read some Ahmed before but never seen her used like that."

Veronica winced. Could Ahmed be used? Could theory be used? Was it a she or an it? Veronica didn't know, didn't care, so she just shrugged. "Thank you. How was your paper?"

"Oh, fine."

Veronica looked away from her three-creamed coffee. She knew that tone of voice for Samantha. It brought her right back to a date the two of them had had at the library, one that turned into giggling and pecks on the cheek, until they were legitimately caught by a librarian. They left the library then because they couldn't stop laughing and secretly wished together that the entire scenario had ended in a porno.

"Just fine?" Veronica asked.

After a big sigh, Samantha said, "Your girlfriend was there."

"What?"

"Stella Flanders. She was at my paper panel. And she was critical. You probably know..."

Veronica's mouth was dry. There were too many assumptions—or accusations—in that statement. She didn't want to confirm or deny anything, so she went quiet. She let Samantha expound on Stella's cutting words about her scholarship. In the past, Veronica would have listed the argument in her head like a map, so she could follow it and jump ahead so she'd know the conclusion, so she'd know how to think, and so she wouldn't be wounded like Samantha clearly was.

Now, she just let Samantha talk. She felt her feelings, her embarrassment, her sadness, the same way she'd felt her laughter and kisses in the library. By the end of her statement, Samantha's eyes had watered over a little bit. "Wow," she said, wiping one tear away. "I really didn't think I'd let her make me cry."

"I'm so sorry."

"No, no, it's fine. I should expect this type of thing in academia. We gotta cite stuff. We can't cherry-pick. We have to be rigorous. This isn't goofing around as an undergrad anymore. As much as I loved that. I just…don't think I'm cut out for this."

"No."

Samantha shrugged. "I thought this was going to be a vacation, you know?"

"Doesn't everyone? I thought that was what conference season was. Academic summer camp."

"Me too. That was why we wanted to go, right? Slumber parties and book clubs. Oh, my God. I was so wrong." Samantha sighed. Veronica put a hand on her shoulder. The room had mostly emptied of fellow scholars. The coffee urn was still there, and a hotel worker—not Bo, much to Veronica's dismay—was clearing out some of the used plates and other cups. He didn't tell them to hurry, though, so Veronica was going to take her time. She wanted to tell Samantha she was wrong. She wanted to tell her that she was cut out for this life and that academic life wasn't how she described.

But she couldn't.

And because she didn't know what else to do

or say, she was relieved when Samantha spoke again. "You know, Stella did say one interesting thing. Or at least worthwhile."

"Yeah?"

"Yes. She said I didn't know what type of scholar I wanted to be yet. That's why I was undisciplined. It was possible to turn my paper around. I just had to decide."

"Huh."

Veronica had never heard that from Stella before. Was that good or bad? She didn't know. Stella's seemingly apathetic attitude toward her own paper confused her now. What was once relief was now complicated acrimony. Veronica realized in that moment she was still sitting on the fence. She hated what Samantha had described about Stella's conduct—yet she had also witnessed her own panel and questioning period. Everyone was nice. Smart. There were no spurs or arrows thrown at her own work. That could mean that her scholarship was better than Samantha's, so they were inherently different. Or it could mean that the people who attended their panels were inherently different people.

One gave Veronica all the power, the other was the winds of chance.

She had no idea who she wanted to be in that moment. What type of woman, scholar, or human being. Everything and nothing seemed like an option; everything and nothing seemed like her choice and also her fault if it turned out wrong. Wasn't that the ultimate quandary of postmodernism? If we are what we do, who the hell are we when we stop doing?

And what happens when we do something so awful we cannot undo it? What happens when something is done to us? Do we let it happen, over and over, or do we decide to be someone else, someone who would not take the pain ever, not once, and only inflict instead? Or disappear into ether, so you never did have to decide?

Veronica's stomach roiled. She hated postmodernism. But she also knew it was sanctioned in this discipline, in her school, in the world. How could you unlearn something? How could you undo an entire movement of thought? You simply couldn't. You had to endure. She remembered Stella's words: you had to survive.

Veronica looked at her coffee. Even her three creams in her coffee now seemed like the wrong choice.

"Anyway," Samantha said. "Thanks for hanging out with me. Are you doing okay?"

"Yes."

Samantha nudged Veronica in the side. Veronica thought it was playful, so she did it back. But Samantha was steadfast. "Ronnie," she said. "You're looking really thin."

"You said that already."

"Did I?"

Veronica laughed. She set down the three-creamed coffee. It was too much now—yet somehow, never enough. "You did. But it doesn't matter because I'm fine."

"You don't seem fine. I'm worried about you."

"Did you not hear me? I'm fine."

"Ronnie. I know you had some trouble in the past—"

"And this is present tense."

"And the past is never dead," Samantha said,

quoting Faulkner that they'd both read together. "It's not even past. The past is present tense."

"I am hardly the racist legacy that William Faulker wrote about. I am hardly big enough to concern American culture."

"But you're part of my culture, and I worry about you."

"You don't need to. Maybe if you spent more time on your discipline, you'd not need to fixate on mine."

Samantha's face fell. Veronica felt her harsh words like a knife against her own skin. Samantha was trying to help. She was only caring about you. *And this makes you mad?* Veronica shook her head. She left the room. She'd blown it, she knew for sure.

But what else was there to do?

Be invisible. Be mean. Or be dumb.

She was in the foyer when her phone rang. She looked at the display and expected to see Samantha's old number flash by. The number was unknown, with an area code in Canada. She couldn't imagine how expensive that call would be. Who would be trying to contact her? Was it really important? She wanted to ignore it. But she put the phone to her ear.

"Hello?"

"Hi. This is Detective Merwin from the Winchester PD. I'm looking for a Marta Allen. Is this her number?"

Veronica's heart rate skyrocketed and then evened out. She put a hand on her chest. She counted the beats. It took her a while to remember that he was waiting for an answer. "Ma'am? Is this Marta Allen?"

"No, that's not me."

"I'm sorry to disturb you. Can I ask who you are

for my own records?"

Cryptically, all Veronica could think about was the Emily Dickinson poem that began: *I'm Nobody! Who are you? / Are you — Nobody — too?* It seemed like the only answer she could give in that moment. She bit her tongue to not speak it aloud. "I'm Veronica," she said. "Veronica Hockmeier."

The man on the other line seemed to pause, shift. A hint of recognition.

"I have to go now." Veronica hung up the phone. She pressed the power button until it shut off. She was not going to deal with this. She was not getting involved. Not Marta Allen. She was not needed. She was no one at all.

She tried to remember the end of that poem, but it had faded. She was sure, though, that in spite of how grim the beginning was, Dickinson had given it a happy ending. As Veronica wandered into the next conference room, this time for Stella, she wondered what would have happened if she'd become Marta Allen. Just for the phone call. Just for a day. What type of scholar would she be? What type of woman?

"Well," she said aloud and recited Emily Dickinson as she remembered it. "Then there's a pair of us!"

Chapter Nineteen

The time is out of joint."
The first words of Dr. Stella Flanders's keynote speech echoed through the banquet hall and caught the audience's attention. All murmured chatter had disappeared as she stepped into the room and poised behind the podium. Her outfit was filled with muted yellows and golds, allowing the aura of her words—rather than her already beautiful face and body—to take over.

And the first words chilled. Veronica was glad she went. She needed to see Stella speak, even if Stella's touch against her skin was starting to feel strained. Stella was a fantastic speaker. Veronica's mind filled to the brim with adjectives, even though they seemed never enough to qualify and therefore, were mostly useless. Beautiful. Cunning. Quixotic. Immaculate. Perfect. A statue she wanted to fall down and worship, but a statue that had a mind of its own, sprung to life like Galatea, and now moved too quickly with abstract theories and concepts.

Stella delivered her lines in crisp, clean words, though at times, what she spoke about seemed as if it was far too speculative to be academic. Her first lines did not actually belong to her but to William Shakespeare in *Hamlet*. They were lines about a ghost. A haunting. When time was out of joint, it was because death punctuated the veil between the living and the dead and threw everyone's clocks out of order. Time was, like Jennifer Egan also stated, a goon that one had to wrestle and fight off, and ghosts were the biggest goons of them all because they represented death—the ending of time—but also the unending presence of life's ultimate struggle. Ghosts made time go backward and forward; it made your memory of life contort; it beat you up and held you down. To have Hamlet confronted by a ghost meant that his time was not proceeding as it should, and it meant that something far larger—like his father's legacy, the kingdom itself—was not working properly.

"And if he did not do something about it, he would die," Dr. Stella Flanders said. "Emily Dickinson realized this, as well. Her poetry about death is also about revenge, like Shakespeare's *Hamlet* is another revenge play about death and ghosts and all the poisonous words they whisper into your ear. Dickinson is Hamlet, as well as Shakespeare's sister. And the room in which she lived her life is that room of her own that Virginia Woolf spoke about, and her poems and hymns   the evidence of a life lived in art and devotion to time's ultimate goon. So I will spend my time analyzing her life in that room and examine just how much of it has become haunted by legacy, memory, and death itself."

Stella marked her remaining keynote address with careful and deliberate steps, orchestrated pauses, and practiced smiles. When she gestured, it was grand and gave her abstract concepts motion and vigour. As she spoke of Emily Dickinson's penchant for only wearing white, the muted yellows and golds of her outfit seemed as if they crafted a poem alongside Dickinson's ghost. Veronica even caught herself looking out the large window in the banquet hall to see if something tapped on the glass, begging for attention.

But no—it was just Stella, Stella, Stella. Like Marcel Duchamp's *Nude Descending a Staircase, No. 2*, Stella became her talk as much as she performed it; by highlighting something out of place, she became a disarray, but that was precisely the point and the beauty of it. When she moved on to the nitty-gritty of Dickinson's life with clarity and accuracy, she gave what was once too speculative firm grounding. There was no doubt she was a scholar, no doubt she was tenured, and no doubt on anyone's faces about why she had been invited to give the last conference slot. The best had been saved for last, even if that meant her audience had thinned, as it always did at the end of a conference. Many people had gone home, skipping the ending celebratory dinner that would also happen tonight. Veronica was sure that Samantha was one of them, and well, good riddance for that.

Listening to Stella speak now gave Veronica a new sense of purpose. She now understood how far she still needed to go academically. Even if the audience had thinned for Stella's paper, it only meant that those who were present appreciated her that much more. And it was clear from their faces that her performance surpassed their expectations. Could Veronica ever reach the level of Stella? She was so poised. So practiced. So artistic in her movements and her voice. Her body was an instrument—so unlike the theremin of desire that they'd once had, Veronica started to wonder if that had ever been real. Perhaps Stella had been a solo piece, an ornate instrument like a harp, heavy and expensive and utterly unique.

Veronica felt like white noise. She spread her fingers out against her knees. She'd gone to the room, realizing she was early for Stella's panel, and put on a skirt. Last year, the skirt had fit and brought out her curves, but now it seemed like she was trying to become a flagpole. She glanced down at her breasts, barely there. She fought the impulse to hold her collarbones. She felt like she was fifteen again, missing several periods and with no fat on her body. She thought of the hair—*lanugo*—that emerged to keep her warm, the bruises against her spine from high school chairs. When her parents had found out about Adele, music lessons were cancelled. When she couldn't approach the piano in her house anymore, her parents thought it was lingering trauma, but it was loneliness. Sadness. She missed Adele. She practiced her piano in her room, alone, using her legs as the keys. She marked herself with bruises she hit herself so hard in an attempt to make music. She marked herself with cuts, the blood becoming ebony keys. When the anorexia took hold, the pathology was no longer hidden under tights or jeans. Her sadness made manifest in the etched cheekbones and frail wrists peeking out of long sleeves.

But everyone always read it wrong. They thought Adele was abusive and this was a cry for help, Veronica's attempt to make herself undesirable so she'd never be touched badly again.

No, no, no. The call of this confession was all in the wrong key. She was lonely and wanted Adele, and if she couldn't have her, she'd become nothing but music instead. Nothing but light and air and sound. Ivory, ebony, black and white. Since her starvation only seemed to make her parents even sadder, Veronica had done the therapy and eaten the food to make the hormones come back. Her period never disappeared again. Her parents were happy again. But instead of not feeling lonely, Veronica had merely learned to vomit confessions, vomit words out, and vomit the food she wished she hadn't eaten. It was a trade-off. She got to leave home, and her parents thought she was healthy. She was an academic, PhD, almost a doctor like the doctors who poked and prodded at her. But it was all philosophy, a mask. All white noise.

She'd always wanted to be the piano.

As Stella finished her talk, Veronica imagined herself as an instrument. She tried to envision herself as a keyboard, small and compact, especially the kind that could record sound bites and replay them at will. That was what she was in front of her class: a parrot, a reference machine. In her room alone and in her dreams, she was a sonata, a jazz riff, something immaculate she'd once played with Adele behind her. A song that was now gone. With Bo, maybe she could be that piano in the basement. *Maybe...*

But she shook her head.

Veronica was roused from her nonsense dreams by Stella's final words. She remained poised, silent, her paper now concluded. Veronica rose from her seat and clapped. Others were already rising and clapping, so she didn't seem like a devotee at the base of a statue. She was just one of many among a crowd. When Stella gave a small bow, she seemed to accept the praise as if it was obvious and yet be delighted by it as a surprise.

One of the moderators took over the microphone. He took only three questions before closing the ceremony entirely, reminding people once again about the dinner in a few hours. People rustled and dispersed, now in a quasi-controlled chaos. Stella walked straight to Veronica through the crowd. Her gaze pinned her in place.

"What did you think?"

Veronica couldn't believe she was being asked. "It was wonderful."

"I stumbled in the second paragraph."

"It wasn't noticeable."

"But it was there." Stella turned away. She looked out the glass windows in the hotel conference room. The sky was overcast; the wind whipped by. The day was coming to an end. They stood in the silence for some time, only punctuated by people leaving and the snapping shut of doors. "We should have dinner with Henry Gable."

"The first keynote guy?"

"Yes."

"I thought you didn't like his paper."

"I don't mind him, though. We should meet. You should meet."

Veronica felt a heavy weight in her stomach. There was no choice in this matter. They were having dinner, and with that dinner meant the conference was truly over. The death of the conference now led to... what? Veronica dreaded what awaited her in Canada. An apologia of her grades and pedagogical practices. Brianna's illness and anxiety. Jonathan's empty office. She'd almost forgotten that she was still in his empty room. It had become so much her own, her dreams the only reminder of his presence, since his name had been removed from the conference program. In good taste, she was sure, but it only added to a trickling forgetting disease she was worried would consume her.

"I'm going to dress for dinner. Won't be too long away," Stella said.

"Oh. Okay. Yes. But..."

Stella paused, gaze waiting.

"Am I coming as your student or as your lover?" Veronica said, changing the last word at the last minute. Girlfriend was juvenile. Partner implied too much sharing of resources Veronica didn't have. But lover...lover was something she could, hopefully, latch on to.

"You are coming as you. Define it how you like."

Stella was gone then, in a blink. Veronica was left empty, filling the room with silent noise.

Chapter Twenty

Dressing for dinner became a simultaneous act of packing for tomorrow morning, when no doubt Stella would want to leave. Veronica still wasn't sure how long Jonathan had booked this room for, but she hoped—prayed—that she could stay in Stella's room tonight. The conference was over. Their dinner with an old friend was hardly a public display. So they no longer needed to draw large lines in the sand, right? Stella had said Veronica could decide who she was now, and Veronica had decided. She was packing for her departure—but they would leave together, as a couple on the road searching for better things.

She was toying with the idea of asking Stella to stop in Love Canal on their return trip when she felt an absence in her purse. She dumped the leather bag's contents on the bed. Gum, keys, American and Canadian money, more gum. Her wallet was there, but the student card was gone. Perhaps she left it at home, knowing there'd be no need to catch buses with her holographic school crest proving she'd paid for more than just tuition that year. But her passport, she also realized, was missing. She checked each secret pocket of the purse and suitcase. Under the bed. Along the lines of the carpet and the bathroom floor. No passport, nothing that would allow her back in her home country.

Her heart hammered. She pressed a hand to her chest, begging herself to slow down. Somewhere, maybe even in a conversation with Stella, she'd heard that the human heart was only capable of so many beats. *You reach the quota, and that is what death is.*

My heart is a goon, she thought. My heart is a ghost. Veronica held her hand over her chest and waited and counted and panicked that she was on a train and heading toward her own demise. When she finally caught her breath, she checked the room all over again.

No passport.

Maybe she'd left it with Stella. Maybe in the car. Maybe it had fallen out on her hike earlier in the weekend.

"Or maybe," she said aloud, her voice hissing in anger, "it's in a damn shoebox."

Veronica gathered her purse together angrily. She slammed the hotel door and walked down the emergency stairs, not bothering with the elevator. Bo was at the front desk, smiling happily as she checked out a couple from the conference. Their clasped hands made Veronica's chest ache but only presented a brief barrier to her confrontation with Bo.

"You," she hissed.

"And you! How did your paper go?"

"Give me back my passport."

Bo furrowed her brows. She wore another bright pink shirt, clashed dramatically under the blue hotel jacket. She was like a bubble gum wrapper, unreal and nostalgic at once. "I don't understand."

"My passport is missing. What did you do? Get a maid to grab it so you could keep it in your shoebox? Just because I'm leaving tomorrow doesn't mean I'm dead. You don't get to keep me."

"Whoa now. Hold on." Bo leaned in close to control the volume. "I don't take what's not mine."

"Please. You're a scavenger," Veronica spat out. Her tone twisted. She felt like a puppet as she remembered Stella's harsh words, and she felt like a plagiarist as Stella's words became her own. "You're even stealing someone else's story, all to suit your own ideas of gender. What is this pink fluorescent nonsense? The brightly coloured nails? Not even real women wear this much fucking pink."

Bo withdrew. Hurt, then anger, etched her face. She whispered, "fuck you," under her breath.

Veronica felt the words like a slap. She blinked and opened her mouth in horror at what she'd just done. Was this the woman and scholar she wanted to become? She was being cruel. She was being *Stella*.

The elevator dinged at that moment, and it was as if she could feel Stella's presence drawing her attention. Stella wore a little black dress—the universal dress, from weddings to fundraisers to a dinner with an old colleague and her lover. Her lover. Not Bo's, not Adele's, not even Samantha's.

Veronica was with Stella.

Nothing could undo that fact. Nothing, moreover, could undo that future.

Stella's gaze was soon set between the two of them. She paused, lingered in a critical assessment but eventually moved to the dining area without saying a word. Veronica swallowed and turned back to Bo. She stomped away, though, into the backroom before Veronica could attempt an apology.

"Bo—wait—I'm…"

Bo emerged from the backroom in a flash, her

black eyes narrowed to points. She held her shoebox in her hands and quickly dumped the contents on the front hotel counter.

"Do you see your fucking passport, Veronica? No? Right. Instead there's this ID, which belonged to my best friend. She laid down on the train tracks when her parents kicked her out. And then this license belonged to a woman I knew from my therapy group. Her doctor moved, and no one prescribed her hormones. She ordered them online, and they were too strong and they fucked her up. So she jumped off a building. And this one—he just thought he was alone, so he slit his wrists. I have their IDs. I have the dead man in room 407's ID because no one ever claimed his body. I have the shoelaces of another person who died in their sleep at the bed and breakfast. Friendship bracelets from a cancer victim. The scribbled notes of another sickness, a death too soon. I have shit. I have dead things. But I do not have your bullshit."

Veronica flattened her face of expression, then her voice of emotion. "I'm sorry."

"No, you're not. You're just sorry for yourself."

"Yeah, you know what? I am. I'm sorry for myself. I'm stuck here now."

"No one is ever stuck." Bo sighed. It was clear she realized she was being overdramatic and soon calmed her tone to the practical. She gathered her items back into her shoebox and handed Veronica a pamphlet from behind the desk. The address for the Canadian consulate was written on the bottom. "It's a bit of a drive to Boston, but there are ways of getting back what you lost, okay? Always."

Including whatever we had before? Veronica wondered but dared not say aloud. Whatever they had with the fiddleheads was thin and tenuous, like her own brittle bones and thin skin from her youth and her current present tense. Something so simple could shatter and bruise, and Veronica was so good at making bruises thinking it was music.

Veronica said she was sorry once again, only as a murmur, as she took the pamphlet. Bo said nothing in return. She fixated her gaze on the computer and clicked aimlessly. In spite of herself, it reminded Veronica of the striking of piano keys.

Veronica wandered into the area where the hotel served breakfast. Coffee was on a hot plate, almost scorching with its heat. She got some and drank it anyway. She flipped through her phone, trying to find directions to the address of the consulate. She fumbled at making plans. She still prayed for a miracle, that her vision was bad and her passport had been found wedged somewhere else, but it was gone. Like the stranger's backpack, it was torn apart by the wind. It was lost to the wilderness.

She opened a new email from Brianna, hoping to tell her that she would be delayed in returning home. But Brianna's words—sporadic and distant in her email prose—made her forget her emergency for a moment.

"A cop just came by the school," Brianna wrote. "He was asking a lot of questions about Jonathan. It's strange, right? Considering he was a suicide. They were tracing where he got the cyanide from. I was the only one in the office, so they talked to me. They did look through your desk, though. It's why I'm emailing—I couldn't stop them since it's technically school property—so I'm saying sorry. But this is what's weird—they thought your name was Marta

Allen. I said it wasn't. So, yeah. Do you know any Marta Allen?"

Veronica swallowed. That call had been for her then? But how did she become Marta without knowing it? She tried to remember if there was or ever had been a student with that name. Was Marta Allen the mysterious girlfriend finally being given a name? No one had been here asking for the hotel room. Veronica didn't even recall anyone at the hotel with Marta Allen on their nametag. She could be anyone; it could be a made-up name entirely, something obscured from time—who knew what had been going through Jonathan's head? Maybe she was another recorded voice on one of his to-do lists. Maybe—

A hand landed on Veronica's shoulder and interrupted her train of thought. She nearly jumped out of her seat. Stella stood there. She lifted her hands as if to show she meant no harm.

"What's going on, Veronica?" she asked when Veronica had set the phone down. "Is there a problem with your room?"

"No. Well. Yeah, sort of. I have to stay another day. I lost my passport." She spilled the rest of the story—save Brianna's email and the call from the detective—in fits and starts. She told Stella about running into Bo, the hotel worker, out on an adventure to find the backpack, eating the fiddleheads, falling over, and sharing more than just a cursory cup of tea with her. She even surprised herself with her own honesty about her eating disorder, the accusations from Samantha, and how it all felt now, stirring quixotically underneath her skin.

"I think I need help. I'm so worried my electrolytes are all off, and I'm hallucinating half the time. My dreams have been so vivid. My dreams—"

"Dreams are a Freudian trip. Nothing more." Stella's gaze grew stony, grey, and chill like the overcast sky. "But I am concerned that you went into the woods. To search for the man's backpack and ate fiddleheads with our concierge?"

"Well, yeah. I think my passport was lost there. Or hell, maybe even the police still have it."

"That is not the case. I would have been notified. But that is a shame that you were so trusting, then you got what you deserved."

"Deserved? From Bo?"

"From going into the woods and looking for a madman's backpack. Veronica, please." Stella shook her head. "You know better than that."

"I just thought—"

"You were not thinking. And that is another shame. I'm sorry you'll be staying another day."

Veronica's stomach flipped. It was clear, like when Stella spoke of academic jobs, that they were not a unit together. Stella was going to take the car and go back to Canada come morning. Veronica was going to stay here. Be trapped here.

No, not trapped. Veronica tried to calm herself down. People lose their passports all the time. *I will get a new one, at the consulate, and things will work themselves out.* They always worked themselves out.

Unless you're Jonathan.

Veronica couldn't fixate there, especially not when she still had her own skin to worry about. She had to get out of this fucking country. She had to get a new passport and leave the goddamn land that made her feel like she was in a novel. She didn't want to feel cartoonlike, a slipshod piece of Americana sold at a tourist trap anymore. She needed the real streets of Canada. The French and English on all the labels. Even the weak Tim Hortons coffee and the dead time of the university campus.

"Are you ready?" Stella gestured toward the dining hall. "Or will you cancel this present dinner because the future is more complicated than you give it credit for?"

Veronica could tell that the clipped part of her tone was an admonishment of Jonathan. *Will you be like the student who cannot stand his random failure, who internalizes it all until it destroys him, or will you survive?* Because she was asking her, Veronica knew that Stella believed she could survive. So Veronica wanted to. She folded away the consulate paper and her cellphone, without replying to Brianna.

"Yes. Let's go."

Chapter Twenty-one

Henry Gable was one of the leading Emily Dickinson scholars, but his approach to academics was different than how Stella—and even how Veronica—worked. He was a text-based scholar, a man of Walter Ong, Harold Bloom, and the anxieties of influence and critical debates. Rather than rising to the occasion, like Bloom did during the 1990s and postmodernism reared its head, however, Gable decided to focus more on the books themselves. Not in terms of truth, he said, but materiality. He wanted to break apart the pages and examine the pulp. Everything to him was a palimpsest; you could scrape away the first layer and then there'd be another. By age forty-five, he'd lost his penchant for metaphors, as he said, and started to focus his attention on inks.

"You can learn a lot about the history of a document if you look at its materials," he went on and on and on about his work. "Much like you can tell a lot about someone from what they're made of—literally. I'm sure Stella knows this the best."

A look was shared between them. It was a slap to Veronica, a breaking of a tree limb after hours of pressure during a windstorm. They knew each other before Veronica had entered the picture, obviously, before Veronica was even born. The cultural debates they spoke about with such familiarity were when Veronica was still a child, still learning the phonemes needed for language. But in that shared, casual look had been an entire history; its own palimpsest of eye contact. Underneath Stella's skin, Veronica saw the rose hue of blush; underneath that, she saw bones that were free of cancer, unlike Stella's mother.

Henry knew about her mother. He knew about Love Canal. He knew everything about Stella, down to the red-covered book of Emily Dickinson poetry she kept on her bedside table. Veronica wondered, with the taste of wine on her tongue, how deep this knowledge truly went. Did he *really* know everything about her, right down to the taste of almonds in her hand lotion and the quixotic smell between her legs?

Stella spoke of the frogs she needed to kill for her biology career. At that school, where Stella had transferred her credits and changed her career, was also where Henry taught and took her under his wing. She was his undergraduate devotee, hovering around his office hours and begging for more information. Henry had saved her from a life of killing wildlife; he'd tamed her citations and made her focus on the biology of breath as one spoke poetry aloud and gave her scansion exercises instead of scalpels with which she could pry poems, not frogs, apart. She learned cadence and rhythm while he, tiring of the metaphors and the proximity of flesh, went on to dissect the vellum pages.

"Without Henry's guidance, I would have never considered Canada as a place to study. It seemed too far away despite being so close. How could someone be an Americanist in Canada? Seemed silly, contradictory." Stella chuckled lightly. "Then I saw their environmental policy and knew it was where I belonged."

"And you will be heading back in the morning while I stay here." Henry sighed mock forlornly. "If only we had more time."

"If only."

Veronica swallowed more wine. Her stomach reeled. She thought of the earlier conversation with Bo, when she'd described Canada as magical, as that mythical elsewhere. Imagine, being an Americanist in Canada while also having been born in Canada, like Veronica. Imagine, being a transgender woman longing for the magicland of gender surgery, while having been born an American to previous immigrants who built the country that exploited them, like Bo. Imagine being Jonathan, from a maritime province, entertaining a ghost inside his stolen research and a bug of suicide inside his mind? *Time is out of joint here, but so is the landscape itself.*

"And you, Miss Hockmeier," Henry said, as if realizing that he was monopolizing the conversation with the past, "Stella tells me you're on your way to becoming next in line as another Dickinson scholar, great among the greats."

Veronica smiled. She would have beamed under this praise two days ago. Maybe even two hours ago. But now she saw herself as a literal line, a species of frogs on a shelf. Stella was keeping her in a glass jar, a wonderful marvel—but wholly a specimen. Hadn't Henry done the same with her, decades ago now, peeling back her ink-black clothing and revelling at her manuscript skin underneath? Was this how all academic study worked? Was this part of survival of the species? We pass on citations and quotations through bodily contact, mouth to mouth, reference to reference.

Veronica shrugged. She thought of the taste of Bo on her lips, maybe, from when she was given mouth to mouth. "I'm doing the best with what I have right now, but I'm flattered to be considered among the greats. Even if I'm a ways away from truly finishing my degree."

Stella gave her a look she did not recognize. A disappointing stare. She turned back to Henry with a heavy expression. "I'm afraid we've been having a bit of difficulty in our program as of late."

"Oh?"

"Yes, a student—a very bright student, one of my best honestly—ended his life before this trip. It was a terrible blow to all of us. He and Veronica both worked as research assistants on an article with me. It's a shame. He was going places."

Veronica sipped her wine. She felt the sympathetic stare from Henry Gable on her body like lechery. Why was Stella sad about Jonathan all of a sudden? She hadn't bothered to go to the mourning ritual, but even in their private moments together, Veronica had not seen Stella's frown or heard her morose words about Jonathan. Veronica had a hard time now, especially after such a performance of Stella's keynote paper, to decipher if this was real or another act. A genuine study of grief or a mask for the night?

"Jonathan was studying the materiality of literary artifacts, as well," Stella mentioned, as if to make his spirit extra enchanting for Henry Gable. "In fact, he was looking at the material history of books and other such texts which go on to form cult-like fascination."

"The Book of Mormon?" Henry asked. "The

elusive but never seen golden plates?"

"Yes, precisely," Stella confirmed. "But alas, I fear that academia nowadays is even more labyrinthine than what you, or even what I, went through. It's not just the contract workers or the sheer number of students now, like a swarm—it's the ideology of the entire construct that has morphed and changed. And ideology fills the vacuum, replacing the air."

Henry nodded as if he understood. Veronica did not. She asked for Stella to elucidate, in her liquid, almost drunk voice.

Again, another withering look. But Stella went on. "Social media, quite frankly, is ruining the academy. It is making the ivory tower walls weak. It's filling it with holes called hashtags. People broadcast their smallest debate, their tiniest issue, and it becomes an explosion. Have you heard about Melanie Knight?"

The name made Veronica's back stiffen. Henry shook his head.

"Suppose it's for the best. But she is precisely what I mean," Stella said and reiterated the situation in clipped terms. "A grad student taped a meeting and then used social media for vengeance. Regardless of who is right in that debate, something has been violated and broken. The walls in which we once put so much strength and honour have been torn down. And for what? Students now see the bureaucracy as identity, as something personal rather than structural. But these are just words on a page. It's just the way things go."

"But can't things change? Surely, things have to change," Veronica asked. "Especially if someone is being caused harm."

"But harm is precisely the issue here. We have

no standard definition. We focus so much on wounds but not enough on treatment or even definition."

"And change?" Veronica asked again. "How can things change, though, if we don't have the diagnosis?"

"We must move on. We will move on. System theory tells us as much—the environment shows us as much. Change always happens, ever present, even if we have no words to qualify it. But to think we are the agents of this change—that we are Melanie Knight— rather than a small speck that has been swept into the wheels, is folly. Pure folly." Stella took a drink. She pressed a hand into a stray hair. "Jonathan Morris was one of my best students. But he got too personal. He became too consumed by the symptoms, by the diagnosis, and refused to progress. Thinking he was responsible, that he could be the sole agent of change... it was his downfall."

Veronica stared. She wanted to pry apart the words and insert meaning inside of them. The tone of "too personal" sounded like something else, something more than academic folly or even the whispered rumours of his plagiarism but instead a pattern of kinship that had been occurring for decades. If Henry had been with Stella, and Stella had been with her, then what if she had also been with Jonathan?

And what if Jonathan, in another backward attempt to pay it forward, had been with one of his students? Was that what it meant to be too consumed in the symptoms, the diagnosis? Was there a line that even they, as graduate students, were not supposed to cross—and was that precise line the definition of *harm* itself? The act of defining harm? Melanie Knight, broadcasting her pain, was the villain in this play, wasn't she? Even if her recording was the only way to treat the wound, she was still cast aside for it. Jonathan's words—*I will not apologize*—rose in Veronica's throat. The thought pressed against her once again: had he recorded something, too? And had it been another meeting behind closed doors, one where Stella had given herself away and given away whatever survival kisses and caresses she'd also given her?

Veronica wanted to throw up. She wanted to wash the thought from her brain. But once there, like a virus, it spread. Was she not singular in this matter? Was she not the only person Stella had fucked?

Was this what Jonathan had been trying to tell her, over and over again, all along?

She wanted to ask Brianna. The country seemed so far between them. Brianna wasn't gay, but did sexuality even matter anymore, when you broke it down to parts and only focused on the power? The camera, the cellphone recorder, the recording bug evened the scales. Archival works, tapes and tapes and tapes of meetings, peeping into windows when she was twelve. A material history of violation, sexuality, and citations, spread out before her eyes. Was that Jonathan's hunger? Was that what made him drink poison?

Veronica wanted to throw up.

"Excuse me." Veronica folded a napkin over her food. She was no longer hungry. "I'm not feeling my best. Thank you for having me for dinner, but I should go."

Stella rose, concern etched on her face. "Are you sure?"

"I am."

As Veronica turned to walk away, she felt their

gazes on her back. She felt foolish, like she was reading too much of herself into these conversations all over again. When she turned to look over her shoulder, though, there they were. Still staring. Still there.

She slipped up the stairwell. The farther away she got, the better she felt. Maybe she had been silly. Maybe she was overthinking this. *Hunger warps the imagination*, the therapist had told her at fifteen. *It makes everything become food, and food becomes everything. Your hunger, even when you don't feel it, is a parasite. It's why the tapeworm is a ravenous creature. Your disease is a tapeworm, and the worm is in your brain.* Veronica's recall muddled the meanings. The memory was warped and tinted by hunger. Her corpus callosum was the labyrinth, and Ariadne had fainted before she could get inside to help Theseus out. Veronica laughed. She was insane, wasn't she? Her hunger had taken her over.

Marta Allen, she remembered. *Marta Allen, Marta Allen.* There were police in Canada, and they were looking for her. The name was like a bullet. Was she a student who had killed herself? Was she the student Jonathan had slept with, if that insinuation was true? And now she was the key to unlock the entire mystery?

Veronica was getting so sick of chasing ghost citations, so sick of Googling words and coming away with nothing but an endless forking etymological tree. There was no Facebook for Marta Allen. The name throbbed in her brain, familiar but not, like snow in the winter. She gave up. She was just so sick. When she saw the package in front of her hotel door, she was relieved. It was something concrete. It was something real.

She picked up the stack of books. The covers were cheesy, a green forest filled with evergreens and the title *Curious Wine* in handwriting font beneath it. She thought of the poem the title was from. *I had been hungry all the years / My noon had come, to dine / I, trembling, drew the table near / And touched the curious wine.* She went to the next book and found the note stuck between the pages as a bookmark.

Dyke lit about Emily D. Figured you'd need this, as you will be waiting around a lot tomorrow. From, Bo.

Veronica held the books to her chest. Oh, something real. Something real, something real. She did not deserve such sudden kindness. She wanted to reject the books based on that fact alone. But she also remembered the lines of the poem. Curious wine was the curiosity of lesbianism, she was sure, but it was also the desire to trust someone you shouldn't. That poem was about watching someone else's house, realizing there was a feast on the other side of the door and suddenly realizing you are being invited inside. It is not just about food or about sex; it was about belonging; it was about love.

Veronica had been an utter and deplorable asshole to Bo, yet she was still showing her love. *The kindness of strangers*, Veronica thought of the Tennessee Williams line from *A Streetcar Named Desire*. She remembered that one professor who liked paintings, yet again, and how she had said that Blanche in that play was supposed to be a gay man. Blanche was supposed to be Tennessee. "But of course," she went on, "you could not talk about that back then, so he changed himself into a woman and wrote a different work. A beautiful work. But different than what he wanted to do. Like this work called *The Naked Maja*." She'd then flashed an image of a nude woman, so common in the art world, but also so different this time around because the woman's gaze met the viewers. "She stared back. And so it was censored."

Veronica could see the painting so clearly in her mind—yet she still struggled to remember the professor's name. She needed to know it almost as much as she needed to see Bo and thank her over and over again for treating her kindly when she could have been mean, too. Maybe even more than that. She needed to know more than she needed her passport.

Veronica powered up her phone and found Samantha's old number. It would cost her a fortune in roaming fees, but it suddenly didn't matter. She thought of how much money, really, she spent on binges. She always thought it was worth the two hundred-dollar shopping spree to eat in three days since she had not eaten anything at all leading up to it. But that was a lie, wasn't it? There was always a cost far greater than she could see on the surface. She texted Samantha without worry of the cost or the return response. She knew whatever it would be would be said in kind.

Do you remember the first-year prof who used to always have paintings in her lecture? I can't think of her name. Let me know when you can.

Veronica let herself in the hotel room. She sat at the desk where her laptop was. She opened the first book, smelled the inside cover, and read the first lines when Samantha texted back.

Isabella Stanton, Samantha wrote. *Though I do believe he goes by Iggy now. Just so you know, in case you decide to ask for a reference letter or something else.*

Veronica smiled. In her dream, that professor's face had blurred with Bo's, with Jonathan's, and she'd felt bad for mixing them all up together. In a way, though, her dream knew more than she ever could fathom. She set the books aside—if only for a moment—to find Iggy Stanton online. He was working out of the university down the street from her now. How had I never seen him before? Veronica wondered and then realized. He was a completely different person. Even if she had walked by him on the street, she may not have recognized him, nor him with her. They were new people now. They were so close, a ten-minute walk away. A ten-minute walk, she thought, and maybe, her life could change.

She sent an email. She closed the laptop. And she read into the night, the faint hint of desire on her pages.

Chapter Twenty-two

There was going to be no goodbye from Stella, but Veronica still wanted to show up in the morning.

Veronica had spent the night reading romances. At first, they seemed utterly frivolous and poorly written, but she soon realized that they were simple and serious. Just because someone had used three words to express a sentiment and not sixty-five like some of the academic papers she'd read didn't mean they were dumb. It didn't mean that what they were talking about wasn't important, either. The more Veronica read pages and pages of descriptions of toothpaste or the shade of blue on a car, the more she realized she wanted to know every last damn detail. It wasn't that toothpaste or cars were the only thing these characters had going on or the only things that these authors felt were important. No, not at all. It was that they treated life so seriously, a page and a half could be devoted to something utterly inane yet absolutely necessary. Chapters of prose could be devoted to something like going to a carnival, going canoeing, or going hiking—but all without hidden meaning or symbolism, only fun, fun, and more fun.

What luxury! What expansiveness!

The first novel reminded her of the feeling she got when Jonathan had emailed her for coffee after classes. Not because something serious was going to happen (though it did) or because it was a romantic connection (because he'd expressly said no to that possibility); it made her feel the same way because it was nice for niceness sake. It was kind.

And that kindness, Veronica was learning, could also extend to herself. She could treat herself well and take care of her body, her mind, her soul. She had a soul, right? Academics would dither about it, and the rhetoric of postmodernism had destroyed it as a concept, but these books confirmed the soul's existence for her. She deserved toothpaste and to talk about the colour blue because it was what enlivened her soul. More than piano, she thought, but she didn't need to choose anymore. She could have everything, these books said. She could be in love and free to move at the same time. She could play piano, badly if she wanted to, and she could enjoy the colour blue.

As soon as she awoke from the few hours of sleep she did get, Veronica went to the vending machine and bought Rolos for breakfast. She popped them in her mouth as she followed along between sex scenes and waited for Stella to come down to the hotel lobby. Veronica had dressed in jeans and a bright yellow shirt, complete with shining sun on it. She'd found the old camp T-shirt in her packed clothing, accidentally taken out from the bottom of a drawer when she decided she wanted to have a sweater in Amherst just in case. She liked the fact that the camp shirt still fit her. It was a youth small, something she wore at thirteen, and something she could still fit her tiny breasts into now. The shirt made her feel better while she ate candy and then Danishes in the hotel lobby, keeping all of it down. She was so determined to keep it all down. The shirt made her feel even better when Stella finally emerged from the elevators. Her gaze hovered over Veronica's barely there breasts, took in her entire outfit, and then she walked past her to the parking lot.

Veronica followed, not minding the silence or scathing look. It made her feel oh so real all over again. As real as the sex scenes and the scent of Rolos still on her fingers, as real as the toothpaste she'd used this morning and the coffee she'd put three creams into later. She was real, real, real. And she was going to be kind to herself, no matter the cost.

"What are you wearing?" Stella asked after she'd put away her suitcase.

"The only clean thing I have."

Stella waited, knowing there was more. When Veronica said nothing, only smiled, Stella sighed. "You should dress professionally."

"This is professional."

Stella tilted her head, asking a silent question of "how?"

This time, Veronica decided to answer: "Well, you could say in a lot of ways that I'm wearing nostalgia, which is from the Greek words translating to painful homecoming. I long to go home so much it pains me, but I can't right now, so I wear bright yellow sunshine instead. The shirt will be in my new passport photo, too, which I find ironic. Don't you?"

"You look like a child."

"So?"

"So," Stella said, mirroring her gaze flecked with anger, "don't be so insolent. You'll start to sound as hollow as your paper."

Veronica smiled through Stella's harsh and inconsistent words. Stella had helped Veronica with her paper all night, yet it was a bad paper? She was either lying then or lying now. It didn't matter, though. All that did was show that Stella believed it to be hollow, like a tooth with a cavity. Worse than being perfect on the surface, Veronica was nothing but a candy-crunching child, arms waving in the air for more, a complete inability to follow what her mentor wanted her to do. She thought of Stella's words to Samantha. Had they been meant for her, as well, a message passed through a game of broken telephone? *You don't know what kind of scholar you want to be. You don't know what kind of woman you want to be.*

Granted, that was all true, of course. She was dressed like a child because she was still a little afraid of who she could become. But she knew now, after seeing Iggy Stanton as a professor so close by, that she could be a different type of scholar. One that respected the body as much as the mind that housed ideas, one that would let her live her life exactly as she wanted to, even if it meant eating Rolos for breakfast and licking her fingers to turn the pages of a well-worn romance novel.

Stella waited. And waited.

But Veronica said nothing in response. She pulled the shirt down tighter over her torso. It was too small around the belly, so it rode up like a 1990s crop top. Even more nostalgia flooded her. While Stella and Henry were fucking around with in-text citations, the 1990s made Rachel's *Friends* haircut famous, along with Ring Pops and Pearl Jam. Suckers and chokers and bedazzled jeans. Veronica was only a child, not understanding any of these fashion statements aside from the bright colours that sparked joy, but it didn't matter. Joy was all that mattered. She knew what she was good at now. Suddenly, Veronica wished she had gum—not the mint kind that covered the vomit aftermath—but the bright pink cherry kind, so she could snap it in Stella's face. Make her confront how much like Lolita she'd become.

"Do laundry," Stella said. She slipped a five-dollar bill into Veronica's hands. "Turn that into quarters. You'll need it."

Stella drove away. Veronica walked back into the hotel and purchased more candy with the five dollars. SweeTARTS, Skittles, and American brands she couldn't get at home, along with the bright pink bubble gum. She ate it all in the hotel lobby, finishing the last novel in the pile and feeling better than she had in years.

Chapter Twenty-three

Veronica wasn't sure how to do this. With Stella gone and herself now sick of candy (but thankfully still keeping it inside herself), she knew she had to go to the passport office. A quick round of Googling led her to realize there was no direct bus route and that cabs would be extraordinarily expensive, especially since she didn't know how long all this would take. She would need to rent a car. She had to make some gesture toward getting out of the U.S., but to do that, she first needed to face Bo.

Bo stood at the front hotel desk and smiled at hotel patrons as they checked in or out. Most of the conference crowd had now vacated, but Veronica recognized a handful of their corduroy jackets and elbow patches, their nametags, and bad haircuts. She recited lines of Emily Dickinson to herself as she tried to work up the nerve to approach the small line, but she eventually replaced the stark verses with lines from romances she'd liked. When Veronica spotted Samantha getting out of the elevator, Veronica took the friendly face as a way to mitigate her fear of approaching Bo at the desk.

It was a bad choice. The moment Samantha saw Veronica, she turned away. Her gait was stiff and so was her speech as she checked out. She'd already paid in full and had the receipt that someone had slid under her door, but she insisted that she needed an itemized receipt for her breakfast on the first day. "It just says breakfast," she said, her tone tired and angry. "I can't submit it to my department when it says that. I need it itemized. Please."

"I don't know if we can get that since so much time has passed."

"You have to. It's the only way."

Bo didn't flinch as Samantha continued to repeat her point in any number of ways, her angry tone mounting as she did. Veronica waited behind her, tension mounting in her chest. This was bad. Had she caused all this? Her snubbing of Samantha's care had now led to the cold shoulder, even though the text message she'd written to her had seemed friendly. But was it? Samantha was a loyal person, through and through. She'd once stopped talking to a potential adviser because he'd told a racist joke. Maybe Veronica had only read the text telling her about Iggy as a kind gesture, but it was really full of the starts and stops of someone pissed off. Veronica had just opened the message again on her phone when Samantha turned around and crashed into Veronica's shoulder.

"Ugh," Samantha said. "This is—Oh!"

Veronica was about to move herself away, go another direction, and hide her face behind her hair, when Samantha grasped her thin shoulders. "It's you!" she said in her jovial and friendly voice. "I'm so sorry. I didn't recognize you. Oh, wow! What are you wearing?"

Veronica's face relaxed. Samantha hadn't seen her. All the worry and tension faded, and for a moment, Veronica even forgot about the fact that Bo was watching them as she caught Samantha up on the last few hours. She explained about her passport being lost, Stella leaving, and how she was wearing the only clean clothing, haphazardly packed before the trip without considering that she'd need to stay beyond her original plan. "And I think I expected to wear my PJs on the road home. But now it's…this."

"Well, I'm sorry to hear all that," Samantha said. "But at least you have a beautiful day outside for your troubles."

Veronica nodded. "Are you okay? I didn't upset you at all, did I?"

Samantha furrowed her brows, not understanding until it suddenly dawned on her. "Oh, don't worry. I got a shitty email before I checked out. Apparently, I get to go back to Canada for a grade contesting."

"Really? Me too!"

"Yeah? Maybe it is as common as my supervisor says." Samantha put a hand on her chest. "Oh, I feel so much better. I was beginning to think I was paranoid, that I did something bad, and I was going to go to teacher jail the moment I stepped on the campus."

Veronica laughed. She liked that idea: teacher jail. It sounded cute and funny, but it also struck at the heart of the issue that plagued them both. Who teaches the teachers? And what happens if what we'd known all these years was just wrong? They commiserated on that point for a little while, mentioning Melanie Knight, but coming away with a better sense of where they stood. Even though Veronica still had to deal with the mess of her missing attendance, and the grades she'd given her ghost student, she was sure she could handle it now.

"I gotta jet. Literally. Good luck, Veronica."

Veronica hugged Samantha. It felt nice, so nice

that she wanted it to linger. "See you, Samantha."

"Sam, please. It sounds nicer."

"It does." Veronica toyed with her lip before she added. "And call me Ronnie, too."

"Ah, yeah? I thought you preferred Veronica now?"

"I did. I do. In some contexts... But this, this is better."

After another nod, Samantha grabbed the handle of her wheelie suitcase and left the front foyer. Veronica still had her phone open, and while there were several emails now from so many different people who she was convinced would help her in Canada when she returned, she knew she was not done with her business today. She turned to face Bo. No other clients were around. Bo stared at a computer screen, seemingly absorbed.

Veronica took a deep breath and approached. "I'm sorry."

"Hmm?"

"I'm sorry," Veronica said.

Bo furrowed her brows. "For your friend? That happens a lot."

"Oh. Well, yes, I'm sorry for her, too. She got a bad email, and then she just wasn't focused."

"I know." Bo shrugged. She wore the blazer for the hotel over a navy blue top. Veronica wondered if it was deliberate, if she had been avoiding the pinks since she'd said what she said. "It happens a lot. I don't take it personally."

"You don't?"

"I can't. I mean, you know how many grudges I'd hold if I did? Bah." Bo waved a hand. "That's too much energy. So I learned a long time ago to figure that everyone was doing their best when I met them. And if they're mean, well, that's their best for the day. Has nothing to do with me."

Veronica was flummoxed. How could someone being rude to you, calling you names, have nothing to do with you? She thought back to her words. She realized that, in spite of what she'd said, and Bo's curse back at her, she'd also given her the books. In spite of how shitty she'd been, Bo still delivered on her promise of lesbian lit, and Veronica loved her for it. Loved? Veronica brushed aside the word. Now that was too personal.

"So can I help you with something or…?" Bo asked, letting the sentence dangle.

"Well, yeah. Yes. And no. I'm just. I'm sorry. I don't understand." Bo was quiet, so Veronica took a moment to try to gather her thoughts. It was made somewhat difficult as the cleaning staff went into the breakfast area and started to put away mugs, dishes, and cutlery, and banging echoed down the hall. "I said some mean things to you. And you're okay with that?"

"That's not what I said," Bo corrected. "I know you were doing your best. That's what it looked like that day."

"And now?"

"Now you're better. Probably because Stella Flanders is gone."

Veronica tilted her head, Bo matching the sentiment. Veronica sighed. "You knew?"

"That she didn't like me? Oh, yeah. That's her best forever. I won't deal with her, though, outside of this context, so what do I care?"

"And me?" Veronica asked. "Will you deal with me outside of this context?"

"Depends." Bo leaned on the counter, her smile genuine. "You like the books? Wanna talk Katherine V. Forrest or grab another couple more recent ones? I think you'd like Ann McMan's *Jericho*. It's about a small-town librarian…Oh, or maybe Melissa Brayden! She's funny."

"Am I funny?"

"When you let yourself be. I think you'd even be downright fun, too."

Veronica wondered what her best really looked like. Weeks ago, she would have considered it to be when she was teaching, when she was empty, when she was all light and knowledge. Years before graduate school, she would have considered it to be when she was all music, all empty, all piano and the songs of the classics. Now she wasn't sure if those were really her best of all time or best in that moment. Was the best still yet to come? Was it more than just Rolos and romance for breakfast?

"Can I help you with something, though?" Bo asked. "I have you checked in for another couple days, but do you need a different room, a view, something else?"

"I wanted to say I was sorry," Veronica said.

"You should rephrase it then."

"Hmm?"

"Saying I'm sorry is too self-focused. You say you're sorry, and that's good, but it's also kind of a 'so what' statement. Like okay, cool. That's only half the equation, though. Like when you're hungry, say as much, but what you really want to say or what you really mean is let's go get food."

Veronica's stomach rumbled. She wanted food, even though she'd just eaten. She wanted to say she was sorry, too. She wondered about Stella's term *apologia* and Jonathan and felt caught between two poles. "What about an *apologia*?"

"A what?" Bo made a face. "Wait, you explained this before, right? Was I being a bad student and not listening? Probably."

Veronica laughed. "So I should explain it again?"

"Well, yeah, especially if there's gonna be a quiz."

Bo was teasing her, clearly, but Veronica wanted to explain again anyway. "*Apologia*. It's where the term apology came from, but it's more about a defense of a way of life. You know, Socrates? When he drank poison because he didn't want to renounce teaching the students of Athens?"

"Yeah, and that was dumb."

Veronica blinked. When Bo shrugged, she went on. "But it's the foundation of philosophy."

"I know. And that's good. But your friend isn't Socrates, and she may be a teacher, but she was losing her mind over individualized toast and butter on a receipt." Bo huffed. "What I mean is that an apology shouldn't be about a defense. It should be about the other person. The sentiment…Ugh. I'm just so sick of defending myself, you know? I just want to exist."

Veronica understood but didn't want to speak. After some strained silence, she suggested, "Should I say something like…Will you accept my apology then?"

"I suppose I'm partial to the phrase 'please forgive me.' It lays out your sentiments bare. It doesn't turn it into a question, either."

"Please forgive me, Bo." Veronica bit her lip. She was shocked at how revealing this was. Like being naked, hiding nothing. More revealing than any kind of defense would ever be. "I'm sorry I said those things. Please forgive me."

"I do. Already have." Bo smiled. "And well done, by the way, for not even trying to tack on the ifs and buts at the end. Bravo. You ask for forgiveness well."

Veronica nodded, though she wasn't so sure about that. She suddenly saw all the places she needed to make amends, almost as if her life had been X-rayed and she'd found all the hairline cracks. Through that kind of knowledge, all the lingering pain in her life and body made sense. *Please forgive me. Please forgive me. Please forgive me.* She wanted to speak it to her fingers and her toes. Her rib bones and her collarbones. *Please forgive me, please forgive me, please forgive me.*

Veronica was awash with emotions. "How do you know so much?"

"About life?" Bo said, her tone teasing. "Ah, you mean about forgiveness. Well, I can tell you that I got a lot of practice myself."

"Because..."

"You can finish the sentence, you know. And you don't have to talk around me. I'm trans. Yes. I have made some mistakes in the past, many of which required apologies, but I also had a father who was a raging alcoholic and spent my fair share of time in AA circles. I also had—and still have—a lot of friends who do and did the same."

"I know the steps," Veronica said, suddenly pulling knowledge from the deepest parts of herself. She recalled one other anorexic in her treatment centre, her roommate for a handful of days, who was also a drunk. Her anorexia was secondary, really; it helped her to get drunk faster, so she worked the steps while most people worked the dessert bar to get out of the hospital faster.

"Good. The steps are nice. Doesn't always work, but it has taught me a lot about forgiveness. So." Bo folded her arms on the hotel desk. More workers had gathered in the front area, a vacuum cleaner out and spray bottles of Windex for the windows. Veronica was taking up too much time. Too much space. She had accomplished one goal, but now she needed to face the rest. "How can I help you?"

"I need to get to the consulate today. For my passport. Is there a shuttle or bus? I was thinking of renting a car, but would they accept my Ontario driver's license? I've never done this alone. I don't really—"

"I have a car. Well, it's the hotel car."

"Yeah?" Veronica gave a shy smile. Bo mirrored it and confirmed Veronica's suspicions.

"It's a slow day today. I could drive you, take my dad's car, call it hotel business. I could even get my own passport, too."

"Yes." Veronica beamed. "Yes, let's do that."

Bo was already typing something into the computer. She shrugged her blazer off her arms and grabbed a jacket from off the back of a chair. She was about to go into the backroom of the hotel, then turned to Veronica. "You ever read Denis Johnson?"

The name sounded familiar, but Veronica shook her head. The answer seemed to be the right one because Bo's smile grew. She dove into the backroom and came back out with a new stack of books. "No romance," she said in an apologetic tone, "but something from my father's AA days."

Bo handed over a slim book called *Jesus' Son*

by Denis Johnson. Again, there was an inkling of familiarity in Veronica's mind. Perhaps a lecture where he was mentioned in part of the American fiction canon. While Veronica read the back of the book, Bo informed the hotel workers where she was headed and grabbed a new set of keys. *Jesus' Son* was a series of interconnected short stories all revolving around addiction in some way. "But it's not your standard addiction narrative," Bo insisted as they slipped behind the wheel of her father's hatchback. "There is no dwelling in the minutia of drug addiction, the spirals of despair. The descent, you know?"

"I do." Veronica wanted to add that every single eating disorder memoir or novel she'd ever come across did exactly the same thing. The pages were stacked with the descent, the skin and bones in exact weights and measurements, the binges documented in meticulous detail. She hated it. She lived it. Why would she want to read it? She wanted to tell Bo this, but she held off. She wanted to hear her excited chatter instead.

"So, yeah, Johnson does some of that, but it's not the point of the book. The point is recovery. Redemption, you know? But a realistic redemption arc. The title is *Jesus' Son*, so he's being pretty heavy-handed there with his intent, but he's also subtle with it, too. The narrator is never given a name—he's literally only called Fuckhead—but by the end of it, he's healing. He's redeemed through recovery, and through his own sense of that healing and recovery. He wants to get better, you know? And he gets there. It's good. I like it a lot."

"I'm sure I will, too. Thank you."

Bo brushed off the thanks. She rolled down a

window when they reached a light and tied her hair back with an elastic band. With the blue sky outside, it was so picturesque that Veronica wanted to keep it forever. A postcard from the other side.

What is the other side, though? It couldn't be Eden, Veronica realized. Eden was the drug addiction; it was her strange eating habits—or on better days, Eden was the time before those coping mechanisms were even necessary. Addiction was the forbidden fruit. So what was next, after the apple or banana or whatever it was? And what did that place really look like?

Before she could ask any of these questions, Bo spoke again.

"You can learn a lot about someone when they read it. What stories they like tells you, more or less, where they are in their own recovery. If you like the zany antics of Fuckhead, well, you're not quite ready to get better. You're still in love with the drug. Even if you're not actually drunk or high, you're still wishing you were. But if you like the last story, *Beverly House*, you're going to be okay. That's why I like the book. It told me so much about my dad as I read along."

"Now I really want to read it."

"It won't take you long. It's short. But if you need to keep it, then please do."

Veronica nodded. The book was less than two hundred pages, shorter than even most of the romance novels she'd been reading. She knew she could read fast, but this work now seemed to bear the weight of something much larger, like a Victor Hugo masterpiece. Bo's words also made her sad: *Keep it.* She didn't want to keep the book because it would mean she was leaving. Even though that was the goal today—get the passports to leave—Veronica was still overwhelmed. Overcome. She didn't want to go yet. She didn't want to leave.

So she focused on what she had right now: Bo, the road, and a new exploration of Amherst.

"Whoa now," Bo said. "You got real quiet there. You okay?"

Veronica nodded. Bo's gaze was hot on her side. She could feel it. She wanted to simply let things pass them by, but that was not going to happen. Even when Veronica insisted and insisted, Bo did not relent.

"I'm going to tell you about one of the stories then," Bo said. "In Johnson's collection. Because it reminds me of you. At one point, there is a car crash, and the two guys hit a rabbit. It dies, but they realize it was pregnant, and they try to take the bunnies out of the belly." When Veronica made a face, Bo nodded. "I know. Gruesome. But that's the point. Fuckhead tries to hold the bunnies to himself. He tries to keep them warm. He wants to protect them. But his actions only kill them."

"Oh. Oh, wow."

"Yeah." Bo was quiet for a while. "It reminds me of what I do with the dead people in the hotel. I want them to be alive so badly, so I hold them to my chest. I drive around like everyone and everything's okay, but I know it's not. It's hard. It's hard to be alive like that. When you try to be alive like that, you crush and kill what's weaker."

Veronica nodded. She didn't want to say anything anymore. It wasn't just about preserving the moment, it was about preserving herself. So much of her façade was crumbling. So much of her own internal landscape of Eden was fading away.

She leaned forward and turned up the music.

"Sorry," Bo said. "I didn't mean—"

"It's okay," Veronica said. She put a hand on Bo's knee. "I'm fine. Are you?"

"Yeah," Bo said with a nod. "Yeah, I think I'm good."

❧❧❧❧

An hour later, they arrived at the consulate. The building was awash in grey and black slabs, completely sterile. Cars seemed to be parked in every single space in the lot, which meant that they had to walk around the block after feeding quarters into a meter. Everything that had once felt soft and flowing between them, so much like a postcard image, now became circuitous and concrete, a Rothko painting shifting to the Russian avant garde's sharp lines. Veronica remembered the works of Natalia Goncharova, Lyubov Popova, even Wassily Kandinsky from one of her early undergrad classes, but she now saw them in her mind's eye, drained of colour. That was what this placed looked like: bureaucracy run amok. Veronica thought of Cyrillic letters from an old manuscript she once read in her Master's; all accents had been familiar from French but spoken so differently in Spanish and then Russian; and then she conjured the ideographic translation of her student's name. Jiang Zhang, Jiang Zhang, Jiang Zhang, her ghost. Veronica asked Bo about her student's name as they waited in line, found out his entire origin from his first and last name. Then Veronica wanted to know what Bo's last name was— Wu—and what that meant in English and in Chinese, the difference between the sounds and the stories they provoked. Bo told her it all as they waited.

Bo seemed to want to tell her everything.

The photo for Veronica's passport had to be taken somewhere else. But they believed her story about the passport being lost, about her academic conference in the U.S., and her quasi-job back in Ontario. Even if no one had heard of her university before, they still believed she worked at one. She was not a threat, not an issue on the paperwork. They gave her another round of forms to fill out, places to visit, and fees to pay. Bureaucracy run amok, she thought again, but she didn't internalize it. She kept it far back. The black lines and oblique sounds became a beetle on its back that she needed to flip over, not because she felt she had to, but it was cruel to not care otherwise.

Then it was Bo's turn. She waited for Bo to be done. It took longer. Much longer. She tried to read some of *Jesus' Son* as she waited, but she got to the scene about the bunnies almost right away, and it upset her. It made her think of all the girls she'd ever known with eating disorders and how different they were from her, but also how similar they were to her. And she didn't want to think of any of them as dead bunnies, held tightly to her chest, too weak to be saved.

Finally, Bo emerged. She seemed exhausted but triumphant as she held up the forms she needed. It was as if they were a golden ticket—*see, here, I am a true live woman*—but she also held them as if they were a curse. If you had to convince anyone this much of your own humanity, it was going to start feeling like successes were still failures in some manner.

"I think I will be two people at once," Bo said when they slipped into the car. "That the photo will make me a woman, but the biology does not."

"Oh."

"That's okay," Bo said, providing her the answer and the out. "This is the very best they can do for today, and since I still get to go to Montreal—eventually—I will be okay, too."

"They don't mind if you don't speak French," Veronica said. "Or so I've heard."

"I thought you've never been."

She shook her head. "I haven't. But I know a lot from books."

"Ah. Sounds like a gossip city," Bo said. "Everyone I know has gone, but I haven't, so it's all whispers and stories. I like that."

Bo's words reminded Veronica of the part in *Walden* when Henry David Thoreau was talking about telegrams. What to do with all the trivia, all that news of the world he'd not been to? It would never be useful, according to Thoreau. But that was because, Veronica thought, dear Thoreau, you are living alone to live deliberately. More than ever before now, Veronica realized one had to live alongside someone else for it to become truly deliberate. Then you had to share it. Then someone had to witness it and speak to you about it. You had to create the gossip cities to make sense of your own landscape. You had to make it with words and hear it with ears.

Otherwise, Veronica now knew, if you did not, it was just like pressing dead things to your chest and hoping they were living.

"What do you think of the book so far?" Bo asked.

Veronica realized she'd been skimming it as they drove. She should have felt nauseated, but she didn't. She wanted to get to the ending. She wanted to see what the hopeful conclusion would be like—but of course, the sentence out of context made no sense when she flipped there first, impatient as a child. She shrugged. "It's sad right now."

"It will get better," Bo said. "It always does."

Silence fell around them again. Veronica shifted in her seat. She put down the book and gathered their paperwork, examined the next set of forms, and looked up the places where they'd get their passport photos. She wondered if she could smile in hers. She wanted to, but she also knew the impassive facial expression required and that these rules couldn't be broken. Some could bend, sure, but eventually, everyone had to fall in line and obey something.

When they arrived at the drugstore, which also did passport photos, a tightness seized Veronica's chest. It wasn't nausea. She was so used to it always being nauseated that every time she felt physically fine, it was strange. Her own body had become a foreign landscape to her, a different country in which she could finally live and feel good about. They walked past the aisle that would have normally held her ipecac. Her ipecac, she realized she was thinking of the illness as hers. Just like Fuckhead's bunnies in *Jesus' Son*.

She turned her face forward. She would not go back. She would not grab the sickly-sweet vial. She wanted to keep everything inside. So she posed for the photo, said nothing, and waited for Bo to do the same. The harsh lights made everyone look bad in these images, but Bo's final product seemed particularly bad on the computer screen and in the printout the store clerk gave them. Her face was like two faces, not necessarily one man or one woman, but one the past and the other the future. Bo was two people at once, two timelines, everything converging in the present tense.

"You okay?" Bo asked. "You got quiet again."

"Yep. All fine. Let's go mail these." Veronica gave Bo back her photos and put on a smile. Bo nodded after a moment and led them to the car.

While they drove and even the silence could not be covered up with music, Veronica realized she had tried to strip away all her knowledge of Bo's biology, especially after she'd said those cruel words and apologized for them.

But that wasn't fair, either, was it? To pretend she wasn't trans was just as cruel. Bo wasn't a blank canvas or some mythical creature, even if her bottom half seemed like a magical trick left unfinished, according to the U.S. passport office. She would be remade in Canada, set against the Leonard Cohen spray-painted landscape of Montreal. It sounded so beautiful that way. So poetic, and yes, magical, when it was probably so intensely painful.

"Can you..." Veronica started. She turned down the volume. "Can you explain how things would work?"

"With our passports?"

"No. You know."

"Ah." Bo nodded. She understood. Though it took her a while, she eventually explained the procedure. When Veronica remained silent, she explained in more depth about the sitz baths and salts and dildos that would stretch and stretch and stretch until she would feel like a kid going too fast and too high on a swing, and she would reach the top and turn inside out. The operation, or a small series of operations, would do the same to her and allow her to become what she always knew she was. "I say 'what' and not 'who' like everyone else," Bo noted pointedly, "because I already am me. I'm not really becoming myself. Just revealing a new category of thought. Or something like that." She was dramatic as she narrated the details, evoking some talk show tell-all. Then, mistaking Veronica's sudden silence for ignorance, she elaborated on terminology, on hormones and trans history in a more serious tone.

Veronica listened, but she was also trying to think of paintings again, trying to find the perfect image to encapsulate this trip and Bo's presence next to her in the driver's seat. Beyond the stock and trade postcards, all she came up with was a Thelma and Louise-style ride and ending vignette into a bloody horizon.

And soon enough, Veronica wasn't even thinking of paintings anymore, but of her time in summer camp. She remembered the first time she'd been alone in a change room full of girls who were becoming women. Puberty ran wild in different shades and spectrums on each one of their bodies. She always compared herself to others, wondering if she was behind. She felt behind. She felt like a boy when she was a kid because her parents wanted a boy, and then her flat chest made her one, according to everyone at school. Summer camp had no history, though. No prior acts of name-calling and vicious taunts of Ronald, Ronald, Ronnie Boy. When Veronica looked around, she realized she had actually started to develop. Next to other girls, she was mature. Next to other girls, she was a woman. A shadow patch of pubic hair emerged and remained visible, followed by budding breasts like tight flowers in pink on her chest. Veronica was older, and that summer, her body shot so full of hormones she felt like a peach and like she'd bruise.

By the time an Adele song came on the radio in the car, Veronica was bruised. But in a good way, she was sure. In the way in which a peach wants to be touched, the fuzz rubbed off through touch and taste and teeth. Adele—not the singer, but the piano teacher—had been twenty-three. Veronica was fourteen. But she looked like Adele a little bit when their clothing was off. Their hands fit each other; their bodies fell into place together like the black and white piano keys—though now Veronica had to admit their cascade together, their series of tangled embraces, were far more like broken mirror shards. So much like the banned painting by Balthus called *The Guitar Lesson*, where a woman has bent her student over her knee and tries to play her like an instrument. The child is used. The teacher abuses. The music is mute.

Quite simply, Adele did to Veronica what someone had done to Adele. And then, of course, Veronica found Stella. Fourteen. Twenty-three. Forty-eight. The nine and then twenty-three-year age differences. It all added up. Numbers and numbers and numbers that remained meaningless because time was always, perpetually, and forever out of joint.

"Are you okay?" Bo pulled the car to the side of the road. "I thought you were freaking out about the stuff I told you, but I don't think that's it. Transphobia doesn't usually come out in tears."

"I'm not..." Veronica touched her cheek. It was wet. Both were. She'd been crying, sobbing silently and without her even realizing it. Her nose was running now, too, and this excessive emotion fell against her face and down over her jeans. It reminded her of her hair, wet from summer camp, falling against her towel and staining it like the blood from her first period, also experienced at summer camp.

Then she thought of the blood from the rabbits in the novel.

"I'm fine," she said. "I just don't want to go home. I don't want to submit the photos."

"Okay." Bo waited. She tapped her hands against the steering wheel, kinetic with nervous energy. "We sort of have to—"

"I know. We will later. But when we do, it means I go home. I just...not now. It happened so fast. I thought I'd be here a while longer. I thought..."

"You thought your vacation could last forever? Huh! Isn't that every kid's dream? Then the last day of summer comes out like a beast. Saddest fuckin' day, other than when you realize Santa's not real. All the dreams are gone. Poof. Then it's just death and taxes."

Veronica laughed. That was exactly it. She wanted to dream a little longer but not the hazy fever dream of addiction. She wanted to stay in the landscape of the dream they'd created, where their futures were like the clouds they used to watch on their backs as kids. And then, maybe, just maybe, they could make those dreams come true in their adulthood. They could recover like people from addictions try to do. Only this time, she was sure they'd be successful.

"Okay, well, we can do that. What do you say?" Bo began, surveying the neon signs and billboards around them. "What about an all-day breakfast at McDonald's, maybe see if I can find a carnival—"

"No, a thrift store. I want to go in the kids' section."

"Well, all right. We will do that. Then we can

mail the passport photos."

"And piano," Veronica said quietly. "Then the cabin's piano? I want to be a song."

"You want to play a song?" Bo asked, smiling. She didn't wait for Veronica to answer. "Oh, are you going to be Anna Paquin for a while? I can dig that. But I bet there is so much trapped in those fingers."

A hush, heavy and pulsating, settled between them. Pain. Longing. Yearning—but not for home this time around. There *was* so much trapped in those fingers. How could she even begin to document it all? To speak it aloud?

So she didn't try. Veronica looked at Bo with desire, the kind she saw inside the pages of the books she'd given her, the one about curious wine. Could this desire be mutual? No way, Veronica thought. She was, like always, a pity case or some prop for an adult with too-big hands. Some narcissist's source of supply, a codependent with bad boundaries, who was addicted to the feeling of being used and calling it love.

But Bo stared at her with a smile. She pulled the car back on the road, their time for exploring about to begin. She didn't say yes to Veronica's desirous stare—but she didn't say no, either.

She merely held her hand. It was everything in that moment. It was enough.

Chapter Twenty-four

As promised, they went to McDonald's for an all-day breakfast, but they also got soft-serve ice cream. A shitty thrift store was around the corner. It looked as if the place hadn't been dusted since 1983, but that meant it was perfect. It was what Veronica needed. There were no corporate logos, no specialty cards or deals. This was a shop where people stole the trash from the street corners and hoped for gold. Pure scavenging. Veronica found a hot pink tank top that fit her around her bust, but the straps cut into her arms like sausage. She discarded it, though the pink reminded her of Bo, an image of her she wanted to keep. When she found a shirt that said *I Had My Birthday Party at McDonald's,* she bought it without trying it on. It would be tight. It would be hers. Nothing else mattered.

Bo disappeared into a circular rack. She oscillated and oscillated and came back with a sequined top. She made a face as she held it to her wide shoulders.

"I don't think it'll fit."

"Does it matter?" Veronica asked.

Bo laughed. She put it back. Ten minutes later, Veronica saw her buy it with a pair of shoes she said she couldn't let go. "Impossible to find anything beyond size nine in women's. This is eleven—perfect for me. Totally a sign."

"A sign of what?"

Bo shrugged. "I guess that we belong here."

Once cashed out at the thrift store, Bo insisted that they mail the photos. "It will still take a couple days for the passport to reach us. So it's not like it's all really *over* over. Only the hours at   the post office."

Finally, Veronica relented. They mailed the package—but at Veronica's insistence, they also went to a photo booth around the corner. Bo easily agreed, and when Veronica recognized the light blue and purple backgrounds, she realized it was the same booth from the shoebox images. Would this be another day for the shoebox? Did this make her like the bunnies in Johnson's novel? She wasn't leaving Bo because of death, but what were the odds she was ever going to come back?

She pushed the thought aside. This was not a mourning ritual, not an activity for the dead time. This was a returning hunger. A hunger for time. For light, for life.

This was the redemption she'd wanted all along. In this context, it was called recovery. Not as cinematic as Jesus rising from the grave—but if you were Johnson who had his own substance issues and got clean one summer so he could write his many novels the rest of his life or if you were like Bo's father, the raging alcoholic who now recited the serenity prayer every damn morning before work—this sort of daily recovery had to be enough.

"All right." Bo held a hand against her chest as if her heart was beating too fast. Veronica mirrored her without thinking about it. "I think I've had enough townie fun. Let's get back."

Veronica's chin dropped to her chest. There were so many more things she wanted to do now, but the sun was setting. Time was flowing away from them. So she nodded, and they headed back to the car.

On the road, they talked about their favourite movies. There was even an adaptation of *Jesus' Son*, but Bo hadn't seen it yet. "I don't want the film to spoil the book. Besides, I already lived most of these stories. I know what each character should look like."

Veronica wondered who she'd be in this movie. Who Bo would be in hers. They were soon dream-casting their own versions of hit flicks, making them gay and trans, by the time Bo turned toward the bed and breakfast. Veronica's heart shuddered with joy. She'd been worried that Bo had forgotten about the promise of a piano. But no, of course not. Bo turned up the dirt road away from the Amherst hotel and toward the bed and breakfast cabin. There were more cars there now. Only one guest booking, Bo insisted, and it was a gay couple in the far-off bedroom. They would appreciate all the racket, she was sure, especially if Veronica knew how to play show tunes.

"I don't know what I remember." Veronica bit her lip to hold back from exploding with sentiment. *I know how to play everything—everything because I am the piano. And I want to be played and played again.*

"Well, I know chopsticks. So let's be horribly stereotypical together."

The descent down the stairs was marked by nervous energy. Veronica held the banister, and her body ached with prior memory. She'd had a seizure right here, so close to the staircase. She could have fallen and cracked her head against the hardwood— but she hadn't. She wouldn't. She'd eaten so much today her body *had to* let her stay upright and okay. When she got to the basement floor, she could already hear the music. She sat on the bench and let herself play, her stomach swelling with hope.

When she looked up, she swore an hour had passed, but it was only ten minutes. Bo was leaning against the staircase railing, a smile on her face. "Very nice. I'll get some tea."

"Why are you being so nice to me?" Veronica placed her hands on her knees. She tapped them like the keys. "Especially after all I said?"

Bo's smile turned rough at the edges. "You weren't that mean. I've seen mean."

"But you're still being so nice."

"Forgiveness—"

"Yes, yes, we had that moment, and you explained how to apologize. And it made sense then… but now I just don't understand how you're still so nice to me. You seem almost saint-like, yet I know you're just as human as me or even Stella."

Bo made a face.

"I know it's hard to believe," Veronica said. "But Stella's lost a lot. She was from Love Canal, you know. Do you know what that is?"

When Bo waved her hand in a so-so gesture, Veronica explained. Bo seemed to bristle under the news. "No wonder she likes to micromanage."

"Hmm?"

"It wasn't just you. I saw her fuss with a lot of people at that conference, hovering over their food and getting all up in their presentations. But it makes sense, I suppose, if she had to be a caretaker extraordinaire in her youth. It gives her purpose. I would not let her near my bedside in my aftercare, but that's just me."

Veronica had a hard time reconciling this image

of Stella micromanaging, but she let it pass. She nudged Bo again. "Still. Forget Stella. I'm having a hard time understanding why you were so nice to me today. I'm just a stranger."

"Maybe. But don't we all start as strangers?" Bo sighed dramatically, clearly quoting from something Veronica couldn't name. Eventually, Bo added, "I do admit that I felt bad about the fiddleheads. Damn near thought I poisoned you. And then when I realized I hadn't, I just thought of Morty. The...you know."

"The one from the box?"

"Oh, so many from the box. But yes, he was the last one I mentioned, in the bathtub, you know. I shouted the story at you, so I don't feel like I need to rehash. But...he was the one I found. It was scary. And I suppose I just don't want to see that again, and if I do, I want the ending to be different."

"You want to be like Fuckhead holding the bunnies together?"

"I wanted that, yes. But it was only through him where I realized I was hurting them and myself, and so...for a long time, I wanted to be Fuckhead but not get in the car. Not have the crash. But that's impossible."

"How so?"

Bo gave her a look. "That's not going outside. You crash. That's just what happened. That's what my Dad taught me, honestly. He's frustrating. He's maddening. But he used to be so much worse." Bo let out a breath and gave a brief snapshot of her father's drinking. "The descent is never as important as the recovery, though. Because it's the recovery that gets you to do the daily shit that used to make you drink, rather than avoiding it. Recovering is that dumb serenity prayer."

"What is that?" Veronica asked.

"Oh, sorry! I thought because you knew the steps, you knew that. God grant me the serenity to accept the things I cannot change, the courage to change the things I can and the wisdom to know the difference." Bo's voice was clear and lucid, a practiced hymn. "Replace God with whatever higher power, whatever it is, outside yourself. But just put your faith in something, so you can endure, you know?"

"What's yours?" Veronica asked. "I mean, if I can ask."

Bo smiled. "I can't say using words. But I do know that now, I like the *Beverly House* ending. So maybe that story is my higher power. I don't know."

Veronica nodded. She noticed that Bo didn't turn the question around and ask her what she believed in. She wasn't sure herself. "I don't think I'll ever get there."

"You will. It's an ending about belonging, about going outside rather than being afraid to leave the house. Everyone wants that. Everyone gets that. So I'm not telling you a spoiler there. One day, you will find where you belong."

"Did you?"

Again, Bo gave a so-so gesture.

"Yeah. Same." Veronica was quiet. So was the piano. She hovered her hands over the familiar keys and added, "So that's why you are being so nice to a wayward lesbian trapped in this country?"

"Someone has to. It seemed like no one had ever bothered to even try before me. But," Bo added quickly, "I can only see so much so far."

Veronica was silent, not correcting. She saw no

need to because Bo was right. Had anyone ever really tried to help her? Maybe, but it was always for their own ends. Maybe, but it never lasted. And maybe, but it seemed to always, always come with conditions. Not even playing the piano could make Veronica feel better now.

"I'll get us some tea," Bo said, realizing that the music was going to need to pause for a while. "It'll make us feel better."

Bo took the stairs two by two. Veronica heard hushed conversations with the staying guests from the upstairs landing, all asking about the playing. Good things, she could tell from tone, but she let the words fizzle out around her. She didn't want to be praised anymore. She didn't want to be cited or approved of or even do the approving. When she'd been with Adele, she could be music. She could be lightness. She tried to replicate the same thing when Adele was gone, but Veronica only scraped herself out from the inside. She tried to put words and knowledge and poetry there instead, but she'd only tried to swallow Stella whole.

She wasn't sure of the right answer anymore. Was there a right answer?

Only recovery, she realized. Only recovery. She still had no idea what recovery could look like. Was it like a romance novel, where the talk of toothpaste was just as important as the big romantic gesture that reunited the protagonists? Was it a postcard that said one day you could be here? Or was it something so much simpler, something she couldn't quite understand yet, simply because she hadn't worked her way through enough of *Jesus' Son* for the ending story of *Beverly House* to make sense.

Veronica took the tea when Bo offered it. It was

sweet, like honey. Not like the artificial sweetness she tasted whenever she was with Stella, from the pink and yellow packets she put in her coffee. How could it be that this woman in front of her presented the most natural option to being, that fully allowed for Veronica to dream, and the woman she thought was her dream for so long only presented a bitter poison?

Veronica looked at the piano again. She set the tea on the floor by her ankles and played another song. Bo moved to the notes this time around, as if it was familiar to her.

"Come sit with me," Veronica said. "Show me what you can play."

Bo set her tea down. Cup to cup, body to body on the bench. Veronica wanted Bo between her legs, like she'd been with her mother learning the keys. Instead, they played opposite parts of the same song, coming together and brushing wrists. She smiled. Bo returned it and shifted closer. Veronica didn't move away, but she paused.

A beat too long. The music was off.

"Sorry, I should..." Bo took her hands off the keys. It was a bruise again. Veronica put them back on and slipped her palms over Bo's wrist.

Bo tilted her head, a chastisement and a question. *Yeah? You so sure now? Even after all that I've told you and all that you now know?*

Veronica swallowed. She nodded.

Bo waited, said nothing.

"I...have never been with a man before."

Bo laughed. "Well, that's good then. Because I'm not a man."

"I know. I'm sorry. Oh, wow. I'm so sorry. I just meant—"

"Shut up," Bo said. Her words were playful, yet serious. "You think too much."

"It's my job."

"Doesn't have to be. Or maybe," Bo added when Veronica must have seemed too sad, "you can think about different things. Either way, you are not at work now. I am not at work now. Just...relax."

Veronica nodded. Bo shifted closer to her on the bench, their hands linking. She was touching, sensing, moving slowly, so slowly that when they did kiss, Veronica's eyes were open. She was so caught off guard it took her another second to blink. She kissed her. It seemed to last for longer than a second, longer than another break in the music. Then she turned her body toward Bo, so she wasn't an encampment for her to climb. She wanted to be open, so she could allow Bo to explore her and she could do the same.

Kissing turned to making out turned to gasping into each other's mouth. Veronica thought of a scientific theory she'd heard from a dietician: *All fat from the body left through breath.* Cardio was good for the body because you breathed out what you no longer wanted. But you could also breathe in what you wanted, too, she realized. It was just like the toxins and pollutants in Love Canal. It altered your body chemistry, but if you wanted something bad enough, you could also take it inside and let it destroy you.

No, you could let it create you. Make you into a song.

Veronica knew she was thinking too much. She tried to live in her body as if it was a home. She tried to allow her breasts to become objects of desire, while still being part of her. She tried to allow her wetness to not seem like an invasion or like not enough moisture between them. When Veronica moved to kiss Bo's neck, she was shocked by the rough skin. Formerly bearded skin, but still no less feminine. She ran her fingers along the edge of Bo's neck, toward her collarbones, and down over her breasts. They felt like her own breasts, yet different. Bo touched hers and soon they were pressed together on the bench, the space between their bodies and their differences eroding and eroding until something new and beautiful emerged.

But there was still the bottom half, Veronica thought. She swallowed. She didn't know how to do anything with...that. She didn't know if she'd be able to do anything. Bo's hands moved along her body, readying her for the eventual outcome—even if Veronica did not know what that would be. So she just spread her legs and allowed Bo to coax moans from her. She allowed fingers, licked with saliva to tease her, enter her, and entice her further and further.

"Not too fast?" Bo asked.

Veronica shook her head.

Bo kissed her again, softer this time. She moved closer. She went underneath Veronica's shirt and cupped her breasts. Veronica did the same to her. But when Bo went to her pants again, teasing and coaxing, Veronica remained on her waist. If Bo noticed, she played it off with another soft kiss that came to form a request, "Do you want to be alone?"

"With you?"

"Yes. That's what I mean. I'm trying to be romantic."

"You do like novels."

"I like you," Bo said flatly so there was no ambiguity. "Do you want to get a room with me?

There's one here."

Her voice almost sounded professional, the hotel worker rather than a lover. Her breath was staccato, her longing evident. Veronica grasped her hands. She nodded. Bo led her to the basement room not a foot away from the piano. The fact that the instrument was so close gave Veronica hope she knew what she was doing.

Bo undressed her first, tugging off the too-tight shirt and working on Veronica's pants. Faint light from a bathroom nightlight allowed the room to glow; it cast shadows against the soft bed filled with multiple pillows and allowed for Bo's body to still be cast in shadows. Veronica was afraid. She didn't want to be, but she was. *Would they have sex like...* she couldn't say "straight people" even in her mind, and she couldn't say "normal," either. What was normal? She didn't know if Bo had a penis, and if that's what you called it or if it was something else. It was so confusing. There should be no words, yet Veronica was all words. She needed them to understand.

She was naked on the bed, and Bo's chest was bare. Her breasts were bigger than Veronica's, which was the first shock. Her nipples were smaller, pointier, directed toward the ceiling fan. Veronica wanted to bury her face in them, kiss them over and over, so she let herself do just that. She flipped their bodies, so she was now leading, and she kissed her way down Bo's neck to her breasts and played with her nipples while she gasped. It was...great. It was...almost easy. Veronica heard the encouragement from Bo's hushed breaths to keep going.

"Keep going. You know what you're doing. Keep going. I'll help. Just..."

Bo was scared, Veronica knew that now. She heard it in that hitch. And so, she felt better. With Stella, with Adele—they always had the upper hand. They had done this before. They were better at it than her. She always felt so bad at sex because of that fact. She was awkward. Gawky. She came too fast and too messily. She loved too deeply and too suddenly.

But there was nothing wrong with her. She was an animal in that moment, only seeking absolution and release. Bo, too, was utterly herself in that moment. A little scared, too. A little bad at sex, too. But they were going to figure it out together. With courage she didn't know she had, Veronica allowed desire to fully take over her body. She slipped the rest of her clothing off as her mouth sought out the softer spots on Bo's body: neck, breasts, and then the sway of the pelvis. She took Bo's pants off, her underwear, and revealed the wetness they both shared. Bo looked different, sure, but she was wet like Veronica was wet, and there was something so relieving in that. Veronica anchored their hips together, allowing their wetness to meet. She kissed Bo on the mouth and rocked, rocked, and rocked.

"I won't...I probably...not as hard to..." Bo tried to say, but Veronica silenced her. She would not get hard in the same way, sure, but that was not what Veronica wanted. She knew that now. In her mind's eye, Veronica saw Bo in all her beautiful glory like a Venus painting. She couldn't even remember the proper name of it now; it was all a vision in her mind. She saw Bo's hair was by her side, her breasts revealed and beautiful, and her genitals laid bare and vulnerable for Veronica. She thought of Bo like the epitome of beauty, and only then did she find the right spot on her body to touch, to flick, to suck, and taste and bring her to several orgasms before Veronica brought her sex to Bo's mouth and let her finish her off, too.

In the glow of the nightlight, Veronica shook. She could not believe she'd been so bold. Bo found her hand and held it close, kissing her fingers with a deep and serious expression on her face. Veronica wanted to hide her body, but she remained bare, like Bo. She imagined herself like the Venus painting until she believed it. "Did I do okay?"

"Oh, yeah," Bo said, laughing. "I just... How did you know how to touch me?"

"What?"

"You did all the right things, in all the right places. If you've never..."

"I've never."

"Okay. So how did you know?"

Veronica thought about this. The answer was obvious: "I imagined you like a painting."

Bo smiled. She didn't need to ask what one. She only leaned forward in the bed, planting another kiss on Veronica's mouth, before they tried to make whatever magic happened between them happen again and again and again.

Chapter Twenty-five

Veronica fell asleep with Bo. They were exhausted from their small adventure, and then from depleting each other. It didn't take long for the few sustained blinks Veronica took to slip into deeper and deeper sleep.

Then she was dreaming of Jonathan again.

She was in the same room where she'd once delivered her paper. The audience was three times larger now, all of them sketchy figures rather than solid forms, as if they were vibrating with colour and motion. Everyone was familiar, though she could not see their faces or know their names. She squinted and realized none of the people in the room was at the conference. This was not a room filled with academics, but normal people. Everyday people. Young, old, and—

Love Canal, she realized. *Everyone here is from Love Canal.*

Veronica gave her paper in the exact same way, except that now she was wearing the clothing she'd bought from the thrift store. She raised her arms in the air, like a child getting ready for her shirt to be put on, and the blazer jacket went over her, helped by some invisible hands. It tightened up around her like a corset. She wanted to speak, but she couldn't.

A phone rang. It was in her jacket pocket. She picked it up but noticed it wasn't her phone. It was Jonathan's phone. Not the office one where his voice was recorded, but his cellphone. She suddenly remembered, as if by some magic psychic knowledge, that no one had found his cellphone. There was a bill for it, along with the cyanide. But there was no cellphone. Veronica knew the detective was looking for that phone. That was why he had called her.

Marta Allen, Marta Allen, she remembered. But who was Marta Allen?

"Will Marta Allen please stand up?" Veronica said in the dream. One of the figures in the back moved, then slipped out the door.

The phone rang in her pocket. It rang like a normal phone, then it sounded like a frog. Ribbit. Ribbit. Ribbit. A group of frogs jumped across the aisle and scattered. They formed a shadow, a body, as if they had once been a person in the audience under a trench coat, but now the jig was up, and they had to leave. The frogs were gone now.

But the phone was still ringing.

Veronica wanted to give her paper, but now she was naked. She was naked, and Bo was behind her. She was covering Bo with her body. The phone was ringing, but it was now on the podium. The anxiety in the room was awful; she felt everyone's feelings as if they were her own, and it was oozing like a thick black sludge. She looked down at the phone. The display read: *Do you see it yet? Do you recognize them?*

Veronica looked at the crowd. Every single person in the audience was Stella Flanders. No shadows, no sketchy forms, just iteration after iteration of Stella. Veronica was naked, but she was smaller. A child. She was naked at summer camp in front of Stella, blood trickling down her legs, and now the podium was too big so she could not answer the phone anymore.

Do you see it? Do you see it? Do you see it?

Do you recognize them?

"Stella," Veronica said in the dream. "What did you do?"

All the Stellas in the audience remained passive. They did nothing.

Then, as if they had sneezed in unison, a sudden gasp ripped through the crowd. They all opened their mouths. Instead of a tongue, there was a key.

An office key. Her office key.

Veronica felt a realization on the tip of her tongue. She grew six feet in a mere instant, breaking through the hotel ceiling. She wore the hotel-like clothing, like Alice wore the house in the Lewis Carroll story. Veronica wandered through the rest of the United States like that, taking gigantic steps, and heading toward home.

The dream faded then. There was no resolution, only a soft light that bled into Veronica's consciousness. When she awoke fully, she realized Bo was discussing something with someone through a closed door. Veronica was alone in the bed, still naked. Shame tinged her cheeks. The dream's sense of failure lingered. The more she tried to grasp the nuances, the more they slipped away.

So she just put on her clothing. It was almost eight at night. This had gone on long enough, hadn't it?

She knew she was going to have to go home.

"Hey," Bo said when she stepped in the room. She put a hand on Veronica's bare shoulder. Veronica fought the urge to pull away—not because she didn't love Bo, but because it would hurt too much to let herself stay in this wonderful feeling. Was it really love, anyway? She wondered. It was so soon. Too soon. But it was the only thing she could think of because it was the ending of the story, right? Love. Belonging. Recovery.

But she couldn't stay here.

"I know," Veronica said. "I'll get dressed. We have to go."

Chapter Twenty-six

Veronica stared out the passenger window as Bo drove. The dirt road to the bed and breakfast was dark; stars spotted the night sky in fluorescent winks. As soon as they turned onto the highway, the stars faded. More houses dotted the area, lights on in their bedrooms, living rooms, and shadows of people indoors. As much as the shadowy people reminded her of the lingering doom of her dream, Veronica knew she'd trade the houses for skylight anytime. She felt like a kid again, peeping inside and hoping for something more.

"Shit," Bo said. "Shit, shit."

"What's wrong?" Veronica asked, still staring at the houses they passed by.

The car started to slow. The engine sputtered. Bo was hitting the wheel with her hand. She managed to navigate the car to the side of the road and hit the four ways before it stopped entirely.

"I'm an idiot," Bo said.

"What's wrong?"

Veronica turned away from the houses to see Bo now. Her hair was tussled, partly from sex and from the current frustration. Her lips were thin, anger tensing her face. Bo repeated her stance of "I'm an idiot"; Veronica peered over to see the empty gas tank icon, and she let out a sigh. She understood now. Though fear gripped her chest at the thought of being trapped in a useless car, she remained calm. She pointed to a house a few feet from them. These neighbouring houses had no lights on, but one a few paces over had a glow from the front window. A living room, Veronica sensed. They were probably watching TV.

"We should ask them for help."

"What?" Bo was on her phone. She was trying to get bars, but it didn't seem to be working. She cursed again before looking to where Veronica gestured. "What did you say?"

"We should ask them for help."

Bo laughed. Then she grew serious. "Really?"

"Why not?" Veronica suggested. In the back of her throat, she held all the objections to her action: no, she couldn't be a bother; no, they could be bad people; no, she and Bo might knock on a murderer's door; no, no, no, this was not how the world worked. All the objections stayed down. She undid her belt and stepped outside. She looked back in through the open window where Bo still was.

"You coming?" Veronica asked.

Bo undid her belt, too. With a shrug, she exited. "Why not?"

An older woman answered the door. Her hair was white and pulled back into a bun. She wore brown slacks and a plaid shirt, a dark-coloured housecoat over her shoulders as if she felt a chill and decided it was better than a typical sweater. She assessed the two women in front of her with a careful eye, and for a brief moment, Veronica panicked. What if she saw the sex between them and made judgments? What if she saw the incongruence of Bo's jawline and leapt to conclusions?

None of this happened, though. After the woman's careful assessment, she merely introduced herself. "I'm Francine. You two havin' some trouble?"

"Yes." Bo's voice was thin and tight. "I'm out of gas. I'm sorry to do this, but—"

"Come in." Francine gestured to the front hallway. "You may as well get comfortable."

Veronica stepped inside first, all fear now gone. The house's front foyer was meticulously swept, each pair of shoes Francine owned lining one side. In between introductions, Francine insisted that they take off their shoes. Bo hesitated but eventually complied. "We just need to use your phone," Bo said, now in her sock feet. "We can get a cab back to the hotel, and then my father can drive me back to get gas. We don't mean to impose."

"Nonsense. No imposition. I like it when people call."

"Thank you, Francine," Veronica said.

"No thanks necessary. Come in for a moment, and we will sort out what the best plan of action is."

Bo took Veronica's arm as they followed Francine deeper in the house. Veronica loved the contact, though she was far less nervous than Bo seemed to be. Was Bo still stuck on the early signs of danger? Was she not yet convinced of Francine and still fearful that she belonged to a more hostile generation? Was it something else altogether? Veronica didn't know, and there was no polite time to ask. She eyed the framed photos in the front hallway, which displayed children from another era, plus grandchildren in more modern clothing. Black and white family portraits were followed by neon shades of a 1980s background clearly taken at Kmart, and then framed images developed from a digital camera, complete with cheap card stock. There were framed paintings lining what seemed to be a dining room, as well, but the canvases contained nothing too exciting or that couldn't be found in a dentist office. They were nice, though, Veronica knew. The carpet was nice, if not worn down. She reached for more adjectives in her brain, but ultimately, Veronica settled on nice most of all. This whole thing, this whole place, and Francine: nice. Just nice.

By the time they settled in the living room and Francine asked if they wanted lemonade, Veronica knew why she was so at home, why she was not afraid anymore.

She'd read this story before. She'd been in this story before.

During one of her first-year lectures, the one taught by Isabella Stanton who was now Iggy, there had been a short story by the American author Raymond Carver. In it, a couple's car broke down, and they needed to seek solace in someone's house. It was an era before cellphones and before mass murder and serial killings were publicized enough to make such acts seem foolish. In the story, while the person helps the couple, they examine the inside of the house. It was a family house, and they were just starting out in their dating life. Without realizing it and only with the benefit of hindsight, that stranger's house became their model for domesticity. It became their model for the happily ever after they wanted.

That was the feeling Veronica was getting now, that strange sense of familiarity, of déjà vu, though she'd not lived here or that story in her own life. In truth, Francine's place was not exactly the same as the one described in Carver's world, but it gave Veronica that same feeling. Hope. Belonging. The future.

As she sipped lemonade and Veronica heard more about Francine's history, that feeling only grew. Francine was an older woman, married once with a husband who died in the war; after his death, she had to move in with her co-worker who also lost her husband in the war to pay the bills and raise their families. From that point on, she and Molly shared the responsibilities of a life together. A shared and intimate life, as up until her death in the early 2000s, they had never spent a night apart. "She was mine and I was hers, you could say," Francine added, her voice sharp with emotion. "So I like it when people call. It reminds me to be nice, as she reminded me to be nice."

In all the houses that they could have stopped in front of that night, they had selected an old lesbian. A Boston marriage, Veronica remembered. That was what it would have been called. Suddenly, the photos in the front hallway now seemed even more familiar than the generic landscapes. They were a possible future she and Bo could have. Children that were biologically theirs, but also outside of the norm in some way. Children that were normal, but also so quintessentially different.

"Anyway," Francine said. She'd moved on quickly from personal history to the history of the house and the area and spoke extensively about her granddaughter's work on biological cancer research as they drank their lemonade. "Thank you for letting me talk your ears off. Now I suppose I should get you some gas from the canister in the garage."

"We can call a cab," Bo offered once again.

"No, no." Francine waved her hand as she stood.

She was old but spry. Her hips were wide and round, her middle soft, but her arms strong. Veronica saw the possibilities in front of her now: She saw what it was like to get old and have that age not be a failure but a badge of honour. She understood that life didn't have to be so rigid, so conforming. It could be like this house. A glass of lemonade. A Raymond Carver short story—like a Denis Jonson short story—only she could be inside of it. She and Bo.

Belonging, recovery. Redemption.

One day, there really could be a place for people like us.

If she could only let it happen. If they could only let it happen, together. If only, like Katherine V. Forrest had done one night, repurposing an Emily Dickinson line, they could create it for themselves.

From the living room, all three of them moved into the garage. The chipper and heartwarming tone continued as Bo spoke to Francine about the history of her parents' hotel, their bed and breakfast, and her own dreams for owning her own place. "Maybe in Boston, maybe in Montreal, Canada, who knows?" Bo said. She was smiling now. What was once all hospitality nonsense became her reappropriated—and more appropriate—legacy.

Veronica was relieved. Even though the garage was darker and made her feel odd in a way she couldn't articulate, she was happy here. While Bo gathered some gas from Francine's spare canister, Francine shared that she and her Molly (she never said wife or even partner, but her Molly) had once stayed at the bed and breakfast. "Long before you were a woman, my dear. You couldn't have been more than eight or nine."

"That *was* long before I was a woman," Bo said. She chuckled, and if the joke was understood, it wasn't dwelled on. Francine said she liked the bed and breakfast and that maybe, one day, she would go back.

"We will keep a room for you then. On the house since you've helped us tonight."

"It's not a problem. Really."

Once the gas was exchanged and the lemonade was consumed, there was really nothing left to do but say goodbye—for now. Even a temporary goodbye hurt. Veronica didn't want to go. She'd been quiet the last ten minutes. Bo eyed her, concern evident, but Veronica just smiled. She reached into her purse and pulled out the Denis Johnson book. With a brief look toward Bo, she gave it over to Francine.

"What's this?"

"A book," Veronica said and then felt feeble. She picked a pen from her purse and wrote on the inside front cover her name and Bo's. "It's us. For later, when you need that reservation."

Francine nodded. Bo and Veronica thanked her again and waved before stepping out into the dark night. The night seemed that much darker and deeper after being in Francine's house. They hurried to the car. Bo let out a great sigh of relief as the car started and the gas tank declared half full.

"Thank God. I was worried we'd be in *Deliverance*."

"Hush. She was nice."

"You're right," Bo said. "She was."

"Good. I like being right."

"I think Francine will enjoy Johnson, too. Though I do wonder if she'll refer to the main character as Mr. Fuckhead."

Veronica laughed. She was caught for a moment by that sentiment, though. As Bo pulled onto the highway and headed toward the hotel, the reality of their situation descended on her. She'd felt like she was in a dream, living in a novel all day. But it was real. It was so real that someone had finally seen her, seen Bo, and now it felt like a future. Was that what Bo felt when she thought of Montreal? The future was another gossip city, a book they had both lived in but never with actual experience to verify it.

She turned to Bo to ask her but drew quiet. A smell from the garage lingered in the air. Car smell— but also more than that. It was familiar. It made her feel sick. She wanted to ask, but she was mute. She tried to focus on the things she did know from today, but she was struck mute again. She wanted to vomit, and that thought made her sad. She wondered if Bo could see it in her expression and hear it in the sudden silence between them.

Maybe she did. Maybe she could, the same way Veronica could understand Denis Johnson without ever being an addict, like she could understand Bo without ever being trans. She understood because she read.

And she read because she wanted to understand and be understood.

"I want to throw up," Veronica said. She balled her fists. "I have bulimia."

"I know," Bo said.

"You do?"

"I figured."

"How?" Veronica wanted to know what exact thing had caused this illumination. When did Bo see the sudden twitch, the sudden need to convert all that sugar they'd consumed in Francine's house into something to expel? "Was it my knuckles?" Veronica asked. "Or my teeth? How skinny I am but how puffy my face is? My thinning hair?" Veronica tried to think of more symptoms. What were her clues, her tells, her personal language? She couldn't think of anything else, and Bo never verified anything. She was quiet.

"How do you know?" Veronica asked, persistent now. "Do you have bulimia, too?"

"No," Bo said. "But it's not like you're hiding it well. It's not like anyone hides anything well. We have all something we're working with, we're dealing with. It's just human nature."

"So I'm not broken?"

"Oh, sweetheart. You're not broken, no, but... You can't do that forever, you know. You will kill yourself."

"I know." Veronica ran her hands over her knees. She thought of Karen Carpenter, the dozens of gymnasts in the news who'd also died of their eating disorders. *Bulimia and anorexia are the most deadly mental illnesses. If your mind does not make it unbearable to live, the treatment of your body will eventually end you.* She knew all this. Yet she also wanted to prove them wrong, all wrong, so she kept doing the bad things and kept living. She wanted to be both. She couldn't choose.

"You know," Bo said suddenly, "I saw this thing on *Oprah* years ago now. It was around the time she had the first trans woman I ever saw before on the show, so I kept coming back to see if I could find more people like me. Anyway, Oprah had this girl with anorexia on. I know it's not the same as bulimia, but—"

"I had that, too."

"Ah. Jack—or Jill—of all trades. Sorry. I don't mean to be blasé, but well, it helps." Bo nodded, and when Veronica squeezed her hand, she kept talking. "Anyway, so this anorexic girl was on the show. She may have even been a woman at this point, in her twenties, so calling her a girl is strange. But she is no more than, like, ninety pounds? Maybe eighty. Either way, she looks horrible. She's been anorexic so long, too, that her brain has stopped functioning well. Like, the glucose that brains need is gone, so when she speaks, it sounds like she's drunk. It's just all mumbling. It was awful. I thought she was having a stroke."

"I know, okay?" Veronica said, voice tipping into anger when Bo dwelled too long on this fact. "If this is supposed to be an intervention, where you tell me she died and I'm supposed to change my ways, I know. I already know."

"I know you know. I know, too. I'm just setting the scene, I guess. I'm sorry." Bo tightened the hand she had on the wheel, a reflex to mitigate her own tension. "This anorexic stayed with me, though. It wasn't just the death, the slow speech, the skinniness. All of that was pretty standard. I knew about it, not too shocking. But much later in the episode, Oprah brought on another girl who had beaten anorexia for a strange coaching session. She was telling the first girl nice things like it was possible to heal, blah blah blah. The normal stuff, you know? Of course you know.

"Anyway, the first anorexic, she was listening. She wanted to hear it. She was paying attention, and you could almost *almost* see her say, *yeah, I want to live. Yeah, this has gone on for long enough. Yeah, please, other anorexic, teach me your ways.* But then a dark cloud moved over her face. She looked away from the one who had healed. She checked out. Gone. Oprah, of course, caught it. She asked what happened."

Bo paused. Veronica, in spite of herself, was on the edge of her seat. She needed to know what happened. So she finally asked: "And?"

"And that damn girl just started to cry. She said she knew what she had to do. Nothing here was new. But how?" Bo affected her voice a little, made it higher, so it was clear she was mimicking the girl on TV. "But how do you eat?" Bo shook her head. "There. Right there. That girl was so far gone she couldn't connect the thought of I should eat more or I'm going to die to the action of eating more food. She had no idea of the how. And damn. I knew that feeling. Not with food. But with this."

"You..."

Bo gestured to her body in a strained, elongated way. "This. I knew that feeling but with this. It was like I knew how to do the boy things. I was not ignorant. I could even do some of the boy things on occasion. But there would also be horrible moments of despair where I'd suddenly lose grip and just wonder, well, how? How could I do this for the rest of my life? It was like looking at a blank wall."

"Wow." Veronica swallowed.

"Not wow," Bo said. "How. That's the killer. It's the unknown *how*."

Veronica felt punched. The how, how, how. Of course. She knew that feeling, too—but it wasn't with food. The food was part of it, sure. The food was the main vehicle for expression, but Veronica knew that she was really speaking about love. That was what she felt when she thought of loving someone, not just having sex with them because that was almost easy. It was the love part. When confronted with the act of love, she always thought, but how?

She could understand the concept. She could even read it in books, books that she was liking more and more, but sometimes, she stopped and realized the *how* of that action was just too hard. How could she love someone without hurting them? How could she be in love without that blank wall of pain?

It seemed impossible. It seemed like a fantasy.

"How did you get out?" Veronica asked. "You know, of... Well... How did you figure out the how? God, that doesn't make sense. I..."

"No, I get it. It makes sense." Bo took a while to think about it. "I realized I had to be the other chair."

"What?"

"You know on talk shows, they have chairs. The first anorexic was in one chair, and the other anorexic was in the other chair. She had gotten better while the other couldn't figure out the how of eating. So I had to be in the other chair, the one that did get the *how*. Eventually, it made sense to become, well, this." Again, Bo gave another gesture to herself, but this one ended with the passport paperwork that she casually flipped open. "I am mismatched, and sometimes, that feels horrible, but it doesn't feel nearly as bad as being in a different body and not understanding the how."

Veronica nodded. She could say nothing, and truly, there was nothing left to say.

They both allowed the quiet to close around them, her confession and their long discussion on Oprah now drained out by music as Bo turned up the radio. They were playing Leonard Cohen; Veronica insisted they change the station. Bob Dylan came up next. Easier to handle but still reminded her too much of the road she would be leaving behind.

Instead of fussing with sound some more, Veronica reached her hand over the seat and grasped Bo's in hers. She realized in that moment she could move herself, change directions, shift, and things would be okay. She thought of herself on the panel from yesterday and envisioned taking a different seat. She envisioned herself with a new supervisor, new research area, new school. She saw it all laid out like the painting of Jesus at the last supper, thirteen people on one side of the table. She put Francine there, along with Samantha, Iggy, Brianna, and several girls she knew from her youth, from that summer camp. She wondered if she should put Jonathan there. She wanted to.

But he was gone. This wasn't a last supper image, she realized, but the beginning of a resurrection.

She thought that resurrection would start in Canada. She dreaded it as much as she loved it. But it was already starting. She couldn't hold it back any longer. She would get back to Canada, yes, and maybe she'd have to cut across the border to visit Bo, or maybe Bo would be the one moving back and forth, it didn't matter. It was going to happen regardless. Veronica was sure of it now—and she was no longer afraid.

All of it would come together. But for now, she wanted to stay here. The hows of the other life were simpler now, she was sure. But the nows were still important, too. Wasn't that another Emily Dickinson line? She wondered, but she didn't need to quote it. She could simply live it.

Chapter Twenty-seven

Joan Baez's *Diamonds and Rust* was playing by the time they pulled up to the hotel. Police and ambulances were there; the lights flashed in time to the guitars. When Veronica turned off the radio entirely, there was no sound coming from the sirens.

"That's not good," Bo said. "There's no urgency. They must have found someone dead."

"A suicide?"

Bo shrugged. "Could just be heart failure. Tick-tick-tock."

Veronica didn't find the words callous; they seemed to be the most truthful thing there ever could be, like the click-click-click she'd heard the first night in her room. After Bo parked, she undid her seatbelt and approached the front awning of the hotel. A familiar set of shoes poked out from an ambulance bay. She'd seen them when Henry Gable crossed his legs at dinner, Italian loafers without laces but buckles that looked like a bracelet she'd worn as a child.

"No..." Veronica murmured. She turned to a paramedic, hoping for the nice one from the dead body on the road. Even the one who had chastised her for her scabbed knuckles would be good. When he wasn't familiar, her heart sank, knowing she'd not be able to pry any information but being too desperate to still ask. "Who died?"

The paramedic ignored her. He closed the

ambulance door, sealing a tomb and the shoes away. He tapped the side, and the ambulance drove while he walked over to disappear into the crowd of people who had gathered. Bo stood out in the centre of them. She spoke in clipped words and hand gestures to a worker, who seemed to say they'd found a suicide. Veronica could read their lips, so persistent and clearly, she was sure.

Old man. Suicide. Cyanide.

"No, no, no."

She walked closer. She placed herself next to Bo, allowing their skin to brush. Their shared act gave her leeway; Bo allowed her access to the inner circle of the hotel. And she'd realized she'd read the lips correctly.

Old man. Suicide. Cyanide.

"What was his name?" she asked.

The woman, eyes red-rimmed from what she'd been through, gasped but didn't speak. She seemed to want to say Henry.

"What was his name?" Veronica repeated.

She swore it was still Henry. She knew it had to be. Henry had yet to check out; Henry had been alone in his room and had taken a lethal dose in his wine. Henry had died. It was always going to be him.

When Bo took Veronica's hand, she was shaking. Bo led her inside, all the while fighting the urge to yell and scream that this was all her fault. They'd left the hotel and gone to the Faraway Nearby, and now this was the price they paid. She'd slept with someone else and now time was out of joint. The viral spread of ideas, Bo's incandescent death box. Had Henry internalized the story of Jonathan from dinner? Had he ended his career because someone else threatened to expose his past crossings with Stella, and who knew how many other students?

"Why fucking cyanide?" Bo grabbed the phone at the front desk and dialed a room. She hung up and tried again, still not getting a response. "What a fucking stupid way to go. We're going to have to check everything now. All the rooms. All the drinks in the fridge. All the food. Jesus, this shit can spread through touch."

"By touch?" Veronica stared at her hands. She expected them to be red. "Cyanide?"

"Not always, but it can. It's strong. And such a fucking girly way to die, man."

"What do you mean?"

"Most old men shoot themselves." With the phone perched on her shoulder, Bo opened a drawer under her desk and tossed her shoebox out. The top askew, she easily fished inside and pulled out a pipe, an ID card, and a thimble. "Dead, dead, dead. The dudes like easy and quick things, while the ladies prefer poison. Maybe gas. Something domestic. Not to be sexist, but—Yes? You're there. In the room? God, is it bad? Are you wearing gloves? Wear gloves. It can spread through touch."

Veronica stepped back as Bo continued to give direct commands. Her mind reeled. She knew what Bo said to be true. Intuitively, deep inside. Cyanide was a weird way to die. Of course it was. Yet she hadn't consciously thought it until now. She didn't want to believe that Jonathan's body had been strange, other than the fact that his action had come out of nowhere. His note had given him reason, the culture of academia had given him reason, and his research filled in the rest. Even if these reasons always seemed perverted, retroactive, and out of touch, not his own. She didn't want to believe that his death spoke of something else, something far more sinister.

But...something was wrong here. Something was not adding up. She thought of the conversation from dinner the night before, the sickly feeling it gave her. She thought of Brianna's email and the detective looking around. Her dream, the one she'd had before waking, and the one she couldn't let go of now. Veronica realized she hadn't checked her email in what felt like so long. Now it seemed like there was going to be more than she could handle.

Nothing was adding up. People in Canada were looking for something. For someone.

Marta Allen, Marta Allen, Marta Allen. A recording? What would he not apologize for? Was there a woman here, in this hotel, dropping ear poison when no one was looking? *Marta Allen, Marta Allen, Marta Allen.* Why was it so familiar?

Do you see it yet? Do you recognize them?

Bo was still talking in a frantic pace on the telephone, so she didn't notice when Veronica stepped around to her side of the counter. She tried to read the guestbook, examine the shoebox. When Bo turned her back, still chattering, Veronica typed the name into the computer for the hotel.

Nothing.

She tried different spellings—still nothing. When Bo finally noticed what she was doing, she threw her a confused look, mouthing, "What are you doing?" Before answering, the phone pulled her back, and she tangled the phone cord around herself in her dual conversations. Bo became a two-headed Janus, looking forward and looking back.

"What are you thinking? You—Veronica—what

are you doing?"

"Did he leave a note?"

"What?"

"Henry Gable. Did he leave a note?"

With a sigh, Bo repeated her question into the phone. "Yeah."

"What did he say?"

"I will not apologize. Pfft. Cheap. Cryptic. Sounds like an asshole."

Veronica's stomach sank. She stopped paying attention to Bo's criticisms. Her mouth opened in a response, but nothing came. Edvard Munch's *The Scream* passed across her vision, but she pushed it away. She didn't want to sit and scream. She wanted to speak.

"I'm so sorry, Bo." She leaned toward her, hoping for a hug, something of which Bo went for instantly. All affection disappeared as Veronica snatched the keys to her car. "I'm so sorry, I will be right back."

Veronica ran out the hotel doors. She got back in the car, still warm, and drove into the night. She was only gone a moment before she remembered that her apology was faulty. "Please forgive me," she said to the air, expecting nothing as a reply.

Chapter Twenty-eight

Veronica arrived at the lone internet café she could find in Amherst. Its yellow sign declared it was open twenty-four hours. She'd already lost all track of time, and her phone's battery had died on the way over. She needed to get to the heart of the matter, and truly, there was no better place than here. She paid for her internet minutes using her credit card and hoped it would still go through. When it did, Veronica hoped that Bo would allow her another hour, maybe two to herself, so she could figure this all out before she had to explain herself. Until she got this itch off her back, this ghost exorcised, she couldn't go on and live the good life. Now that she knew it was possible—so beautiful, so wonderful—she simply had to close this case file.

And what if she couldn't get what she needed in two hours? What if, after all this excavation, there was still no *how*?

Veronica wasn't sure. She just knew that, like one professor told her in class, two hours could yield so much research, more than enough for a paper. The trick was simply getting started.

Her email was the first hurdle. After excluding all the banal and trivial matters from the school—and Iggy, who agreed to have a meeting and discuss potential research topics as soon as she'd returned to Canada—there were the startling array of emails from Brianna. In between trying to follow a seemingly endless chain of Brianna's replies, Veronica Googled the name Marta Allen.

Too much came up. Facebook profiles and Twitter pages spoke of bands and movies she'd never seen, fandom interests that seemed more parasitical than enthusiastic. Not the right Marta Allen. Veronica combed back her Google search and tried again, this time focusing on scholarship. She found academic journals, reference software, keynote addresses, and transcribed audio content. Veronica combed through citations until a pattern emerged, until the meaning in the white noise made sense.

Then there she was: Marta Allen in an acknowledgment section of Stella Flanders's article, alongside Veronica's name and Jonathan Morris's. They were thanked as her research assistants, followed by Marta Allen without giving any indication of her role. Just: *And thank you, Marta Allen, as always.* Nothing else.

Invigorated, Veronica searched more. In another academic article from the 1990s, where Stella was listed as the seventh author, Marta Allen's name came up as a case study. The article was about the aftereffects of Love Canal.

Veronica shuddered. She had her answer. Marta Allen was a girl born with two sets of teeth and no legs. She was Stella's neighbour, and soon Stella became Marta's caretaker when she'd gone home again. Marta Allen had died of heart failure, from the black sludge that still lingered in the soil and in her bones. Like Stella's mother, who was also mentioned in the article. Stella had written this research all without using the words I and me—but Veronica knew. She could see it in the careful poetic tone that sometimes emerged. Stella started to write this article while still a biology undergraduate student (hence being seventh on the totem pole), but she had finished as an Emily Dickinson emerging scholar. By the time the article was published, she had probably changed schools entirely and was being dissected by Henry's material history, rather than dissecting Marta Allen's bones for cancer.

Now Henry was dead, too.

Veronica turned back to Brianna's messages on the screen. As she read from the beginning, she watched as Brianna's messages lost capital letters and syntax as she darted from one dawning realization to the next, each one a cascade of harm.

"It's Stella! It's Stella!" Brianna wrote in one of the last emails. It had been sent two hours ago. "That's why I've been sick. I don't have any type of illness. I'm not gluten intolerant or have food poisoning, and this is not psychosomatic stress symptoms. It's Stella. You notice how we get sick when she makes coffee? When she brings us food? When she's around? I don't get sick alone. I get sick with *you*. I watch you get sick. And I know you are throwing up behind that door. I know, but I never said. But I know."

Veronica turned away, hot and shame-faced. She thought no one knew. She thought she'd been so good at hiding her bulimia. But how could they *not* know? Her knuckles. Her gnarled teeth. Her breath. The gum. But of course, the noise. The retching behind closed doors.

Of course they knew. They all knew.

"But it's not you," Brianna wrote again. "She's poisoning us, Veronica. It's been her all along."

Veronica's time ran out. The internet minutes

fettered into grains of sand, crystals behind a screen that shot through with blue and said she was done. *Please purchase more time at the front.* Veronica looked behind her, sure someone was watching. Bo? Officer Neilson? The ever-present paramedics? Jonathan's ghost?

There was no one, not even Stella.

But Veronica still felt so, so haunted.

She left the computer and grabbed her purse. She stepped outside and followed the red hair of a man in front of her, over six feet tall with gangly limbs, believing it really was Jonathan. She wanted it to be him. She wanted to face him, like she had in her dream, and ask him what his paper was about. She wanted to ask him what he'd recorded. What had he eaten, what had Stella fed him, and what had she told him their love was supposed to do? And when had she betrayed him, failed him, and then stolen someone else's work to staple it onto his? When had she made sure that nothing out of his mouth would be believed because she had been the one who told him what to say and then ratted out his lack of citations?

Do you see it yet? Do you recognize them?

Veronica wanted to shout from the rooftops that she saw it now. She wanted to take Jonathan's hands in hers and tell him that it was not his fault, never once, never again. But that was the point: never again. She'd not seen him at their coffee date, where no doubt he'd had hard recorded evidence of Stella's misconduct. Or maybe just proof to save his own academic career, proof that with any key Stella could open office doors and steal research from one to suit the other.

Jonathan couldn't tell her any of that, though. He'd been gone for more than a month. The dead time had turned all whispers into gossip, and then made an entire city for the students to inhabit.

But students were fighting back now. Veronica saw as much. Brianna was taking a page out of Melanie Knight's books. She was fighting back. Veronica wanted to fight back. But she felt weak at her knees.

When the stranger from before stopped at a crosswalk in front of her, Veronica fixated on the side of his face. She wanted it to be Jonathan, but it wasn't. She stared at the red hand, glowing and blinking, telling her to stop and wait for the lights to change. For once, she listened. She turned around, back toward the car, and confronted what she finally needed to see.

☙❧☙❧

"You know," Stella said during one of their first closed-door sessions, after the reading course but before Veronica had graduated from undergrad, "the first anorexics were women who wanted to be saints. By not eating, they thought they were getting closer to God."

"Oh?" Veronica said, unsure of what she could say. There was always a moment whenever eating disorders were brought up in conversation where she wasn't sure if people were talking to her or about her. Did she respond like a patient? A victim? Or a casual listener? As someone who had also caught that special report on the epidemic of our teenage girls going wayward?

With Stella, though, the answer had been obvious: respond like a scholar. "That's fascinating, actually. I didn't know that. What book is it from?"

"*Fasting Girls* by Joan Jacobs Brumberg. Very

interesting in terms of case studies." Stella picked up the book from her shelf and laid it on the table in front of Veronica. "From these hagiographies, we now get the tell-all nonsense of the confessional narrative, a *20/20* special on Karen Carpenter. It's not as clear or clean a line as that, but the lineage is there. We went from saints to superstars. It saddens me, which is why I suppose I retreat to Dickinson instead of watching TV at night. Her curious hungers are anorexic in that way, and her need to wear white perpetually is quite saint-like. That's a reading I could write about. That's a reading someone should write about."

"Oh," Veronica said again, feebly. She knew Stella was offering her a topic to explore, a way to enter into her academic world, but she'd been sucked into the images in the centre of the book. The bones, the gauntness. So familiar. So comforting. When she met Stella's gaze again, she saw that same sharp comfort in her gaze. Her bones offered her a solution; her experience could be saint-like. They could be the poetry that Stella wanted from her.

If Veronica had to pick a moment, she knew that was the first day she was poisoned.

Veronica thought back to every last morsel of food she'd eaten in front of Stella. Every last drink, be it water, too-sweet iced tea, or rum and Coke and wine sipped after hours. She surveyed every touch after hand lotion was put on, every hint of almonds and sweetness that she could not place. Was it there? Was it then? And how?

The why, though, was obvious.

Veronica knew why, though it had been harder and harder to come to terms with. Stella Flanders, the woman she had loved for so long and whom she still wanted to believe was human in some way, was poisoning her and all her students because it was the only way to prove which ones could survive.

Because, in some odd way, it was the only time Stella felt love.

Veronica called Brianna from a payphone. She picked up on the second ring. "Hello?"

"Hi," Veronica said. Her voice felt flat. "It's me."

"Jesus Christ," Brianna said. "Are you okay? Is she around you? What's going on?"

"I'm alone."

"Good. Do you know?"

"I see it now," Veronica said. "But tell me, too."

Brianna launched into explaining everything, sparing no detail. Veronica listened intently, knowing all of it from her own body. It was antifreeze, apparently, that they'd found in Brianna's urine and blood test results. A biopsy would confirm crystals from the ethylene glycol bonding with her cells, making her sickly and weak. Veronica was sure that if she had gone to the hospital when she fainted and seized, they would have found that, too. She was sure she felt it now; a slight pain in her side, around her back, was probably the same crystals. She wondered if she'd break herself open if she'd look like a geode. The paramedics had probably already tried to find and warn her but only came back to a dead person's ID. She thought back to her sudden urge to vomit around Francine; the smell of the garage; the familiar sight of bottles filled with antifreeze, the antifreeze that her body now understood as bad, bad, bad. She didn't want to purge because she was scared of the future with Bo. She wanted to purge in that garage to keep herself safe.

"The body remembers," Brianna said. "And the body always wins. That's what my doctor said, anyway. I'm going to be okay. You are, too. I promise. It's all treatable. There might be some kidney damage, though, but that's a small price to pay. She used the harder stuff for Jonathan."

"And Henry."

"Who?"

"Never mind. I'll tell you later. I—"

"The detective," Brianna said, cutting her off. "He did say there were probably more. He took our mourning ritual list. He's looking into all of them. Stella's...she's a murderer. A serial killer. We are not the first."

But are we the last? Veronica wondered. She still couldn't speak. She followed along with Brianna's sentiments, all the while watching the clock tick-tick-tick away. She may survive this, sure, but Veronica still felt like her time was running out. She felt stuck at the crossroads, suddenly knowing that she wanted to live for that possible future more than ever before—but also being struck blind and dumb by the near-death experience she'd just had. There might be lingering damage. There was always a cost to survival, especially once you had been corroded inside. The double set of teeth. Marta Allen. Love Canal that could hold no more vegetation. *Because I could not stop for Death,* Veronica thought, quoting Dickinson in her mind. *He kindly stopped for me.* She sighed. Was this poison, too? Did she ever really like Dickinson, or was it yet another way to manipulate?

She wasn't sure. When she closed her eyes, she saw paintings. *The Faraway Nearby, Nighthawks,* and *Venus.*

"I promise, you will be okay," Brianna said. "Just don't eat or drink anything else. Okay?"

"You don't eat or drink in the underworld," Veronica said. "Or else you'll get stuck."

"Exactly. Is that something she told you?"

"No. Just...I don't know where she is, Brianna. Stella. Is she there?"

"I don't think so. We were all worried she'd kidnapped you."

"I got away. I was like the bunny."

"What?"

"Never mind. I have to go. I need to find her."

"Don't drink anything—"

Veronica hated to do it, but she hung up the phone. Brianna was too far away, already in a stabilized world. Veronica needed to use her last half hour effectively. She called the car rental place next. The SUV had not been returned. Stella had not left; she had not gone back home to Canada, which meant that the woods around Amherst became smaller and smaller, a death-grip hug. Most likely, Stella had Veronica's passport. She was locking them into this virgin land, now claimed by chemicals, and she was going to finish them off.

Veronica hung up the phone. Her hands shook. She was almost giddy with the revelation. Despite all this, she'd survived. She was going to keep surviving, though Stella was still here, trying to trap her. She was going to go deeper and deeper into the underworld, back to the empty ghost room of the hotel, and confront the woman she thought she'd loved for years.

As she drove back to the hotel, Veronica started to feel woozy. It wasn't the lingering crystals in her brain she feared, but the scarred words and memories of her mind. All her conversations with Stella became fat and twisted with double meanings. Stella's touches became knife blows. The nights spent making love, only to be topped off with a coffee with a strange taste and a lingering kiss on the mouth, were now erased as romantic interludes and became something fierce, something from William Blake's *The Marriage of Heaven and Hell*. Veronica was an illuminated manuscript, shot through with scar tissue that glowed and glowed and glowed. All her harm was iridescent, and Stella's words became what they really were, too sharp to hold, a parasitic relationship that should have ended before it started but had tasted so much like something familiar.

When Veronica arrived, the hotel front desk was empty. So were the hallways, the elevators. Even the lights were dimmed. She took the stairs and felt as if she was in a disaster film.

At the threshold of her hotel door, Jonathan's former room, was a basket full of muffins. The smell was familiar, cinnamon and sugar, the recipe torn from the pages of Emily Dickinson's diary. Stella baked this every other Saturday. Stella fed it to her. Of course this would be the final confrontation. Not Stella in the flesh, but Stella made manifest in bread. Stella as food. Stella as the eating disorder, tempting her, making her sicker through twisted words and the idealistic visions of sainthood.

Veronica sighed. She remembered the first time she'd eaten these muffins as the first time she'd binged at Stella's place, and then vomited in her bathroom. She'd felt as if she'd sullied the beautiful granite countertop, the pristine porcelain bowl, and the framed image of van Gogh's *Wheatfield with Crows* in the hallway.

But throwing up had probably saved her life. The body always remembered, and the body always won.

Veronica was going to win.

She picked up the basket and took it into the hotel room. She checked all the nooks and crannies for ghosts, for Stella. There was nothing. But there was something in the basket. She removed each muffin with a tissue, careful not to let whatever poison seep into her fingers. She revealed a sheet of paper. A handwritten suicide note? Something to make it all better?

When Veronica turned it over, she expected it to say, *I will not apologize.* Instead, it simply said, in Stella's delicate handwriting, *I am so sorry.*

"Of course you are," Veronica said aloud. "But I do not forgive you."

Chapter Twenty-nine

I think I want to call it the academic mystique."
Veronica placed her hands on the keys of the piano, but the sound was muffled due to the first pedal. Bo nodded along to her words, understanding the reference to Betty Friedan's *Feminine Mystique* right away.

"But you're not second wave," Bo added, a teasing smile on her face.

"No. Not at all. As much as I like a lot of the books from that period, I know they were not too kind to trans women."

"You can say that again." Bo chuckled. "But go on. You were spit-balling."

"Thanks..."

Veronica blushed. She'd been doing this a lot lately. She'd talk out her ideas as she played the piano, washed dishes, or went on walks. The talking helped to get Stella's words about the world out of her brain. At first, Veronica had been afraid that along with Stella, Dickinson would also go, but her presence stayed. Veronica didn't recall all the lines, but the more important ones, the ones she liked, lingered.

"So, yes," Veronica went on. "There is something about academia that empties out all meaning in the daily world. It becomes study, study, study, like the housewives of the 1950s experienced dishes, dishes, and dishes. Your classes, like housework, become a way in which to fill the void of time—but everything has also become mechanized, so there is less to do while also so much more to do. Then you have this blank page of a dissertation, your own research like a baby, but that research is also never fully your own because your supervisor is a shadow, like your baby will eventually become their own person. We claim that we give grad students independence, but it's just another set of rules. Another mystique, another layer. I'm..."

Veronica set her hands on her knees. She heard Stella's voice in her head, still trying to correct all her unclear or inconsistent statements. She heard all the arguments, the counterarguments, and saw the annotated bibliography before her eyes. She understood it so well. And she understood, deep down, that she may never get rid of Stella, like she may never get rid of Adele.

But it was okay to not have it all figured out right now.

The body would eventually win. The hows would take care of themselves.

Bo's interested expression gave Veronica courage to keep talking even if she was still not quite making sense. "It's just an idea Brianna and I have been passing around, trying to make sense of what's happening and what still has to happen. We wanted to raise awareness before, you know? But we had no idea of what. We thought it was all about mental illness in the academy or about the nature of revealing harm like Melanie Knight tried to do, but now we're realizing it's more like a miasma. It's like a poison, and naming the mystique is part of the recovery. Brianna wants to publish already...but I'm more hesitant."

"Can't say I blame you after all that Stella nonsense," Bo said. "Take your time, though. The words will come."

Bo squeezed Veronica's shoulder, whispering quickly that she'd be back with more tea. Veronica took the pedal off and filled the air with song.

Three days had passed since Henry's body had been found and Veronica received the muffins. When detectives showed up at the hotel and told her Stella had been missing for twelve hours, elusive and untraceable, Veronica told them to look in Love Canal. Stella was found then, sitting in the shell of an old house. Not her house, but Marta's. Her motivation for studying what she'd always studied and her first love. The first time she'd felt love in caretaking and caregiving, and then eventually, in the mercy kill. When searched at the police station, officers found vials of cyanide like Jonathan—and Henry—had been given. They also found Jonathan's cellphone. One of their conversations, about his failed exams, had been recorded on the phone, along with the two of them speaking about their relationship. They found nothing else on Stella, not even Veronica's passport.

Veronica didn't like to think about that recorded conversation too much, or the whole ordeal, beyond the mystique that she and Brianna could finally articulate together and beyond the hope that she was feeling for a new life and a new sense of recovery. Veronica had spent a night in an American hospital as they fixed her fluids. She was still dehydrated, her kidneys in a bad way, and crystals, much like Brianna, marking her body like some kind of diamond mine. She was going to be okay, though. She even spoke to a therapist about getting information on bulimia, some psychological treatment. All of it would need to be back in Canada, but she had pamphlets now that she knew she'd read. A lifeline she knew she'd follow.

That night in the hospital, Veronica had had another dream. Jonathan was there—it felt like he was always going to be there—but he didn't stay long. She'd woken up in an Eden, one that looked like her everyday reality back in Canada. It looked like the café where she was supposed to meet Jonathan, except that it was also filled with people like Francine and Bo and Samantha. Everyone had smiles on their faces and listened to soft music from a piano on the other side of the room. Iggy was there, too, even though Veronica had no idea what Iggy looked like now. Halfway through the dream, the room became filled with students. Students she had yet to teach, students she had yet to affect. She realized she was talking in the dream, but it was all coming out as colours. A tie-dye tapestry spilled from her mouth, mixed with the notes, then she woke up.

It was so simple when she really thought of it. Nothing happened. But that was sort of the point, wasn't it? She didn't need to do anything anymore. There was nothing to notice, nothing to see and solve and fight, other than simply enjoy the people, the music, and the colours around herself.

It wasn't exactly Eden then. Eden was what was lost. But it wasn't exactly the Faraway Nearby, either, since that was a future prospect. It sounded more like serenity, from that phrase that Bo had mentioned as part of AA rhetoric. A serenity dream, a serenity nearby.

After Veronica was discharged from the hospital, she took a cab to the bed and breakfast. Bo welcomed her with open arms—but only after demanding seven different kinds of apologies for stealing the car. Veronica gave in easily; please forgive me now rolled easily off her tongue. She felt more and more connected each time Bo kissed her forgiveness into absolution. Then Bo led her to the basement room of the bed and breakfast with an open invitation to stay as long as she needed.

"As long, of course, as you fill the time with music. The last guests loved you. So let this be your music hall."

Veronica eagerly agreed. The price seemed fair. And the piano became the way to work out the kinks of her body, along with talking aloud. Her doctors had feared nerve damage from the extent of her exposure to poison, so she thought she could prove them wrong by playing and speaking and reading those pamphlets and writing down her meals. Write it down to keep it down became a new mantra, one that she knew, eventually, would replace Stella completely.

When Veronica started to play again, she remembered Adele. Just the lessons at first, the correct placement of hands over ivory, but then the other parts emerged. She confronted the good and the bad; she played through the past and into the present moment, and suddenly, it was as if Adele was expunged. Veronica was in the present tense, the present moment, and it was good. She thought of Bo and only Bo now when they shared a bed at night. The two of them, side by side in bed or on the piano some afternoons, reminded her of their road trip to Boston. She wondered if she could talk about that, write an entire dissertation about their days getting passports and what that meant for them as tourists but not. So many people had talked about the U.S., it was hard to believe there could be something new here.

But there was, there always was.

Iggy had said as much, as well. They had a standing meeting arranged for when Veronica returned. Her career was not over, Veronica understood. It was just beginning. It was still unfocused, still rambling, but Veronica would continue to play the piano as she tried to figure out her meanings in more concrete terms and until she could get stronger glimpses of her future between the black and white.

"So this came for you today." Bo put an envelope on top of the piano. It was from the Canadian consulate. Her passport.

Veronica took the envelope in the edges of her hands. She held it with reverence, then with disquiet. She could go home now. She was not exactly sure where that home was anymore. She wanted to remain in this endless stretch of time where there were so many possibilities, and she chose none of them.

"Did yours come, too?"

Bo nodded. "Mismatched but all mine. Guess who else came by today?"

Veronica furrowed her brows. Bo leaned on the piano gleefully. "Francine."

"Really?"

"Oh, yeah," Bo said. "She baked us cookies, too. They're upstairs. You want one?"

Veronica had a brief flash of the muffins. She blinked it away. Francine was not Stella. She wasn't even Emily Dickinson. She left her house, embraced the world, and left sweet things in their wake. Before Veronica could answer, Bo was already grabbing her hand and dragging her up the stairs. They laughed as they got plates and put out the poppy seed lemon cookies. Bo took big bites, and then kissed her on the mouth. Heat grew between them. Veronica's stomach felt heavy. She kissed Bo. She ate a bite. And then she decided she could speak again, knowing exactly what she wanted.

"I'm glad your passport came," Veronica said. "Because we should go to Montreal. Use our mangled French. See the billboards. Marvel at architecture, new and old."

"And Leonard Cohen's face spray-painted on a wall?"

"Of course."

Bo folded her arms across her chest. She lifted a brow. "You're not just dreaming, are you?"

Veronica shook her head. They stared at each other for a long time. Veronica bit a cookie, tempting. Bo leaned closer and snatched the cookie from her hand. Veronica balked, but Bo kissed her on the mouth again, then on the chin, leading all the way to her ear. "Sure," she said in a sweet whisper. "Let's go."

Epilogue

S ay cheese!" Iggy snapped a photo of Veronica and Bo in front of the Leonard Cohen mural in Montreal. He looked down at his phone and beamed. "Ah, perfect! This is great. It reminds me of a painting, actually."

"Shocking," Veronica said. "But tell me anyway."

Iggy tossed some of his darker curls out of his eyes as he spoke about the trans artist Sybil Lamb. "She has an interesting collection I've seen online. I can't remember the title of this one—one of the damning things about the internet is things are never properly cited—but the painting is of a woman holding her iPhone out and taking a picture. Then there is another set of arms folded in the front, posing like someone from one of the first selfies. New and old tech combine. It's neat. It reminds me of you two, honestly, because you're both very professional and yet, utterly...."

"Beautiful? Amazing? Compelling?" Bo asked. She vogued for Iggy.

"Yes, sure." Iggy nodded and laughed. "All of those."

"Thank you," Veronica said. "I must look that painting up later then."

Veronica grinned. Her face felt tight from all the genuflecting she'd been doing this morning and afternoon. She, Bo, and Iggy were all staying in the same Montreal hotel for a conference. Six months had passed from that three-day interlude in Amherst. Everything was different, but everything was also the same.

Veronica was still a teacher, her worry about the students contesting their grade needless and fruitless when one didn't even show up for the hearing. The other retracted the complaint. She was still an academic, too. At a different school, with a different supervisor, and in a completely different field of English literature. She felt sad some days that she'd left Emily Dickinson behind, but she was happy— more than happy—to now be examining addiction literature. Denis Johnson, Raymond Carver, and even her old mainstay Marya Hornbacher, an eating disorder writer who had penned a memoir about her alcoholism in addition to her more famous work onanorexia and bulimia. Instead of the prose Veronica studied making her feel inferior because she couldn't understand it, she now felt like she was competent. Cogent. More than anything, these works reminded her how she could stay alive and what was waiting for her when she did.

Iggy was a great supervisor. Not only did he support her academic vision wholeheartedly, but he also took no bullshit and cut right to the chase during their first meeting: "So tell me about Stella Flanders," he'd said. Iggy had followed the news event, but after having watched the Melanie Knight debacle, he also knew there was always more than one side to any story and wanted it straight from Veronica's mouth.

"Everything still feels like rumour and gossip," Veronica had told him. "But here's my take on the truth."

They'd bonded instantly over shared notions

of truth, the ways in which we sometimes blind ourselves to our own realities and how that plays out in addictions. He'd had his own struggles with alcohol shortly after his teaching contract ran out. He had pulled himself out from the darkest days, however, by finding solace in art.

That was what the conference was about: art and art history. Veronica presented a paper on photographic images of fasting girls (and how that soon changed into anorexic inspiration online). Iggy presented a paper on *Nighthawks* and the American Gothic in the urban city. They both practiced all night in each other's hotel rooms, sharing insights and supporting each other. They had also both attended the other's paper and panel, too. It was great. So inspiring and hopeful, even if the material was sometimes a little dry. Veronica could handle dryness in the academics, as long as the person she was working with would look her in the eye and mean what they said.

Iggy meant it. Iggy understood. Veronica knew that her degree would work out. It wasn't an issue, not in the least.

"I am being serious, though," Iggy added after a moment. He displayed his iPhone and the picture he'd taken of Veronica and Bo. "This is a great image. Author photo material."

"Really?"

Veronica looked closer at the iPhone. She was shocked at her own image. Not only was she happier now than ever before, but her face was also brighter. Her hair thicker and cheeks fuller. She had grown another size in the last six months, and while sometimes that fact bothered her, other times, she was reminded of how human she looked.

With Bo beside her, the photo only got that much better.

While Iggy and Veronica had been talking about art the past three days, Bo had been scouting out her doctor's office, making the final arrangements, and basically getting ready for the last big leap. While she'd visited Canada here and there the past six months, it had mostly been to see Veronica. Mostly to maintain their relationship and set sights on owning their own house—which one day, Bo wanted to turn into a bed and breakfast. Surgery had seemed like such a far-off goal, but now it was happening. Not this weekend, not even within the following six months, since there was a long waitlist and a period of saving and financing that needed to happen, but it was happening. One day, Bo would wake up and set into her body.

Yet Veronica knew, just from looking at the photo of them now on Iggy's screen, that they had already both done that. Veronica had gained weight. She learned to eat again. She learned to think for herself again. Meanwhile, Bo learned to let go of her family history, her box of dead things, and stepped into Canada on her own two feet. On that first trip into Canada together, the one they'd taken when Veronica still felt as if she was half crystals from the ethylene glycol, they'd taken Bo's shoebox and scattered it over the border. She wanted to let her dead things go. Her bunnies go.

The only way to save them, she now understood, was to save herself. And the only way to truly save herself was to move. To live the life she'd always wanted, instead of feeling bad for her friends who didn't get so far.

"So what do you think?" Iggy asked Bo, gesturing

to the photo. "I think you look cute."

"My hair is too long. And, my God, you see the bags under my eyes?"

"No," Veronica said.

"Well, there are bags. It's all the French. It's giving me a headache."

"You don't have to speak it," Veronica said.

"I know. But I sort of like it, too. I want to try."

Veronica sighed. Bo flitted between French and English, like she oscillated her coffee preferences between two sugars and no sugars, between sometimes milk and sometimes cream. Now freed from her past, she liked to move like a whirling dervish in her preferences, and though it sometimes made her long for her to just stay in one place, one country, Veronica loved Bo as she was. She would continue to ask, every single morning, *what type of coffee today?* as long as it meant she got to speak with her.

"Let's try the photo again," Bo said. "But I want to stand there."

Veronica put on another smile. She stood with Bo in front of a museum entrance. They posed professionally, then Bo insisted they vamp. So they vamped. They posed like Charlie's Angels, like Uma Thurman from *Pulp Fiction*, and then stood back-to-back with their arms crossed in front of themselves. Iggy wanted in on the action, too, so the three of them asked a stranger to take their photo.

The woman who agreed to take their image reminded Veronica of Francine. Whenever Veronica had crossed the border to see Bo, though it was only two more times, Francine had been a brief stop—until, suddenly, there was a for sale sign on the house. Bo had brought up an obituary with her on this trip, saved from the local news. Francine had died in October, after a long illness. Neither one of them had been invited to the funeral, of course, because they were passers-by. Someone Francine had baked for. Someone she'd helped one night. It wasn't a lot, but it was something that still made Veronica's heart hurt. Bo hadn't known if she should save the obituary, but Veronica was thankful she did. She had it in her wallet now. It was not a talisman of dead people, of life suddenly cut short. Rather, it was evidence that there was such a thing as a natural death. That caretaking did not have to be violence. And for the last six weeks or so, as the memory of the last conference she attended haunted her, Veronica had needed that periodic reminder.

Now, though, she felt like the paper had served its purpose. It burned in her wallet. She wanted to let it go.

Iggy thanked the woman who'd taken their photo. Her eyes glimmered as she waved goodbye. They all looked at the image on the phone, goofing around and laughing as they added compliment after compliment to one another. *Oh, perfect. Wonderful. Extraordinary.* Their image reminded Veronica of the three charities from Greek mythology. Half the muses. It made her happy, without reference or explanation.

Iggy's phone rang. He sighed as he read the name. "Sorry, gotta take this. Dinner afterwards?"

They all nodded. Iggy stepped aside while Bo took Veronica's hands. "You okay? This weekend hasn't been too intense?"

"I think I've already lived through the most intense weekend of my life," Veronica said. "I'm just happy you're here."

"I was thinking about that," Bo said.

"About what?"

Bo smiled, though it seemed hard. "I was thinking your apartment was too small. We need some space for all the stuff I'm going to bring."

Veronica's heart swelled. There was no question, no debate. Just a statement of fact. *We are moving in together, so you better cut down on the amount of coats and shoes and books you have. Well, maybe keep the books. But it is a fact. We are together. We are moving in.*

"So you're finally embracing the Canadian lifestyle."

"I'm thinking I will have dual citizenship." Bo nudged her. "And you should, too."

"Probably."

Bo's face turned serious. Their mouths met in a tender kiss, one that still felt like the first. Each and every time they met up, it seemed like they were brand new people. Every kiss was the first, every touch and caress still shiny and new. She wondered if holding Bo too long would cease to be exciting. Would everything fade to grey again?

Then she remembered Francine. That house. The photos of the future and the various ways their lives could go, if they let it happen. Veronica unlocked their hands so she could pull out the newspaper article. Bo furrowed her brow until she understood what was happening.

Bo took the other corner of the newspaper. They held it up in the air. And then, like the shoebox that Bo had finally dumped over the border, they let the obituary for Francine go in the wind. It was caught in an updraft, and for the briefest of moments, plastered across Leonard Cohen's face. They laughed. They kissed. And then it was gone.

The future they'd been dreaming of could begin.

"Hi again," Iggy said. He checked his watch. "Is it too early for dinner?"

Veronica eyed him with Bo. She shook her head and took her arm. "No, it sounds perfect. Yes, this is exactly the right time."

About the Author

Eve Morton is a writer living in Ontario, Canada. She teaches university and college classes on media studies, academic writing, and genre literature, among other topics. She reads tarot, has a lot of tattoos, and loves all things occult and supernatural in nature. She also loves true crime, especially the forensic side of it, and is often swayed by a really good podcast (even more when it's funny). She received a PhD in 2019 and continues her research work on LGBTQ communities and film, in addition to other topics related to addiction and mental health. Find more information on authormorton.wordpress.com.

IF YOU LIKED THIS BOOK...

Share a review with your friends or post a review on your favorite site like Amazon, Goodreads, Barnes and Noble, or anywhere you purchased the book. Or perhaps share a posting on your social media sites and help spread the word.

Join the Sapphire Newsletter and keep up with all your favorite authors.

Did we mention you get a free book for joining our team?

sign-up at - www.sapphirebooks.com

Check out Eve's other book

Survival – ISBN – 978-1-952270-18-5

After surviving a school shooting, Mona Ouellet moves from Montreal to Peterborough, switches her PhD discipline from English Literature to Psychology, and tries to move on with her life. Unfortunately, her nightmares follow her—and so do a host of "bad men" who seem to appear around every corner to make her life difficult. Her only escape is to fall into her research completely, where she soon becomes obsessed with retelling true crime case studies and enamoured by a waitress at a local diner.

Kerri Reznik is a waitress by day and horror writer by night, where she turns elements of her two-month long captivity in the wilderness with her survivalist father into stories to scare others. Though over a decade has passed, Kerri is still haunted by her brother Lee's absence in her life and her inability to reconcile with it. She seeks camaraderie with Absalom Lincoln, a detective on Peterborough police's force, where the two bond over mysteries, both true and imagined.

As Kerri and Mona's connection becomes stronger, their past traumas begin to intertwine and both of their worst nightmares begin to evolve and intensify. Each character must struggle to negotiate how to live in a world where survival is never guaranteed, and even when it is possible, there is always a cost.

Greenish - ISBN - 978-1-952270-44-4

Harley Hewitt is living the dream. She's about to wed her fiancée, Tracey, when her best friend suddenly bails as her maid of honour. Her night job as a nurse and her lack of contact with anyone in her hometown make her realize that she has no friends of her own, so she goes to a speed dating event in hopes of catching a maid of honour, rather than a future bride-to-be.

Denise North thought she had everything. Her own home, a good job with great friends, and zero debt. At her best friend's wedding, she soon realizes that her aspirations of being someone's one and only have been put on the backburner. She throws herself back into the dating pool, expecting to find the perfect man of her dreams but accidentally shows up at a lesbian speed dating night instead.

When Denise and Harley cross paths, it seems like the stars have aligned. Denise needs to get out of her shell, and Harley needs "someone borrowed" for her big day. They both have similar interests and senses of humour. What could go wrong? As the wedding approaches and Harley's best friend returns with a secret, both women find out just how green they've been at love and life so far.

Other books by Sapphire Authors

Broken, not Shattered – ISBN – 978-1-952270-22-2

Even when it seems hopeless, there can always be a better tomorrow.

Jill Bishop has one goal in life – to survive. Jill is trapped in an abusive marriage, while raising two young girls. Her husband has isolated her from the world and filled her days with fear. The last thing on her mind is love, but she sure could use a friend.

Alex McCoy is enjoying a comfortable life, with great friends and a prosperous business. She has given up on love, after picking the wrong woman one too many times. Little does she know, a simple act of kindness might change her life forever.

When Alex lends a helping hand to Jill at the local grocery store, they are surprised by their immediate connection and an unlikely friendship develops. As their friendship deepens, so too do their fears.

In order to protect herself and the girls, Jill can't let her husband know about her friendship with Alex, and Alex can't discover what goes on behind closed doors. What would Alex do if she finds out the truth? At the same time, Alex must fight her attraction and be the friend she suspects Jill needs. Besides, Alex knows what every lesbian knows – don't fall for a straight woman, especially one that's married…but will her heart listen?

My Home is on the Mountain - ISBN - 978-1-952270-

40-6

You can make your life extraordinary, if you have the courage.

Cecilia Howison, the rich and well-known daughter of a prominent East Tennessee family, appears to be the perfect Southern girl, cultured, gracious, virginal. The actual lesbian she is feels restless and ready for something new. She finds it in a high mountain meadow: a girl, wearing nothing but overalls, asleep beside a violin. Cecilia accepts the challenge.
Airey Fitch is the mainstay of her family's hard-scrabble hill farm. She has no love for the Howisons or any their kind, who now, in 1931, are evicting the mountain folk to create a new national park. Despite them, she will hang on, despite them, she will seek a life in music. When Cecilia offers to make that happen, Airey dares to trust her. And wonders at Cecilia's hold on her thoughts.

Cecilia understands all too clearly the risks she runs by wooing Airey Fitch but cannot stop, lured like a moth to Airey's flame. Airey wants more than the passion Cecilia gives her—wants her heart. But the world they live in forbids it, and Cecilia is faced with a choice that only love can make.

Curtain Call - ISBN - 978-952270-42-0

What do you do when you come from a long line of dancers that spans the globe and generations, yet you can't tell your right foot from your left? You fall in love with a dancer, of course!

Gray Rickman is an awkward seventeen-year-old when she first sets eyes on Christian Scott at the dance studio/theater Gray's parents own and run in Denver, Colorado.

Though only a handful of years older than Gray, Christian carries herself with poise and wisdom far beyond her years. A woman of few words, she speaks volumes with her body.

Before Gray even really knows what her type is, Christian stars in endless daydreams and even fulfills a couple of her fantasies before vanishing out of thin air, leaving Gray in an empty bed with nothing but bittersweet memories and broken dreams.

With no choice but to move on, Gray attempts love, even moving with her college girlfriend to New York City to pursue a career in journalism. But her standard has been set, the bar way too high for any other woman to reach or clear. It's an unexpected encounter in an obvious place when Gray sets eyes on her dancer again. Will the bright lights of Broadway illuminate the way back to the woman of her dreams? Or will they blind her to any other possibility of happiness?

Break a leg, Gray. The Great White Way calls.

Laying of Hands - ISBN - 978-1-952270-49-9

Nestled in the Adirondack Mountains of upstate New York lies a picturesque retreat for the conservative young women of the Sanctity Covenant religion, surrounded by crisp, pine-scented breezes and the endless blue shimmer of Coyote Lake. But dark secrets lurk behind closed doors at Valley of Rubies, and what emerges from the summer shadows is nothing less than terrifying.

Adel Rosse, an investigative journalist for Vanity Fair looking for a way to stand out in the cutthroat world of Manhattan journalism, has just been handed an assignment that will catapult her career—if she can survive as an undercover Creative Writing tutor at Valley of Rubies and get the scoop on what really happens there. Just as she starts to uncover the gritty truth behind the shadowy cult running the organization, she falls in love with the one woman who holds the key to the story.

Grace Waters is an old maid at twenty-six, at least by Covenant standards, and her annual idyllic summers spent teaching at Valley of Rubies are suddenly imperiled by the news that she must marry the man chosen for her at the end of the session. If she refuses, she risks being excommunicated—or worse—but a mysterious new writing instructor at camp makes her wonder what would happen if she dared to write her own story.

Pushing their boundaries in search of answers, Grace and Adel seek to redefine themselves to save their futures—and maybe each other.

Keeping Secrets – ISBN – 978-1-952270-04-8

What would you do if, after finally finding the woman

of your dreams, she suddenly leaves to fight in the Civil War?

It's 1863, and Elizabeth Hepscott has resigned herself to a life of monotonous boredom far from the battlefields as the wife of a Missouri rancher. Her fate changes when she travels with her brother to Kentucky to help him join the Union Army. On a whim, she poses as his little brother and is bullied into enlisting, as well. Reluctantly pulled into a new destiny, a lark decision quickly cascades into mortal danger.

While Elizabeth's life has made a drastic U-turn, Charlie Schweicher, heiress to a glass-making fortune, is still searching for the only thing money can't buy.

A chance encounter drastically changes everything for both of them. Will Charlie find the love she's longed for, or will the war take it all away?